James McCormick Dalzell, John Gray

Private Dalzell

His Autobiography, Poems and Comic War Papers

James McCormick Dalzell, John Gray

Private Dalzell
His Autobiography, Poems and Comic War Papers

ISBN/EAN: 9783337307318

Printed in Europe, USA, Canada, Australia, Japan

Cover: Foto ©Raphael Reischuk / pixelio.de

More available books at **www.hansebooks.com**

HIS

AUTOBIOGRAPHY, POEMS AND COMIC WAR PAPERS

SKETCH OF

JOHN GRAY, WASHINGTON'S LAST SOLDIER, Etc

PART I. MY AUTOBIOGRAPHY
PART II. MY WAR SKETCHES, Etc
PART III. JOHN GRAY

A CENTENNIAL SOUVENIR

CINCINNATI
ROBERT CLARKE & CO
1888

To the Soldiers of the Union Army,

OFFICERS AND MEN, BUT ESPECIALLY TO THE PRIVATE SOLDIERS, MY DEAR COM-

RADES ONE AND ALL, FOR WHOM AND WITH WHOM THE POOREST OF GOD'S

POOR, THE NOBLEST AND THE BEST, MY LIFE HAS BEEN SPENT, FAR

TOWARD THE SHADOW THAT SHALL SOON ENVELOPE IT AND

THEM, THIS BOOK AND VOLUME OF MY POOR HUMBLE LIFE

IS AFFECTIONATELY DEDICATED, TO THEM AND THEIR

SONS' DAUGHTERS AND SONS, AND THEIR

DAUGHTERS' DAUGHTERS AND SONS,

FOREVER AND A DAY.

PRIVATE DALZELL.

CALDWELL, OHIO, *April 4, 1888.*

CONTENTS.

(3)

PART III.

JOHN GRAY, OF MT. VERNON.

PRIVATE DALZELL.

PART I.

MY AUTOBIOGRAPHY.

PREFATORY.

I promised the public my autobiography, and here it is. The book and volume of my life is too humble a part of history to be elaborated in any detail, and I have not the vanity or egotism to do so. I was born as others are born, and shall die as others have died, and that's about all there's of it. The proper time for a man's "auto-biography" to be written is when he is safe in heaven. The gentle reader will not murmur nor complain, there-fore, if I cut it short in righteousness.

It's all a mistake that I alone put down the rebellion. I had the able and valuable assistance of Generals Grant, Sherman, Sheridan, and several other gentlemen whose names and rank are too tedious to mention, including— and, as history has neglected to refer to them in any manner whatever, I beg to refer to them in passing—sev-eral privates!

This fact seems to have fallen into oblivion and sunk to the bottom. They all ably and equally rendered me—

that is, the country—valuable assistance in crushing the
hydra-head of treason and rebellion. I believe if it had
not been for their presence with me in the field I might
possibly have failed and seen the Union divided and the
flag dishonored.

This is a concession which no other memoir writer has
yet ventured to make. But I want to close the history
of the War. I shall close the history of the revolution
in the Life of John Gray; and, while I have my hand
in the closing up business, I would be proud, indeed,
to close out the whole war business! It needs closing
pretty badly just now, I vow! It runs riot in all our
papers and magazines of fiction, together with no end
of "war histories," so-called, and is like to run on, like
the ancient river, forever and forever.

I think this book will close the business out, and perform for modern carpet-knighting somewhat of the service which Cervantes' Don Quixote accomplished to bring
into deserved contempt and ridicule the absurd romances
of chivalry and knight-errantry of the Middle Ages.

It is time to beat swords and all warlike weapons into
plowshares and pruning-hooks, and usher the dawn of
much-needed rest. If this humble volume shall accomplish this, or the half of it, I will hang up my pen and
write no more "histories;" but if another dose is needed
I will administer it until this craze for war romancing
under cover of history of the war is completely cured.
With the pen I have stormed the redoubts of buncombe
before and won laurels there.

I am cautioned by judicious friends that this is a rash
and foolish undertaking—a rush upon the thick bosses
of the almighty memoir makers. This battle of the

books must some time cease. Why not here, and now, and forever? It was no easy thing, I assure you, to end the war. It took all I could do—sometimes I feared I was going to fail; and, indeed, I should have been discomfited had it not been for the assistance aforesaid of the several generals aforesaid, together with the said privates aforesaid!

Yet it took but four years to end the war. It's like to take a thousand to end its history! It's so much easier to write than to fight battles!!

Of late, especially from the comrades of the Grand Army of the Republic and the gentlemen of the daily newspaper press, with whom my life for a quarter of a century has been largely passed, I have had numerous requests for my autograph and photograph, neither of which is a thing of beauty. And they have even asked me if I really existed at all except in the imagination and the newspapers. To all these inquiries I have replied according to the facts, and whenever I could afford it I have uniformly sent my picture to all who sought it.

This has stimulated me to believe that public curiosity is sufficiently awakened to require the present effort. And here it is—my life—on paper, where all who run may read it, and from which all who do not like it may run as fast as they can; but in the chase of life none can run so fast as to outstrip the heart of kindness and affection which shall follow all men every-where so long as it beats.　　　　　　JAMES M. DALZELL.

CALDWELL, O., *Feb.* 14, 1886.

I.

My father, Robert Dalzell, of Huguenot descent, was born in County Down, Ireland, May 2, 1802; my mother in County Tyrone, May 9, 1799. Father left Ireland with his widowed mother in 1809, and removed to near Greenock, Scotland, where he lived until 1832, when he emigrated to Pittsburg, Penn. There he met and married my mother, Anne McCormick, and there, in 1838, on the 3d day of September, I was born. I say Pittsburg, but I mean Allegheny City, just across the river from the old Smoky City. My father had been a distiller in Scotland, and for several years in Pittsburg, but, convinced that liquor-making was wrong, he abandoned it and started a new and untried business to him— carpet weaving. I spent my early years in the loom shop winding bobbins and cutting carpet rags. Thus I began life in rags, as I am likely soon to end it.

In 1847 we left Pittsburg and settled on a farm near where I now live, in Ohio. In 1868 my father sold the farm and removed to Fayette Springs, Pa., but I remained here.

It is a most ungrateful and callous soul that does not turn reverently, and affectionately, and often to parents and schoolmasters—for one has called the early teacher "the father of the mind."

My father and mother were both cast in the same mold. I can not think of one without thinking of the other, so like were they in mental trait and habit, so harmonious in affection, aspiration, and hope. I never heard a jar between them in opinion or counsel. Both

Seceders, afterward members of the United Presbyterian Church, trained from childhood in the severe but logical discipline of the Calvinistic creed, their home was quiet, serene, and rainbowed over and lit up with a faith that no cloud of sorrow or poverty could dim or darken. The Westminster Confession of Faith, the Shorter Catechism, and Dr. Pressly's church paper and a Bible were our entire library.

The simple truths of Holy Scripture, the daily sacrifice at the family altar, reverence for all that is accounted holy and good, and aversion to all that is wrong or mean, were the atmosphere that I daily breathed from the dawn of my life until I crossed its sacred threshold in maturer years to pass out into an atmosphere not so full of airs from heaven as blasts from hell. I never saw a card or a dance, a novel or a fiddle, or heard an oath or a rude jest in that house.

Struggling with poverty, a plain, homely, honest pair, they toiled on to old age, turning neither to the right nor left, unaffected and unabated in their pious devotion. It was all one whether the world outside behaved itself well or ill, the smooth current of their simple lives ran on without a ripple or a murmur. I was taught not so much to talk as to think, and feel, and act. Action was the supreme ideal there—not of words, for these my parents knew but little. Their words were few and well chosen. I have sat in the awe of the solemn silence of our sitting-room for hours, while father quietly read the Bible in one corner of the room, and my mother read Rouse's version of the Psalms in the other, neither uttering a word, except now and then, at long intervals, pausing to slowly and reverently read some passage that

had thrilled them through and through with its portentous meaning.

Neither of them was educated beyond reading and
writing. Their lives had been spent in hard labor, and
even now the picture of my mother reeling or sewing
carpet rags in Allegheny City, forty years ago, rises up
to my memory like the vision of an angel, as I know she
is now.

They taught me my A B C's. I had no brother—
one sister only. There was no public school. At five
years of age I was started to school in an abandoned
store-room, north of the Diamond, in Allegheny City,
then taught by a lame Englishman, named William Turner. He kept a select school for a pittance. It was
our only school. With him I slowly learned to write
and figure a little—for my parents had long before
that taught me to read. I have no recollection of learning to spell and read, except by that sort of recollection
spoken of by Goethe—such a mixture of memory with
what my parents told me after, that I can not discrim-
inate recollection from tradition. Mr. Turner offered a
prize for the boy in our spelling class who should be
head the most times during the term. I won it. I remember with what pride I bounded into the loom shop—
father on the loom, mother at the spinning-wheel, both
pausing in their labor to look up and smile, the greater
prize after all, as I almost screamed with delight, " I've
got it!" It was a beautiful white card with my name
inscribed on it in copper-plate, as we called it then, and
this card fastened to a blue ribbon and suspended from
my neck.

No champion ever returned crowned from the Olympian games with greater pride, and no one ever received more generous and heartfelt applause than I did there in that dingy old loom shop. It was the turning point of my life. I had to maintain the reputation of being the best speller in the school, and I did ; and from that day to this I have never allowed myself to misspell a word.

One day—it was in 1845, on the 10th day of April— as I was returning home from school, the fire-bells suddenly began to ring, the engines were drawn out with ropes, and the whole town was in a state of alarm, as if it were the last day, and judgment coming on all. Pittsburg was on fire. I could see the smoke rising in dark volumes, hear the flames hiss and roar, and smell the fumes of the conflagration just across the river. I was terrified and ran home. My father was out with the old Washington engine all that day and night. It made an awful impression on my childish fancy and memory.

But, as distinctly as I remember the great fire, quite as vividly, but with pleasure, instead of pain, do I remember seeing General William Henry Harrison, in 1841, when I was scarcely three years old. He was on his way to Washington. It happened that, in passing over to Pittsburg to the carriage in which he rode, he stopped in front of our door. It was an open carriage drawn by four white horses with plumes. There sat the white-haired old hero, whom my father worshiped, for he was a' whig; and my father proudly held the boy up in his arms and gave him this his first lesson in hero worship. Not a railroad, not a lamp, not a telegraph, not a school-house in Allegheny City then. When I was about seven years old, along came the talk of the telegraph. I was

in the loom shop. Alderman Hayes, who often called in
to chat with father, was descanting on the telegraph.
He announced that it would soon be along in Pittsburg.
" Why," said he, " they can send news along a string
up on poles from Philadelphia here in less than no
time." " Less than no time," thought I; " that is pretty
quick." 1 have thought about it, and how they could
work such miracles with a string on poles, and I have
thought a good deal about it since, and understand it
now about as well as I did then, and so do you, if you
will confess it!

One day—it was the 1st day of April, 1844—our school
was dismissed, every factory and mill closed, and the old
schoolmaster took us little fellows down to the Mechanic
street bridge, on the Allegheny side of the river, to see
a miracle. All Pittsburg and Allegheny were there on
either bank of the Allegheny river. I had never seen
so many people. It had been announced that a man
would fly from the Mechanic street bridge to, and under,
and over the Federal street bridge and back at 1 o'clock.
It was in all the papers. We all thought then that
the newspapers could not lie, and some of the people
who were not present that day may still think so, but it
disenchanted me. I believe they can lie now, though
they seldom do.

Promptly at one o'clock, a man dressed in tights, but
with a great cloak over his shoulders like wings, suddenly appeared on the bridge. A hush fell on the
mighty concourse of people. In my childish credulity,
I thought the hour and the man had come. You could
have heard a pin drop. The simple-minded old Irish
and Scotch, of which the Pittsburg of that day was

composed, and their still more simple children, would
have believed any thing. Yes. any thing that Munchausen could have told them.   They all—ten or twenty
thousand men and women and children—with equal faith
expected now to see the apparition on the bridge spread
its wings and fly : and it did—but it *was a goose !*

Pittsburg had the latent element in it which, three de-
cades of years after, made its railway riots possible—a
curious community of people as you can find anywhere,
with all that is good wrapped up by strange contradictions with all that is evil. in the whimsical human nature
that fills those twin cities and a roar of rage like the
shout of an army went up along those crowded banks, as
a rush was made to kill the man who had duped two great
old babies of cities, as they really then were.   But the
mountebank escaped. and the audience dispersed, some
cursing and threatening vengeance, but the greater part
laughing at the way they had been sold.

Imagine the effect on my childish thoughts of the announcement of the war with Mexico.   The young men
around us were enlisting.   I could hear the fife and drum
day and night, and could see the recruiting office just
across the street.   It was my first glimpse of war, and,
like the serpent that it is, charmed me even while it terrified me.   What is there in human nature that makes
what is so repulsive and abhorrent as war, attractive to
the childish fancy?   It must be the dregs of that old
barbarism and brutality come down to us from that
brother who slew his own brother in cold blood, in the
beginning of time.

It is more than an intimation that the instinct of strife
and bloodshed is man's most natural, indeed his predom-

inating instinct. I saw the Irish Greens embark with Colonel Sam Black, who, nearly twenty years afterward, fell on one of the fields of the great civil war. I heard the children screaming, and saw the wives and mothers clinging to their husbands and sons, as they went on board of the steamer that was so soon to take them away forever. It was a sad sight—to a child, terrible.

Soon, however, my father bought a farm in Ohio, and in 1847 we bade adieu to old Pittsburg. got aboard the Mingo Chief, and floated off down the Ohio with all our wordly possessions. It took us ten days then, to reach our destination in Ohio. It takes less than ten hours now: I shall never forget that steamboat ride down the Ohio, and up the Muskingum to McConnelsville, Ohio, before the days of railroads and telegraphs—in the old, old days. Times were slower; men were slower; the very planets seemed to move slower than they do now. for did the days not seem longer? Travel was the slowest of all. Disembarking at the sleepy little country town of McConnelsville, my father found a couple of old road wagons, which started next morning over the hills to our new home, a log cabin in the woods. I remember that long April day's toiling through the mud. It was in 1847, and I was but eight years old—my education finished!

I saw the first log cabin that day I had ever seen, and no other human habitation did I see, except log cabins at long distances apart. in all that trip of twenty miles.

It was night when we reached our destination. We were soon installed in our new home—the log hut—a blazing fire on the hearth, and roaring up the stick chimney, which was almost the biggest, certainly the most conspicuous part of the dwelling.

It was a new life to me. The men, strong, robust, cheery and communicative; the women, even more so, plain of speech, frank of manners, and all anxious to help the new comers all they could. The men crowded in to chop our wood, and show father how to perform farm work, of which he had no knowledge or experience. The women came to show mother how to pick wool, pull and spin flax, cut and dry apples and peaches, and make soft soap. It was a new world to us all, that life in the cabin. The transition from the cozy brick house in the city to the log house in the deadening, surrounded by the primeval forest. Think of it! But we soon "got de hang of de barn," and the years rolled on with us much as they did with our neighbors. Still I look back to those days, and sigh when I think of the honest, true hearts, and the willing hands, that surrounded and helped us until we learned the ways of the farm. That genera- tion is long since in the grave, and is one of which this might well be proud. Inviting as the theme is, I must not pause to moralize. The reader can do that at his leisure: and contrasting the generous men and women of that day with the selfish ones of this, is a gloomy task which I freely delegate to any one who can endure it patiently, for I can not.

There were frolics of all sorts, quilting parties, husk- ings, dances, wood choppings, raisings, merrymakings of all sorts, in which the whole country-side joined; plenty of whisky in every house, and out on all such oc- casions; no drunkenness among the men, no scandals among the women, nothing to bring the blush of shame to any check. Locks and keys were unknown. Promissory notes were seldom required for any loan or other debt. For years and years I knew of but one or two arrests, and not half a dozen civil suits in all my childhood there. Men and women stood upon their honor, and it was a Rock of Gibraltar that required the sanction of no law to strengthen it. There was no caste. All were of one class. All were on visiting terms. No one ever went to the poor house from our settlement—not one, none to the penitentiary, none to jail, not one to the lunatic asylum. Money was out of the question. Exchanges were carried on mainly by barter. We traded our wheat and live stock mainly for sugar, coffee, whisky, and other necessaries. Nobody would help you raise a house, or clear a field, or roll logs, until you set out a gallon or two of whisky. I remember, once at a neighbor's I saw two big strong fellows walk into the harvest field with their scythes on their shoulders. The farmer told them he had no whisky. "Then," said they quietly, and as a matter of course, "we will cut no grass," and off they went. Had he told them he had no money, they would have laughed and cut his grass all the same, provided that he had whisky. The mercenary spirit had not yet appeared.

There were no misers, no usurers, consequently no contention or litigation, no pride and no envy, no idleness, drunkenness, or vagrancy. I have seen six months pass by in my father's house and not a cent of money in it, and he was about as well off as his neighbors. Even those who owned no land of their own were held to be on an equal footing with the best of the land-holders. You could see no difference between the boys and girls, the young men and women, of the landlord and the free-holder. They romped together, worked in the field to-gether, sat on the same bench in the church and at the log school-house, courted each other, intermarried, and in all things were on an equality. I grew up as other farmer boys did—and I need not repeat the old story, now so familiar to all.

In 1855, my good mother had got together $100, and sent me off to Pittsburg, where I entered Duff's College. There I learned somewhat of bookkeeping and penman-ship. In the spring I went to Ohio University, at Athens, walking all the way, and carrying all my effects in a handkerchief. I worked for my boarding. At that time the gorgeous young men of the South were there in large numbers, affluent, proud, and generous. I confess I then acquired a prejudice in favor of these noble youth that even three years in war with them never shook off. Poor as I was, almost ragged, working night and morn-ing for my boarding, I remember with gratitude their kindness and generosity to me.

The next year I taught my first school and earned the first money near Allentown, Vinton county, Ohio. It was the year of the Banks' contest for the Speakership and of the election of Buchanan. It was to me a long winter—so anxious was I to earn the money to go back to college. I got $65 for seventy-two days' teach-ing, and started home thrilled with joy and hope. I was in my eighteenth year. What joy realized in manhood can be compared with the dreams of youth indulged in such ecstatic moments! I had never in my life owned an overcoat, overshoes, or underclothing of any kind. I had no habit that cost me one cent. To-day I looked at my diary kept that winter, and it was a terrible winter, as you will remember, the winter of 1855–6, when the snow fell at Christmas and lay at great depth till April. I walked a mile, built my own fires, and never thought of an overcoat or a glove. My entire expenses for the winter were seventy-one cents. I was not different from the other young men of that day, who, like me, were pushing their own fortunes; but what would the young men of to-day think of seventy-one cents allowance in money for the entire winter? I thought more of Latin, Greek, and mathematics that winter than of money, and I do yet.

There was a slight thaw as I started home on the first of March. It rained a little, and the ice began to break in Sunday Creek. It was swollen and dangerous looking, but it lay between me and my mother and college, and I could not brook delay. I got off the horse that had been sent me to ride home (nearly 100 miles), started him into the stream, swollen like a river, and full of broken ice. By dint of hallooing and pelting him with pieces of ice, I managed to get the poor brute over. I then ran up the creek to see if I could find a place where the ice was whole that I might cross myself. At length I found one where the ice seemed unbroken to the other shore. With the impetuosity of youth, not minding the adage, "Look before you leap," I sprang down the bank onto the ice, and through it, and almost under it. I got a thorough wetting in that chilly air, but scrambled out, still on the same side. Approaching it a little more cannily, I found a better place, got safely over, got my horse, and rode home, wet and shivering with cold, for I had not a change of clothing in the world. Nor did I take cold by it.

In a few weeks I was back at the Ohio University, which I was soon forced to leave on account of fever and ague contracted there. I returned home sick and discouraged; spent a miserable summer, alternately burning and freezing, until at length in August youth and strength prevailed and threw off the disease, and I was myself again, but my money was all gone but ten dollars. The doctors had got the rest for doing what nature had kindly stepped in and was doing for nothing, as usual. Since that I have found that if the vigor of the constitution, pleasant and healthful surroundings, and a conformity to the simplest rules of living do not cure you, you need not call the doctor. Call the undertaker when this fails, but not the doctor!

For some years then I taught school of winters, worked with father on the farm in the spring, and attended college at Sharon, Ohio. It was a quiet, unpretentious school, but some of the best men and women I ever shall know here or hereafter were my classmates. The college seat was an inland village, forty miles from any railway, but to me as pleasant and beautiful in memory as Auburn was to the poet, Goldsmith. I remember the faculty: Rev. Randall Ross, president, and Rev. W. W. McMillan our only professor. Since leaving that little country college it has been my privilege to attend Washington College, Pennsylvania, and Columbia College at Washington City, four long years, and there enjoy the ample means of education afforded by those two colleges, yet I never in my life met the professor in any college who holds the place in my estimation which my heart and judgment ac-

cord now while my eyes are flowing with tears of gratitude to Randall Ross and William McMillan. In my affections they are without a rival among all my schoolmasters. With the modesty always linked with great persons, vast erudition and profound piety, if our schoolmasters, Ross and McMillan, did not make a deep and
lasting improvement in all the young men intrusted to
their care, no man ever could.

On the breaking out of the war, the president entered
the army as a private soldier, the other students mostly
following his example, and the professor removed to a
western farm, and that was the end of Sharon College.

In 1861, I entered Washington College as a Freshman
half advanced, and continued there till August, 1862,
when I enlisted as a private soldier in defense of the
American Union in Company H, One Hundred and Sixteenth Ohio Infantry. I had just entered the Junior
year, after a hard struggle of fitful and irregular at-
tendance at college from 1856 down to 1862. If my father
had had the means to pay my way, I should have graduated long before the war, but I had to manage that myself the best I could. Many a time, returning home from
the school or the plow, as the case might be, with my
air-castles all seemingly crushed by the rude hand of
circumstances, I would have given up in despair but
for the gentle voice of my mother, her sweet, sad
smile irradiating the darkest passages of my life, and
kindling a hope in the gloom of the future. She had
carried me, her only son, in her arms into Dr. Pressly's church, at Allegheny City, and at the baptismal
font dedicated my life to God. She desired me to be a
preacher in the Presbyterian Church, to which I had be-

longed since I was eighteen years of age. But for the
war I certainly would have been some sort of a preacher,
if for nothing else than to gratify her in whom my life
was bound up. She followed me on with her deep and
matchless love, until she had nearly reached her eightieth
year, and had dandled my little ones lovingly on her
knees, when her spirit took its flight, peacefully and still,
to the world that her faith had long beheld shining in
glory behind the stars. Her form rests under the shadows of the Alleghenies—a sacred spot to me. If I had
no other incentive to a pure and blameless life, and a
faith that knows no hesitancy or fear, it would be that when
life's fitful fever is over I may meet her with my son,
James Monroe, over the river under the shadow of the
tree of life.

II.

Transferred in a day from the peaceful shades of class-
ical learning to the camp of war, from the companionship
of innocent, aspiring, hopeful young spirits, to that of
soldiers, restless and noisy, eager to march to the front,
and try the fate of battle, I found myself passing my
first night in camp at Marietta, O., August 22, 1862. It
was Sunday night. The profane oath, the obscene jest,
the questionable story, rang round the camp, and all was
so unusual that, stretched on the hard boards of my
quarters, I could not sleep. As I looked out into the
night, and up at the stars, and in fancy still on toward
the future, then vailed no less for my country than for
me in gloom, a sadness came over me that I could not
then understand, and now have not the power to describe.
And was this the end of all that struggle to obtain an

education which a hard destiny had seemed to have denied me? What was to be my fate, and what was to be
my future? And these noble young men around me,
what was to become of them? Ah, was it not kind in
God to leave the answers to be unfolded in his own good
time? If, as the thunder follows the electric flash, response had come in a moment then to all my question-
ings of the future, and I could have foreseen the fate of
us all, the young, brave, and patriotic spirits about me
that night, flesh and heart must have fainted and failed,
and reason itself deserted its throne forever. "God is
his own interpreter," and man must wait until his plans
are unfolded.

I was destined to live to see one after another, class-
mate, room-mate, friend, neighbor, old acquaintances
and new, descend into the dark valley of death one after
another—some on the red fields of war, and some in the
loathsome hospital, some in camp, some by the roadside
—but to me that night no voice spoke out of the future
to reveal it.

Whether fortunately or unfortunately to me, I can not
yet determine, two things seemed to be in my favor from
the outset of my military life. First, I was conceded to
be the best penman and accountant in our company.
Second, when I was a schoolmaster, my present captain—
as gallant a soldier as ever drew a sword—W. B. Teters,
now at Boulder, Colorado, had been a student in my
school years before, and we were intimate friends. As
I was not as robust and strong as most of the other
farmer lads in the company. Teters kept me at his quarters to do his writing, keep his accounts, and make out

his reports, until the following May, when I was promoted to sergeant-major.

I have no disposition or desire to repeat what has so often been better written than I can write it. I shall pass by the winter of 1862–3, when we entered West Virginia, marched to Clarksburg, across to Buchanan, Beverly, the Cheat Mountain region, returned to the Baltimore road, and joining Mulligan at New Creek, made a forced march to Moorefield, and received our first baptism of battle. It was a complete victory. From there we went to Romney, and in the spring to Winchester. About two months after that, we had a three days' fight with Ewell's forces, and were completely routed and defeated, and forced to find safety—all of us who could—in the mountains. We brought up, after a long chase and a hard march, without provisions for three days, at Hancock, and went from there to Bloody Run. Though at hand and in sight of the field, we never fired a gun at Gettysburg, the Waterloo of the war.

That winter we spent in winter quarters near Antietam. Next spring we took the field with Siegel, and were badly drubbed at New Market, and forced to retreat to Cedar Creek. Hunter next took command, and the long retreat from Lynchburg followed. Then came Sheridan, and no more retreats.

I had been disabled, and was no longer fit for field duty, when Colonel Washburn, my gallant commander—who was ever a father to me—was shot through the head in the fall of 1864, and recovering as if by a miracle, ordered me to Wheeling with him, where he assumed command of that important post. He and I remained there until the war was over.

3

I had seen over two years of hard service at the front,
with which I could fill a book, but the last year of my
enlistment I was destined to serve in the inglorious capacity of a military clerk, until May 26, 1865, when I
was discharged, and once more a citizen.

Where was Bier, the head man at my college in 1862?
Where McCollum, who always sat beside me in the class-
room? Where McIntosh, with whom I used to spend
the long winter evenings at home when we taught ad-
joining schools? Where a hundred other far better men
than you or I? For the best men of the North and
South, remember, died in that war, almost to a man.
Where? Died on the field of battle, starved in the
prison pens of the South, dying at home or in hospitals
of disease. Alas! All, all gone. Not one of my old
chums survived, not one. Others of my comrades, less
dear to me, good men and true as they are, remain, but
who shall ever fill the vacant chairs of those brilliant and
promising young men who went with me to the war?

III.

In the war I had met most of the men who were destined to be the central figures of the future in this country—all officers, no privates. Then, as well as now, i
knew that the American people despise private soldiers.
They have never elevated one to any office and never
will. The fact that a man was a private soldier is taken
and held as final and conclusive evidence that he is a
worthless, good-for-nothing. The most and best he can
do is to keep it from being known—as if he were an escaped convict. The reasoning is this: a private soldier

is a worthless man, a coarse, brutal, vicious man; you
were a private soldier; *ergo*, you are coarse, brutal, and
vicious. The logic is bad, I grant you, but it is universally accepted as good. I saw this before I was in the
army a month. I have never had any reason to change
my opinion and never will. If I had a score of sons, I
should warn them against entering the ranks of the
army as private soldiers. Thanks, they get none; pay,
little; bounty and pension, grudgingly, and as if thrown
to beggars; and the people who stayed at home and
made money out of their blood despise them and their
children's children to the third and fourth generations.
As well kick against fate. It is destiny. It can not be
helped. There is but one escape from the odium of
being a private, and that is death, with the certain pros-
pect that the grave itself will be desecrated with sneers.
This discrimination invades every walk of life. Nothing
can shield the private soldier from this storm of con-
tumely and scorn. Is he a lawyer? It will keep away
clients. Is he a doctor? It will keep away patients.
Is he a preacher? It will divide his flock and empty his
pews. Is he a mechanic or laborer? He can never rise
above it, and will be kept in poverty and held in contempt all his days. So, of all other professions and call-
ings in which he may engage—Nemesis follows him still.
He can not escape it. Ask any private soldier what his
experience has been for the past twenty-five years, and
he will corroborate every statement I make, and illus-
trate it by a hundred doleful examples.

Out of this sprang the *nom de plume*, Private Dalzell.
Seeing no escape from the reproach that must pursue me

for being a private, and not depraved enough to try to lie
out of it, I boldly took the bull by the horns, announced
the odious rank to the world, and asked them then and ask
them now, what are you going to do about it? To be
sure, too many of our poor fellows, by their profanity,
drunkenness, and other vices, gross and notorious, give
some excuse to the people for lumping us all together as
a bad set, yet I must say that as good men, as good
fathers, brothers, husbands, neighbors, and Christian
gentlemen as walk this earth were only privates.

It ought not to be so, but it is so; and fool indeed is
that private soldier who for one moment believes any
professions or promises to the contrary made by any
clique or class of politicians, in any party, church, or
society in the United States.

The die is cast. The evening draws nigh. Death is
at hand. By patience in well-doing, by faith in Jesus
Christ, you and I may earn the approval of Heaven and
admission to its portals; but, wherever it is known you
were a private, expect the confidence and esteem of
men, the *entreé* of good society—*never.*

IV.

It was reflections like these with which the last doleful chapter closed that caused me to assume the *nom de
plume* of Private Dalzell, a quarter of a century ago, and
endure it ever since. It was the leap of Horatius into
the gulf; the acceptance of the inevitable; my bow to
destiny. But I should not advise any one else to do so,
for I always envied the good fortune of Private Miles
O'Reilly, who died soon after assuming it.

The war was over. What was I to do now to earn a living, was the question that troubled me most. The great question of the reconstruction of the dismembered Union was undergoing public discussion, but the reconstruction of my finances and the shaping of my future was a question that pressed more closely upon me, and demanded immediate solution. Like half a million other young men, the war had torn me up, turned me inside out, and left me penniless, with broken health, gloomy forebodings, and without occupation. I sat down by my mother, and we talked it all over. Her faith in her son and his future had been undimmed by all the clouds of war, and she encouraged me to start out and begin again. I had three half dollars in silver—all the money I had on the earth; half a dollar a year for my military service to the Great Republic—and these I punched and strung together with a wire. They are here in my desk now. I often show them to my children as an object lesson in patriotism and a warning to keep out of the ranks of an army. I had taught school. I had written for the papers before the war and during the war. I have seen my war letters bound up in Frank Moore's Rebellion Record, copied from the Philadelphia Press, of June, 1863, and written while *en route* for Gettysburg. I thought this all over, but, as I had never received one cent of pay for my irregular and spasmodic contributions to the press, I saw no encouragement there. As Coleridge said of poetry, so I said of newspaper writing, from 1856, when I commenced, down to 1865, it had been to me "its own exceeding great reward" —nothing more.

In an old sugar-tree camp, on my father's farm, on

February, 1856, I had sat down on a log and read aloud
to my father, by the blazing fire and the boiling kettles
of syrup, my first published contribution to the newspaper press, printed in a local paper here in Noble
county, Ohio. From that time on my leisure moments
had been employed on this most unremunerative toil.
Poetry, sketches, letters, and tidbits of all sorts were
continually appearing over my name in all the leading
daily papers of the United States, for which in ten years
I had not asked or received one cent. But that would
not do. I must find some sort of work that I could get
an honest dollar out of to meet my crying needs. So I
taught a country school that winter, at $30 a month,
and in the spring had $120 of clear money, for my fa-
ther boarded me, and necessity had taught enforced
economy.

My old major was elected county clerk in 1865, and
entered upon his new office in the spring of 1866, making me his deputy at $2 a day, a princely income to me,
and I took up my abode with him in Caldwell, Ohio,
where I now reside.

I remained with him until the August following, when
my friend, Hon. John A. Bingham, our representative in
Congress, procured my appointment to a clerkship in the
Customs Bureau, Treasury, Washington City.

My father then lived on the old farm. On receiving
my designation to the clerkship I saw the avenue of escape from the drudgery of the life I was leading in the
little village, and the future seemed once more lit
up with the radiance and beauty which I had long
supposed to be eclipsed forever. I mounted my major's
horse, the same that he had rode at Cedar Creek and at

Lee's surrender, and, in such heroic companionship, in
the cool of the morning, dashed off up the road and over
the hills to bid my father and mother good-by. They lived
eight miles from Caldwell. I had to pass through the
little village of Sharon. There resided two noble
girls whom I had known before the war, the Misses
Aikin; and, turning my horse off the road, up a lane to
the house where they lived, I was at the door in a minute. They met me like sisters, sang the songs of the
war to me, chatted pleasantly, and, wishing me Godspeed, I remounted my horse, rode down the lane, out
into the main road, and off for home once more. It was
a pleasant incident of my life, and one that rests in
my memory like a lovely picture yet. And there is reason for it. Just before I reached the main road, I had
to cross a bright stream of crystal water that ran across
it. As I did so, I heard the steady tramp of a horse's
hoofs on the road just ahead of me, and, turning my
eyes in that direction, saw the closely vailed figure of
a young girl on the horse. As my horse stopped to
drink, the apparition passed the end of the lane, and on
west, the road I had to travel. Something of the impudence and curiosity that I had picked up in the war
made me resolve to see who the strange young lady
was, and, if possible, make her acquaintance and flirt
with her a little to pass away the time. I reined up my
old hero, touched him slightly with the spur, and he
soon carried me out into the highway, west along the
road, up to, and past the lady on horseback. As I
passed in a gallop I lifted my hat and said, "Good
morning." No reply came. My effrontery had over-
shot the mark—met its just rebuke.

She was so closely vailed I could not see her face, but there was such a mystery surrounding her that my determination was renewed, at all hazards, to form or force her acquaintance. And this is how I succeeded, and it may serve as a hint to all bashful young men in the future who may be like situated. Two or three hundred yards further on a little creek crossed the road. There I stopped just a few rods in advance of the mysterious equestrienne. My horse was restive, and the old fellow didn't like the foolishness of standing there in the water when his thirst had been so lately fully quenched at the other stream. He seemed to divine my stratagem, and in his playfulness tried to defeat it. But I held him to it until the lady rode up beside me, and her horse eagerly stopped to drink. The situation was awkward. Country-girl, as she must be, she could not but see the game I was playing, for if I had succeeded in concealing it myself the major's horse was cavorting the secret out in his tramping and splashing and eagerness to get away. Not a moment was to be lost. "How far are you going this way?" I ventured to ask, trying in vain to peer through the thick vail which hid her features from me. "Eighteen miles," she quietly answered, in a voice of such low, sweet melody as I had never heard before. " I am going six miles in the same direction," I replied, and, without giving her a chance to repulse me, impudently rode beside her as her horse raised his head and rode up out of the water. I was fascinated by the voice, and I had at least seen her hand and her form, both of the most exquisite beauty.

The tone of that voice had captivated me, and thrown me out of my senses. If I had had the world at that moment I would have freely thrown it away to see that face. I had set out to flirt with her in a kind of boyish, devilish way, but that voice had knocked all such nonsense out of me. I was dazed, bewildered, thrilled through and through with an emotion I had never felt before. I was madly in love with the strange, quiet little horsewoman, whom I had never seen, and whom I was destined to chat with for an hour that day as we rode along, and whose face I was not to see for a year to come. But all things come to an end, and so did that morning's ride.

When I bade her good-by at my mother's door, and she rode away through the green woods west, I had no knowledge of her name or residence, and had not obtained any clue to either, though by every device of which I was possessed I had endeavored to discover it. Every question was so delicately parried as to increase my curiosity and deepen the mystery into which she had taken refuge. She rode away from me, and had left me nothing but the music of her voice.

By a chance I met a good woman, near my father's house, who told me that the young lady had been visiting a sister near Sharon, and that she lived near Des Moines, in the State of Iowa. She was probably crossing the country to see another sister who resided at Rix's Mills, Ohio. Her name was Hettie M. Kelley.

I felt the hopelessness of ever seeing her again, and tried to banish her from my thoughts, but, do what I might, her form floated before me and the music of her voice thrilled me still. I had ventured into the camp of the enemy and was made captive myself without an effort on her part.

But time was pressing. I must leave for the city of Magnificent Distances next morning, and there was no time to indulge day-dreams of love. I put it aside as a strange, inexplicable episode of my life, bade father, mother, and sister good-by, returned to Caldwell, and next morning left for Washington City with barely enough money to take me there. Arriving there, I stopped at the Washington House, where Ben Wade, Judge Bingham, Henry Wilson, and other celebrities were then boarding.

It was a new world to me. I had met all the men of the war who have now or had then any name in history, and formed an intimate acquaintance with General Sherman, General Logan, General Leggett, General Banks, and others almost equally distinguished, but of the politicians or statesmen I knew as little as they did of me—nothing.

It was a new life to me now to live in their presence. I was dazzled with the splendors of the public buildings, parks, statues, and all the profuse and bewildering beauties of art at the Capitol. But, charming as these were, I realized what Emerson said, that what delighted me most was the *men*—Sumner, Stevens, Wade, Chandler, Bingham, Colfax, Wilson, Chase, Stanton, Raymond, and all the celebrated statesmen of the century; the greatest men that time ever brought on the stage of action.

Andy Johnson was President. He had not swung the circle yet. All the capital was then engaged in the worship of military achievement. Grant moved about like a god, worshiped by all. When Custer rode down the avenue every one ran to the door to see him pass. Statesmen vied with each other to see who could do the most or say the most for the soldier. But I was not there a day until I saw that all this worship was meant for the generals, and by no means for the privates. I happened to look like General Custer. Arriving late in the evening, an entire stranger, I noticed all the idlers about the hotel office staring at me. As I did not register, one or two belated musicians came in pretty well befuddled, with their big brass instruments under their arms. "They stared at me a moment, then stepped aside and spoke together in a drunken whisper, which is not far removed from a sober conversational tone of ordinary pitch. "S'r nade 'im; s'r nade 'im, hic, at's it!" I heard one of them mumble, and the other fellow nodded assent profusely, and they started off down stairs.

The gentlemanly clerk, who had noticed the affair, with a smile, stepped up to me, and, with the politest bow in the world, handed me a pen, and asked me to register. He knew Custer well enough, of course. I wrote my name.

"See here," he said, with a smile that only a hotel clerk with a bold heart need ever try to copy, "those fellows think you are General Custer, and are going to serenade you."

I laughed outright; and if I had not been three years in the army, it would have gone hard with me, but that I had added a blush. Just then toot, toot went the horns below, on the pavement, and the confused noise of a dozen of oxfollicated youngsters, all talking at once. Toot, toot, preparing to play, the hotel clerk, alarmed at what might happen, rushed from me, down the steps, and while I stood back in the shadow of the stairway, I heard the following not very flattering colloquy:

Clerk.—" What the —— are you fellows at, any how ? "

One of the band.—" Hic ! goin' to blow up ole, hic ! Custer—'s all right."

Clerk.—Custer, —— the ——. That fellow is not Custer. It is only Private Dalzell."

I heard a few oaths muttered out in a maudlin fashion, and the rattling of instruments and drums, as they staggered together and off down the avenue.

The clerk came back wreathed in the smiles out of which, to say nothing of his big ring and false diamond breastpin, he made his salary, and with the ready wit and complete absence of a conscience characteristic of his class, explained that the band was about to serenade Colfax, but he had explained to them that he was not in, and they had gone off. I seemed not to notice the lie, and went to bed, thinking of the difference between my rank and Custer's. Custer was a glorious fellow, and I had seen his yellow locks flying on the field of battle more than once, and now was not displeased to have been mistaken for him.

Nevertheless, I had not failed to observe the discrimination of rank in Washington in this my initial lesson in that wonderful heterogeneous society—a lesson that was afterward repeated to me in a thousand ways. I passed the examination and was installed as clerk in the Treasury Department. My chief was Nathan Sargent, known to our grandfathers by his newspaper *nom de plume* of Oliver Oldschool. He was thin and cadaverous, mettlesome and nervy, a typical officeholder, indeed. Always in office till he died, often holding two offices at a time; judge of the Levy Court, whatever that was, for it was like Ben Butler's cript, no one knew, and Commissioner of the Customs as well, the blessed old soul was as happy as a clam at high tide, with his two salaries drawn at once. The drudgery of the desk there for two years took but little of my time or attention, and I managed to draw my $120 a month regularly, until, at last, disgusted with the monotony, and helplessness, and hopelessness of an existence a little less endurable than a private soldier's, I resigned it, in September, 1868, and left the city, and came back to Ohio.

I could write a book on what I saw of Washington life. But, as I said of army life, it has been written threadbare, and the subject is repulsive to me. My personal friends, Hayes and Garfield, respectively, while President, tendered me a clerkship there at $2,000 a year, but I declined both, with thanks. Reduced to the alternative of taking a clerkship again, or taking a mattock and a spade in the fields, I should not hesitate to embrace the latter as a means of support.

Washington said no man worth the powder and lead to kill him would be a soldier in time of peace. That is my estimate of a clerkship there. The most wretched, dissatisfied, depraved men I ever met outside of military life, I met in the corridors of the departments in Washington. Always poor, often drunk, always pressed for money, in debt, without hope, without a future, generally they were the most wretched set I ever knew. I never hated a man bad enough since to desire to see him become a Washington clerk.

Of course, there were exceptions, but they were few. Andy Johnson was President. I saw him and his

drunken set of official rowdies start to swing the circle
in 1866, and saw them return drunker still.   I know it
is the fashion to slur it all over, and lie about it, but I
know a drunken man when I see him, and a drunker set
I never clapped eyes on.   Whisky since sent most of
them to their graves.

I attended the impeachment trial, and reported it for
a provincial paper, and received no pay.   I did the same
afterward at the trials of John H. Surratt and Guiteau.
Somehow I always got admission to these great state
trials—the only ones of note since the trial of Burr—
even when thousands of other men were denied admission.

At night I attended Columbia Law School, graduated,
and in the summer of 1868 was admitted to the bar.   I
had seen all the great men of the Nation—for they all
get to Washington, either to Congress, or to see it, and
say they have been in Washington.   I published my
first book there, "The Life of John Gray, the Last Soldier of the Revolution."   It is in all the libraries of the
world, but never brought me a cent.   Its only effect was
to deplete my purse of all my savings, and procure the
passage of a bill which gave the old hero $500 a year
his last two years, when he died, and with him the last
man of the army of Washington.

In the final audit of affairs, I hope to find this to have
been the best act of my life, and now believe it was.

But, as the spinners of yarns say, I am a little ahead
of my story.   In the summer of 1867 I got a leave of
absence, went home, managed to find that vailed lady on
horseback, and we were married.   She returned with me
to Washington, and we kept house there a year, as happy

as happy could be. She still survives, and the music of
her voice, with the rhythm of her footstep, is to me still
the divinest harmony of this life, and the sweetest promise of a life beyond. In sunshine and shadow, buoyant
with hope, crushed with sorrow, standing by me at the
cradle or at the open grave of our child, in prosperity
and adversity, ever the same loving faithful wife—but for
her, life would be one long hopeless agony to me. In all
the dark labyrinths, hers is the only hand of affection
left to lead me on to the light, and hold me back from
stumbling into the gulf of despair.

Once and long I loved the wine cup, drained it to the
dregs, and when there seemed nothing left but utter ruin
for me, after the world had turned its back on me, with
our children in one hand, with the other she gently took
hold of mine, and led me up and out of the darkness,
until again my feet were firmly planted on the Rock
Christ Jesus.

V.

It was a chill December evening—December, 1868—
my wife, infant daughter, and myself, arrived at the little
inn at Caldwell, Ohio. Fifteen hundred dollars was all
the money we had in the world, and that was hers. We
immediately bought a house—the house we yet live in.
It took all our money to pay for it, and we had a hard
winter. I had no practice yet at the bar. I kept writing
schools of nights in the country, and so earned a few
dollars. We did not make ten dollars a month, but we
managed to get along. An economical wife can make a
little go a long way.

The next fall (1869) I was elected prosecuting attorney of my county, and from that on we had no more trouble, financially at least, for many years, until I entered into politics.

I determined, during the two years for which I was elected, to close every liquor shop in my county, and after a hard struggle I succeeded; but it cost me a second term, for the liquor men banded together, and spent money lavishly to defeat me in 1871, and they succeeded. I had now to depend on the practice of law alone, and applied myself closely to it.

I pause a moment, here, to relate the pleasantest incident in all my career as a lawyer these twenty years. I was called to Washington county to defend an old schoolmate of mine, Dr. Devine, in a case brought against him by a carpenter who had built his house. It involved all my old friend, Dr. Devine, had in the world. It was for less than $300, yet a judgment would ruin him, and turn him out on the streets with his devoted wife and eight small children. I stayed all night with Devine, and we never slept a wink—talked all night over his case. The next day we tried it before a jury in a justice's court in the woods. All the merits were on my side, and the trial was a bitter and protracted one. I was worked up to the highest pitch, and won the case. The bystanders gave me three cheers, and resolved to build a town there, which they have since done, and it is called Dalzell to this day—one of the handsomest villages in Ohio.

Forming a partnership with Judge Knowles, of Marietta, my practice grew, and was soon worth $3,000 a year. I saved something, purchased a farm, and had nearly $4,000 in money, and owed no man in the world a dollar. And so life ran on smoothly and prosperously for four golden years—the flower of my life—until, in an evil hour, in the summer of 1875, I foolishly accepted a nomination to the legislature, was elected, and there ended my prosperity. After the election in October my name was in all the papers, congratulations poured in on me from every quarter, and I was invited to take the stump in Pennsylvania, which I did, at a great waste of time and money. I thought nothing of it then. It was only when, years after, I looked into an empty flour-barrel and hungry children's faces, and felt in my empty pockets, that I fully apprehended my folly. Four years I now spent in the maelstrom of politics, whirled and tossed about at the caprice of fortune, without any power to control it. I look back on it with pain. If a man can make a large figure like Blaine, Garfield, or Sumner, in politics, let him pursue that profession till he dies. He can work out his destiny there better than elsewhere. But for mediocrity, I know of no calling that offers a more certain ending in disappointment, remorse, poverty, and despair, than American politics. It is a grand game, and none but grand men need try to play it. Let men of moderate abilities like myself keep out of it, if they would escape the chagrin and mortification of failure, accentuated with the pangs of poverty.

Four years in the House of Representatives, though I was a member of the Judiciary Committee all the time, and Chairman of the Committee on Military Affairs, on the stump every fall, not only in Ohio, but in Massachusetts, Indiana, and Pennsylvania, and in the councils of the leaders of the Republican party, its Presidents, Senators, and Representatives in Congress,

4

on terms as familiar as I was with comrades in the army, yet all this was but a poor compensation for the loss of my law practice, my farm, and my money.

Hayes was governor. I admired him then and I admire him yet. I determined he should be the next President, and so wrote him in the fall of 1875. His reply I printed in all the newspapers in the United States, for at that time I had easy access to all of them. This started the ball rolling that finally landed him in the White House next year. I was one of nine members who were on his special train on that perilous journey to Washington, and there, amid the cries of the mob, I saw my prophecy and hope fulfilled on the 5th of March, 1877, and I returned to the legislature determined that Garfield should succeed him. Garfield and I had often stumped together, and I so admired him that I began to write him up for the Presidency. As in the case of Hayes, the wise-acres made merry over it, but I kept right on. There is nothing so advances the prospects of a politician as to keep his name constantly connected with some great office. At that time, besides having access to all the dailies as a contributor, I had the free use of the telegraph. I kept prophesying that Garfield would be President, until at length in 1880 I saw the prophecy fulfilled.

Garfield and Hayes have often referred to all these matters in the presence of leading statesmen, and I have of their letters bundles that will confirm it.

By the way, at sixteen, I began to write to prominent men, and have kept it up ever since. You can not name a statesman of the past quarter of a century who has not written to me, and whose letters I have not here in my desk. Their publication by my children, when the writers and I are dead, and their publication will wrong no man, will make plain many things that now seem very dark to the uninitiated.

General Sherman's letter to me, in 1875, when I was exploiting Hayes for the Presidency, was published at the time in America and Europe, and produced a profound sensation. It virtually made Hayes President, for before that the papers would not notice him at all as a Presidential possibility.

General Hayes' letter to me on the same subject was extensively published, and Howard copied it into the campaign life of Hayes in the year after.

General Garfield's letter before his nomination, the one written by him to me, also, the evening after his nomination, and the one inclosing his photograph the night before he was shot obtained an extensive publication at the time they were written. But the great bulk of my letters from celebrities have never seen the light. Charles Sumner, Henry Wilson, Horace Greeley, Samuel Bowles, Governor Morton, and Zachariah Chandler, wrote me almost from their death-beds, as did also General Grant. They are especially valuable to me. Longfellow, Bryant, and Holland wrote to me up to nearly their last days. I have some of the last utterances of the greatest men that ever trod the planet. They will fill a large volume.

There is no way to get at the interior secret and mystery of events but in this way, early adopted by me, and pursued without cessation now for twenty-five years and more. These were not the days of senseless scrawls or typewritten letters from nobodies who had mistaken their calling.

One of the first signs of decay which I observed in our statesmanship was the substitution of the type-writer and the clerk for the good old hand-written method universally employed by our men of note. A man who can not muster the courage to write a letter, and boldly sign it with his own hand, but tries to shield his imaginary rising greatness behind a typewriter, never was President or any thing great, nor in the nature of things can be. Nothing reveals character like an auto-graph letter, and the celebrated man whose greatness is not purchased with money, and is not the caprice of ac-cident, from Cicero to Sumner, always wrote his own let-ters with his own hand, and so gave them a value beyond that of gold

The paper that such a hand touches is transmuted into a possession forever, to be treasured and prized like the gifts of a king, while the wretched scrawls of clerks and the idiotic splutter and splash of machines have no more intrinsic value than rags, and my uniform custom has been to burn them the moment I received them, and that for two reasons :

First. It was conclusive evidence that the writer was nobody, and, like all nobodies accidentally in power, anxious to conceal his nonentity.

Second. Because I never wanted to correspond with any man but on equal terms, and I therefore abruptly discontinued all correspondence with a self-confessed fool.

23° Aug 1880

Dear Sir:

The Soldier's Reunion at
Columbus on the 10th 11th and 12th
of this month impressed me as one
of the most enjoyable and notable
gatherings of veterans of the war
that I have ever attended Perhaps
it was taking it all in all, the
most satisfactory affair of the kind
that has yet been held   Its

leading features were the great number
of old soldiers who were present
the encampment in tents for several
days, the interest taken in it by

the Citizens of Columbus and their from topal and abundant decorations of the Street, dwellings flowers of business &c &c. the procession of veteran Soldiers with their old flags tattered and torn by shot and battle, and the large and Enthusiastic meetings of the veterans, Soldiers especially. The deeply affecting and interesting meeting of the Survivors of the Rebel Prisons

I think this was the Seventh, of the general Reunions of the Prisoners Soldiers of Ohio. The first I remember to have heard of was called, as I now recollect by Presidt Dalzell and was held at Coldwater

Worcester County. The book of Poor Reviews which I attended was at Worcester in 1877. General Diaries of Massachusetts and San. Council of Massachusetts with many other well known Charities. they were Indians. I think think there is no doubt of the humanity of these institutions, and think the am—Annual meetings of the Ohio Society of the Union will continue to grow in Cleveland as heretofore.

Very truly yours,
Rutherford B. Hayes

VI.

I had observed that from most of the army societies the privates were left out, as if they were no part of the army which suppressed the Rebellion. So, in 1873, I determined to call a soldiers' reunion, to be held at Caldwell, Ohio, September 16, 17, 1874; and it was held here then, with 25,000 people present, and General Sherman and staff, in full uniform, on the platform. It was an immense success. The Associated Press spread its proceedings before the whole world every morning. It at once became National, and known and read of all men. Sectional strife was never more heated and bitter than then. The bloody shirt was waving in all its terror, North and South. It was the only stock in trade of both parties. In the name of the Lost Cause the South was kept solid. By the same sign, a solid North confronted it with a fierceness little less intense than that which had characterized the war.

I determined to try to see what could be done to soften the asperities growing out of this ugly state of feeling, and so, in issuing the call for the National Reunion of 1875, at Caldwell, I added a strong appeal to the men of the Blue and Gray to meet there on a platform of friendly and patriotic equality.

At the roll-call in September, in the umbrageous forest which I had rented for the purpose, twenty-eight states responded, but three men in the Gray—one of these, General Cockrell, now the distinguished senator from Missouri.

The press commented variously on all this. Not a

little ridicule was aimed at me by the clever gentlemen
of the extreme partisan daily press, but, with the wiser
and more patriotic editors of the leading daily papers,
my novel experiment met with unbounded praise, and my
idea was a success.

A third reunion, of tremendous proportions, at Caldwell, in 1876, crowned my work with success, General
Kilpatrick himself making response to my address,
and giving my idea unqualified approval. So my reunion was National, and the idea which I had launched
floated on over the Republic under the smile of popular
indorsement. I was president of all these reunions.
I paid nearly all the expenses, and it nearly ruined me
financially. But I was young and ardent then, and
stopped at nothing to make it go. The newspapers were
very generous to me then, and gave me the free use of
their columns to explain my project and purpose. Reunions in imitation of mine sprang up every-where after
that, and now there is one at every cross-roads every
fall.

The first year I held my reunion in the woods near
the little village where I live. Over twenty states were
represented; and, while the crowd was largely made up
of privates, General Sherman, and some of the leading
men of the Nation, were present, and spoke. The proceedings would fill volumes.

I have been at scores of reunions since these, which
sprang out of this rural beginning, and no one rejoices
more than I at the growth of the idea which I had the
honor to originate and plant in American soil, even if
it did cost me years of hard labor and all my little fortune. And it would be ungenerous of me to forget that

Congress passed bills to help me carry out my programme; and the War Department, under General Grant, freely gave me guns, ammunition, and other materials, without which I should have failed. The Legislature of Ohio did the same thing. The two men who were so soon to be President—Hayes and Garfield—honored it with their presence, and were my guests. Not a man of any note, in war or peace, then living, but what sent me a generous Godspeed, and the letters containing these messages of good will and encouragement I have laid away with my other epistolary treasures, and they will be the best if not the only inheritance that I shall leave my children.

In 1877 and 1878 we removed the reunion to the city of Marietta, and President Hayes and cabinet were present in the former year.

In 1879 it was located at Cambridge, and was one of surpassing interest, both in enthusiasm and numbers. It had no rival on the continent. Annually the greatest statesmen in both sections vied with each other as to who should speak the loudest in its praise. Congress annually paid it the compliment of yielding it the approval of both Houses by the passage of bills in its favor, and the newspaper press indorsed it with great fervor. And then I dropped it, after six years of untiring and unceasing labor, a labor of love, out of which I never received a penny, and never shall, though it cost me thousands of dollars and the flower of my life. My object was attained. The rank and file, the poor, nameless private soldiers, had commanded public attention and asserted their individuality. The Nation had applauded the effort to compel the public to respect the rights of the

rank and file, and at the same time recognize the fact
that sectional hatred no longer existed between the men
who did the fighting North and South. My idea had
won its way to popular favor, and there I dropped it,
knowing well then, what all know now, ten years later,
that the little leaven of patriotism and peace which my
hand had put in the first call for the first reunion, away
back in 1873, was destined, ere long, to leaven the whole
mass of our politics, and rebuke and put down forever
the petty cry of placemen who kept fanning the dying
embers of war in order that they might boil their little
pots it its blaze!

VII.

During these reunion years I had my duties in the
legislature to perform every winter, several weeks every
autumn I was on the stump for the Republican party,
and I had my full share of practice at the bar. I suppose from 1874 to 1882 I made a thousand speeches,
such as they were, and scores of them were eagerly
sought and printed in the papers. I never had any great
opinion of them myself, but, such as they are, they are
to be republished yet ere long.

I saw my delegation, elected by an honest people, melt
away under the talismanic touch of money freely given
as bribes. I saw no private soldier ever could be elected
to Congress. I saw no poor man had any business in
politics. I saw that bribery was the power behind the
throne, greater than the throne itself, and I then and
there, growing old and poor and worn out in the service
of my country, abandoned politics forever.

In 1878, I was freely offered the nomination for Con-

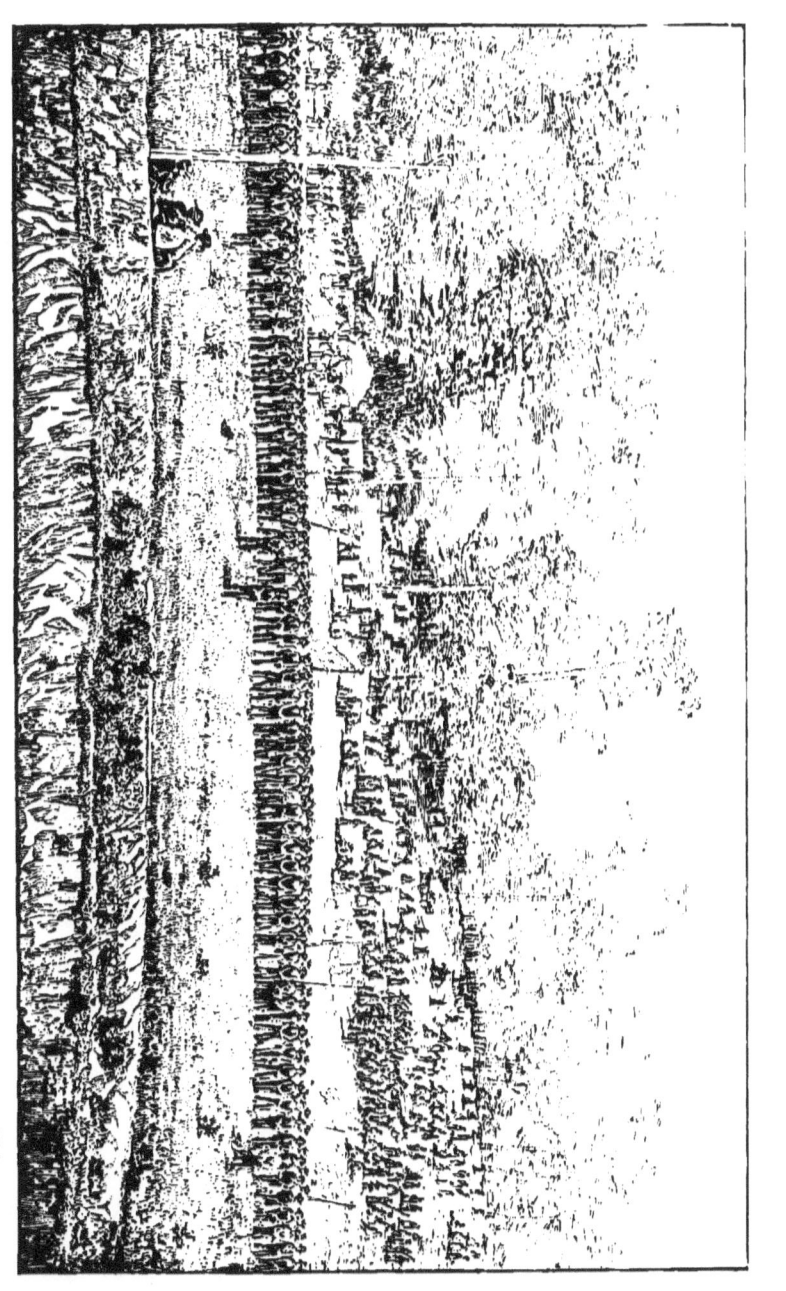

FIRST NATIONAL SOLDIERS' REUNION, CALDWELL, O., SEPT. 15, 16, 1874.
J. M. Dalzell, Chairman. Gen. W. T. Sherman and staff present. 28 states represented, with their old battle flags. The first and the model of all reunions since held.

gress, as I had been once ten years before, but I declined it, because I thought Colonel Van Vorhes, our then Congressman, had a prior claim on the honor—for that is all it was in a Democratic district, in which General Warner was elected that year. But in 1880 I was silly enough to be a candidate for Congress, and saw myself balloted for nearly three hundred ballots, and then withdrew in disgust, and then and there withdrew from politics forever. And from that time I have devoted myself wholly to my profession of the law. What mattered it to me that the Garfields, the Hayes, the Kilpatricks, and Douglasses and I, had traveled and stumped together on terms of equality, and together had received the cheers of thousands, from Boston to Cincinnati? What mattered it that I had spoken with all the great men of my day, and for ten years had seen my name in every paper that I picked up? What profit that I had been for ten years in daily communication with the wisest and most powerful men of my day?

One thing—for I must hasten on to the close—let me pause to say in this hurried resumé of the events of my life. The newspaper press, I love it, its editors and reporters. Among them I have found the best, the most enlightened and generous spirits I have ever known. It is the power behind the throne. Of all things outside the shadow of my own roof-tree, I most love the daily newspaper press. The best years, the best moments of my life, have been spent upon it. No one can know the rapture of the soul over print, who has not reveled, as I have, with delight, for thirty years, writing for all the daily papers.

I had begun almost rich, and I was now very poor in-

5

deed. I had not a dollar in the world, was loaded down
with debt, covered with rags, and broken in health. For
myself, I could have borne all this without a murmur,
but here were my wife and six children; and, with one
mighty effort turning my back on all the illusions I had
so long and so fruitlessly pursued, I resumed the practice of the law once more. It was a hard struggle. At
times I felt like giving up. But a sense of my obliga-
tion to my family and my creditors, and a little of the
old pride—a saving grace in a fallen or broken man—
held me up and pushed me on to moderate success, and
on to solid ground once more. The four years from
1882 to 1886, with only occasional efforts in the press,
the remains of the old habit, glided on swiftly and
smoothly in my dingy little law office. It was the
quietest and pleasantest period of my life, without a jar.

VIII.

During these years there were born to us six children,
four daughters and two sons—James Monroe Dalzell,
born November 26, 1870, and Howard Hayes Dalzell,
born July 4, 1878.

Monroe had the dark eye and hair of his mother, and
resembled her in all her most excellent qualities of mind
and heart. From the time he was five years old, he was
sober and reticent, and busy with tools of all sorts that
he could lay his hands on. He was a natural mechanic.
He had the patience, application, industry and ingenuity
which must combine in large degree to make the successful operator with tools. Even for toys he preferred
his little plane, hammer, hatchet, and miniature saw.

PRIVATE DALZELL'S CHILDREN.

He watched the men on the streets breaking stone, and at once began to look about for the means to do the same in his mother's yard. He improvised a little hammer of his own by driving a stick through a top, and with this went to breaking stone, "napping" them as skillfully as if he had worked at it for years. At five or six years of age, in this way he constructed a walk to the back door of our dwelling-house, which will be good for a hundred years.

He took to his books much the same as other boys, and never neglected his studies for the sports and out-door employments for which he early discovered such a relish. I do not think he was seven until he was a good reader, and fond of books adapted to his years.

He came to his mother, one day, and said: "Mamma, I want you to draw a paper for me to sign, that I will never touch tobacco or liquor while I live." His mother drew it up in his own childish words, and there at her knee he signed it, and, what is better, he kept it as long as he lived. Soon after, he asked her if she could write a pledge that he would never use any bad words. She turned the temperance pledge over, and wrote the promise as requested. He looked at it gravely and thoughtfully a moment, and, looking up into his mother's earnest, loving face, said: "Mamma, put in there, 'Not if I can help it'"—so careful was he of the solemn vow he was about to sign. And so it was put down, and he put his name to that also. This was his own suggestion throughout. He had never seen a pledge, nor had he ever seen any one sign one. He had been thinking of the evils of tobacco, cigars, liquor and profanity, and came to his

mother, as all good boys do, with childish candor and
faith, to get her help in building up the noble character
of which thus early he had been led to form a true concep-
tion from the talks he had had before that with his mother.
Other boys, drank whisky and beer in his presence, and
when where older persons could not see them, often tried
to induce him to break these solemn pledges, as some of
them have told us since, but he kept every one of them
faithfully until his pure unsullied soul returned to God.

In a sacred corner of the family sitting-room to-day,
that mother's written pledges, with the childish signa-
ture, is framed and hung, and bears its solemn testimony
to the character of the noble boy, now gone forever.

He had a passion for raising chickens, and soon became an adept in the business. Nothing delighted him
more than to feed and water the chickens, and with his
little hands he would gather the eggs, and lay them away
softly and carefully. He attended to the brooding hens,
and watched the advent of the little chicks with childish
delight. He always had money—seldom wasted a cent.
The little presents of money that he got, the money obtained for running errands, and for the eggs and chickens that he sold, he carefully laid away, instead of wasting
it in foolish purchases. I do not think he ever asked me
for a cent after he was six years old. He always had
plenty of money. When his mother or I needed a nickel
or a dime, he always gave it to us cheerfully, for he always had it to spare. He seldom missed a day from
Sabbath-school, and I do not think he ever went without
the penny for the little basket; a penny, too, that he
had earned himself by some honest employment adapted
to his age.

He studied all the best methods of raising poultry. knew all the diseases to which they were subject, and the best remedies that were known to the editors of the poultry papers with which he was always supplied. He constructed coops for them with his own hands, so skilfully that, while they were clean, bright and airy, that no rot or other enemy of the little chicks could ever enter or molest them. Little metallic troughs supplied the little ones with water without danger of drowning.

His house for the larger chickens was always a marvel of comfort and cleanliness. I have seen old men and women taking lessons of him in this useful art long before he had reached his teens, and of all the boys in his native town, he was the only one who had ever regarded the matter of sufficient importance to care to study it and attend to all its minute details. He drove his mother's cow and attended her garden. His vegetables were the earliest in the town and the best. He had a natural love for all that kind of work, and his whistle and song never had a happier sound than when he was at work with a spade or hoe in the garden. With this, as in all he laid his hand to, each year showed improvement. He read the agricultural papers that came to our house, not as I do, but carefully, studiously, and for practical purposes. He studied the nature of plants, and soils, and trees. Not a tree that his dear hands ever planted but is growing to-day. Thrift followed his hand every-where, and still his studies were not slighted. He could play on the piano and the harp. The last tune I ever heard him play was Sweet Home, as he passed out of the front gate. playing it on his harp, as he went sweetly and all unconsciously to his

death.   Much of his time he spent in my now lonely
office.

If there was vacation, on Saturdays, or during bad
weather, he sat at the table with me.   For hours together—long before he was eight years old, often afterward, and down to the last—he would sit, and spell, and
read in Webster's Unabridged Dictionary.   Of all the mass
of writing and printing in his desk here beside me to-
day, thousands upon thousands of words, not one mis-
spelled—not one—the effect of that sort of study.   He
bought a small printing press with some potatoes he had
to sell, and often amused himself with it.   He could set
type like an old printer.   He had inks of all colors and
a decided artistic genius, loved to draw, and paint, and
sketch, and print letters.   I have them all by me yet,
just as they dropped from his hands into the drawers, all
evidencing the existence of pure and noble aspirations,
gone to rest now with him forever.

If such things were possible—music, painting, printing—in the unfolding character of a youth of fifteen,
what would they not have flowered into at twenty, or
grown to at forty?   He had no teacher in any of these
things.   Indeed, his companions and parents had neither
taste nor ability for any such pursuits.   He took to
them as Pope took to poetry—because they came to
him.   Every step he made was a surprise to us.   New
faculties were continually unfolding without warning.
Now it was the harp, then it was the brush, next it was
the stone mason's hammer, or the carpenter's plane, he
was using, and all with a skill and confidence which, to
the ancient Greek, would have been evidence that he had
learned it in some other sphere and in a former life.   He

gave no warning of what was coming. He talked little—
never of himself or his plans. Their first announcement
was his work upon them. He wrought in silence and in
calmness, no noise, no haste, no confusion, generally
alone.

If he had known that his life on earth was to end at
fifteen, he would, I think, have acted and looked as he
did. Unaccustomed to censure or punishment, he was
as little concerned about praise. If his work pleased his
mother, he was happy; but I never saw such indiffer-
ence to praises of others as he always manifested. He
was always usefully employed. While he could romp
and play like other boys, when the hour came for him to
follow his self-appointed tasks, he dropped every thing
else, and went to work like a man who knew what he was
doing. Some of his beginnings in all these things were
crude and unfinished at first, but that never discouraged
him; he persevered until, at least, the point of utility
was accomplished.

He built heavy stone walks around the house and one
of brick. This was within the last year or two. Of the
thousand and one things about a house and outbuildings
that get out of repair one time or another, there was
scarcely one noticed until his willing and skillful fingers
were at work making necessary repairs. His mother
having no servant for years and years—on from a small
boy, indeed—her every wish was anticipated by the boy
who worshiped her and received worship in return, of
the purest sort, the only remuneration he ever sought.
Water, coal, kindling-wood, every thing, not one day
only, but every day, wet or dry, cold or hot, there his
hands had brought them, where his mother could reach

them with the fewest steps. No errand proper for a boy
could I ask him to run, however busy at play or work he
might be, but his little feet were ready to run the moment that I spoke.

His kindness of heart made him friends. He had not
an enemy in town. The best mothers held him up constantly as a model for their boys to imitate in industry
and morality. He could skate, and ride, and walk on
stilts, play base ball, play checkers, swim and leap equal
to any boy of the town. He could not bear to be beaten
at any thing. Strong, active, wiry, and spirited, he
sometimes frightened me with his daring feats in ska-
ting, swimming, and riding. He absolutely knew no
fear, and only refrained from laughing at my appre-
hensions of danger because of his respect for me, which
never once failed to show itself, whether I was present
or absent.

He was a universal favorite in the village. The retired
farmers sat in their doors, and with pleasant smiles
cheered the little man as he trudged along with his hoe
or his spade on his shoulder going to his work. I had
no taste for gardening or outside work or sports of any
kind, so he just took it up himself. His mother bought
a farm and several vacant lots near town, and it was his
delight to cultivate these with his own hands. He had
an old head on young shoulders. When the land was
to be paid for, he ran to the bank and got out $60, which
from his small earnings he had saved to help his mother
pay for it. He was not a miser. He was ready to give
his mother or me his last penny cheerfully, but he would
waste no money. He was not ashamed to be seen on the
streets in plain, dust-stained clothes, often patched, too,

with his hoe on his shoulder, and Frank, his favorite
dog, trotting at his side. It was a picture of industry,
contentment, and thrift that formed an example which
all the good mothers in the village constantly urged their
boys to emulate.

He helped make hay in the beautiful June days the
week before he was hurt. That hay since sold for the
money which his mother put into the monument at his
grave. Could any monument in all history tell of a
nobler origin than his—literally built with his own hands,
the fruit of his industry? Though not fifteen when he
ascended the skies, he had over $25 in money besides all
this. He seldom joked, never trifled, had little taste for
fiction. He so loved the truth that he was averse to
any the slightest exaggeration or perversion of it, even
in amusement. He tried Gil Blas, Don Quixote, Gul-
liver's Travels, and Paul and Virginia, but I only got
him to read them because he wanted to please me. He
preferred travelers' tales, history, and matters of fact.
His tastes were refined, but eminently of the practical
sort. A lie was a lie to him, even if invented for
amusement, and he preferred truth above all things.

Next to the pleasure of using his hands and brain in
devising and constructing little wagons, carts, chicken-
coops, and the like, he most enjoyed reading pure, good
books. He would often ask me, as I read aloud some
wonderful story, "Is that true?" It was his constant
question. If I could answer in the affirmative, he would
listen with rapt attention. If, however, I was compelled
to say that it was the creation of fancy, that was enough.
He was off in a trice, and would not hear a word of it.
With the development of his æsthetic nature, swiftly un-

folding itself in his growing love of music and the work
of the pencil and brush, which he wielded so gracefully
and naturally, I looked for the awakening of his imagination and fancy and a corresponding love of literature
of the poetic and romantic sort. But that faculty had
not yet developed itself. What might have been the result of education and maturer years in this direction I
can only conjecture, but I doubt not it would have been
all that I desired. I never saw him idle a moment.
His brain and hands were busy from morning till night,
and he slept sweetly at my side with peace and innocence
for the companions of his dreams. He never closed his
eyes in sleep until he had asked the God of the night as
well as of the day to bless him and us all. He seldom
talked about religion, but when he did it was earnestly
and thoughtfully, and with a faith that was clear as a
star. He rather acted than spoke religion. He had all
his mother's gentleness and tenderness of conscience,
and saw nothing in the world to compare with character.
His only care was to be good, to shun evil thoughts and
evil companions, and beyond this he had little to say
on moral or religious subjects. Duty was his delight,
and the only pain he ever seemed to feel was when he
thought he had deflected in the least from the path of
duty. If I could paint a perfect character I should be
successful in describing that of my boy, and no one who
knew him would hesitate to indorse it. He was not brilliant. He had to work hard to learn what he wished to
know or do, but once at his task he never would quit
it, never think of any thing else, and above all things
ask no one to help him, until he had gained a compara-
tive mastery of it. I wondered why he did not go to

the printers to learn to set type. His mother smiled as I made the suggestion, and said, quietly : " Did you ever know Monroe to ask any one to show him how to do any thing ?"

No, that was not his way. He had eyes and hands and a brain, and a will that knew no discouragement and that laughed at obstacles. He worked in a sincerity and sadness, as I see it now, that was almost supernatural, and I believe that it was the work of a genius that I could not fully appreciate until it set in death. He had trained his dog, Frank, a large, intelligent, and beautiful fellow, to work like a horse in his little wagon. He contrived and made both harness and wagon, and the first we knew of it was when he came up the lane, with his dog drawing a load of sods which he was bringing to beautify his mother's yard. Frank was his constant companion, and did whatever he was told to do. The friendship and devotion of that dog for his master formed one of the most beautiful pictures I ever saw, with which presently this chapter will close.

But, alas! all things in this world come to an end, and pass out of view, except as they are retained in the memory of the surviving and bereaved.

It was a beautiful afternoon in June, the 28th day, 1885. The family had all dined together, and no one around the sacred board was more cheerful, healthy, or happy than my darling Monroe. Verging on manhood, strong, buoyant, and full of youthful fire, he sat at my side, and often looked up into my face and smiled. I see his dark eyes, and his honest, manly, confiding face of innocence and beauty yet, as it shone with angelic beauty in that final hour.

If I had known then, as I know now, that I was sitting with my dear boy at what was to prove soon to be our "last supper," how my heart would have throbbed with emotion no tongue can express. But the future is all hidden from mortal vision. Not all, after all. Glimpses of the coming fate steal over our souls in such supreme moments, but without the key which heaven holds in its own keeping and refuses kindly to give us them, we feel the shadow coming without understanding its terrible import and signification. The mystic pulse of my spirit that day felt the throb of coming disaster, the first faint, mysterious thrill of a fate that was nigh at hand.

"Who is that at the door?" I inquired, as I heard a footstep on the porch near where we were sitting. Why I asked it I could not then tell; now I know. The portentous shadow was approaching. It was death at the door. An awe like a passing shadow of the shifting clouds of a summer's sky came and went in a moment— a moment that I could take hours now in describing and still fail to make any one understand. "It is Carl," answered one of the family, "only Carl."

Carl Martin was a sweet, noble lad, as good as he was lovely in form, feature, and disposition. He lived near us, and had dropped in, as he did at all hours, always a welcome visitor, for he was about Monroe's age and a fit companion every way. He had come to take a walk with Monroe—a walk that was to be his last. Thus we conduct each other to the grave in our shortness of vision, weakness, and helplessness, one way or other, in all time. Lightly rising from the table, catching up his hat and his French harp, Monroe tripped out, and in a moment the youths passed through the gate, my son playing "Sweet Home" as he went. They were both clean and well dressed, for it was Sunday.

I sat down to read, but somehow felt restless. I now can understand why, though then I gave it scarcely a thought. Thought furnishes no key to the mystic meaning of such a spell. It transcends all human scrutiny and forecast, and lies far beyond the reach of speculation, conjecture, investigation, analysis, and exemplification. It mirrors itself in darkness, and is the shadow of a shadow. An hour had passed—one short hour since the boys had left. I was sitting in the family sitting-room; our children, five in number, and my dear wife sat beside me. It was three o'clock, a summer afternoon, bright and hot. The door on the street was standing wide open. In a moment, like a flash of lightning from a clear sky, a boy sprang into the room, white of lip and face and out of breath. "Monroe is hurt," he gasped, rather than said. "Where? Will he die?" I cried, as I sprang up and staggered to the panting lad. "At the turn-table: he is badly hurt," stammered the poor little fellow; and away he went, frightened almost to death himself, and alarming all whom he met as he fled for home in his terror. It was half a mile to the turn-table of the railroad. I sprang through the door, out onto the street and across the field, without waiting for hat or coat or shoes. My wife followed me closely, weeping with me as we ran. As we neared the fatal spot, a great crowd appeared to be gathered there, and in a moment I found my boy stretched out in an arm-chair and bolstered up by kind hands. His face was as white as the paper on which I am writing. His brow was marble—as white, as cold. Not a tear was in his dark, beautiful eye, not a

moan on his lips. His garments were saturated and
heavy with blood. It was all plain in a second. He and
Carl and the gasping messenger above referred to had
been whirling the turn-table, and it caught my poor
Monroe across the hips and crushed the last drop of
good blood out of his body.

His heroic mother came up, knelt before him, and
kissed him as only a mother can. One glance was
enough.

She wept.

"Mother, do not cry," softly murmured the boy in his
weakness of body and in the strength of his love.

She saw he was gone.

I saw he was gone.

The brave, good man who had taken him from the
table and borne him in his arms told his mother that
when he picked up the broken and bleeding form of the
boy, the only words he uttered were, "Do you think I
will live until mamma comes?" "Yes, indeed, no danger
of that," returned the good man, and the boy smiled
and was silent, and spoke no more until she came.
Tenderly he was taken up by the strong arms of kind
friends, and carried home and laid on the bed of suffering from which he was never again to rise.

A week of untold agony followed. All that affection
and skill could do was done for him by friends, neighbors, and physicians. He was subjected to several severe surgical operations, one of them lasting for over
two hours, and his heroic conduct, patience, and meek-
ness under all these trials surprised the surgeons and
filled us all with wonder and increased admiration. He
scarcely moved—never was heard once to complain.

Through the long, weary watches of the nights that followed, his faithful pastor sat beside him and prayed for his recovery.

The pastor's wife and numbers of other noble women ministered to his wants, and endeavored by all their sweet and gentle words and smiles to sustain and comfort his sinking and suffering soul.

He wore a pleasant smile to the last moment. He recognized the boys and girls of his own age, and had a word for every one who called. Every eye that met his swam in sympathizing and sorrowing tears, but he never wept or expressed a fear.

Calm, gentle, growing weaker day after day, the habitual smile of his pure and happy life was still on his lips as the supreme moment came on. Wan, weak, almost helpless, he had a " thank you " or a " please " for every one who smoothed a pillow, waved a fan, or cooled his fevered lips with a cup of water. The whole country-side came to see the pale sufferer for miles and miles around. Hundreds had to be excluded toward the last, but they would linger in the yard and street adjacent to the house, and with grave faces full of anxiety and voices subdued and sorrowful inquire how he was. There was no lack of nurses, no lack of kind friends, for Heaven had him in its keeping, and sent its messengers there, the reward of a brief but blameless life.

The Fourth of July dawned at last, and he still breathed and was conscious, but we all saw the end was nigh.

It was the birthday of our son, Howard Hayes, just seven years old that day, and instead of laughing and playing, the little man was celebrating this birthday, the

brightest holiday of all the year to those who are happy—
he was celebrating it with tears and lamentations. The
kind parson knelt and prayed for him. Monroe closed
his eyes, now dim with the shadows of approaching
death, and folding his pale thin hands over his manly
breast, he reverently joined silently in the prayer.

The night before, in great agony, when his mother and
I were sitting by his cot, he had folded his hands in the
same way and uttered these words calmly and with deep
reverence, " O, my God, be with me." It was not a
second until he was asleep His prayer was answered.

Though I felt all unfit to do so, when all hope was
gone of seeing my noble boy restored to health, I had
asked him if he could trust the Lord, and if he saw his
way to Heaven clear, and he had told me, in his earnest
laconic way, that he did—I could say no more. I was
overwhelmed with grief. How could I?

Up till noon on that Fourth of July, his suffering was
very great. In the afternoon he began to sink. O woe,
woe what a day! To sit there and watch that beloved
boy breathing out his life, and not to be able to rescue
him from the grave.

What a Fourth of July! In the village all that day
the children stood in silent groups about the house all
thinking of Monroe; all anxious to hear the latest news
from his bedside. They left the sidewalks and marched
up and down the street for fear of disturbing the boy
they all loved. It was a Sabbath in our town. Of the
hundreds of boys there was not one gave a shout or fired
a cracker that day. No sound of cannon or guns, no
revelry, no music, no speeches; the town was awed into
silence and dread, and had only one thought, and that

was of Monroe. Never had a human character received
a more expressive eulogy than the silence and respect of
the village gave Monroe Dalzell that day.

As the sun set at the end of that long weary day
of pain and anxiety, quietly, peacefully, without a struggle, as if resigning himself to slumber on his mother's
breast, our darling ceased to breathe. And us—how could
we realize it? How could we bear it in the chilly embrace of death? O, what darkness entered that house
then never to depart! The greatest loss that can befall
a human being, the loss of a darling son, our hope and
pride, had befallen us, and our grief was not a transient
shadow but the very darkness of despair and mourning
that only deepens still as the years roll on.

His funeral, attended by all the best men, by rich and
poor, old and young, the country round, testified the esteem in which he was universally held. He was sincerely
mourned by all who were witness of the beautiful life he
had lived, and even those who had never seen him were
attracted to the obsequies by the fair report they had of
him from his neighbors or playmates. The school children
wept—they had lost a friend. His Sunday School teacher
and the teachers in the day schools, the gray haired
judges, the learned lawyers and physicians, and the good
honest farmers all around, no less than the poorest in
the village, followed the hearse that bore his mortal part
to the little country graveyard.

If he had lived to fifty years and realized to the full
all the hopes that he had indulged of the bright career
that seemed to lie before him, he could never have come
to the grave with greater honor. But above all the sat-
isfaction and comfort which we derived from this re-

flection, infinitely above the good opinion of men, desirable as that good opinion is, is the consolation that we find in believing that his soul is at rest in Heaven.

The day of his death was the birthday, as I have said, of our only remaining son, Howard, and strangely enough to seem to me a warning from Heaven to us all, the day of poor dear Monroe's funeral was our daughter Annie's tenth birthday, the fifth of July. Farewell, dear Monroe. We shall meet in Heaven.

PART II.

MY WAR SKETCHES, ETC.

.

I.—DAVE SHEPPARD, THE FORAGER.

Dave Sheppard was in our mess, and a merrier lark never fought with Milroy, ran with Sigel, or stampeded with Hunter. Long-legged, gaunt, hungry, and as long-winded as a hound, a chase of a dozen miles at any hour of day or night was nothing to Dave, if it only ended in bringing in a box of honey, a pair of chickens, or a canteen of mountain dew. He was seldom present except on pay-day. The captain, good-humored, and as big a rake as any of us, scolded and cursed poor Dave all in vain. He was so jolly and good natured that the captain could not find it in his heart to punish Dave, especially so, because every time the fellow came in he had a leg of mutton, a full canteen, or a bunch of honey, to appease the captain's wrath and conciliate his good will. These things were very soothing to official anger in those days, and the boys understood it so well, that they never went out on a French of their own but they came back loaded with peace-offerings of some sort for our headquarters. That made every breach whole. There was nothing bad about Dave. In his midnight predatory excursions beyond the picket line, of course the harum-scarum youngster, for he was barely eighteen, always carried his life in his hands—and his musket, and always brought both back undischarged. Like the dove let loose from the ark, he generally brought back something more than he carried away, too.

He improved every opportunity for plying his favorite amusement, and nothing afforded his genius better scope than the frequent stampedes and retreats, when every fellow went it on his own responsibility, and the officers were so busy taking care of themselves they had no time or inclination to look after us, or enforce military discipline. Besides, even on ordinary occasions, like the old Roman, he would either find a way or make it to steal beyond our lines, in more senses than one.

There wasn't a hen-roost or pig-pen, a bee-hive or a still-house, within ten miles of our camp, that Dave would not manage to discover and visit by hook or by crook. He was sly and reserved, and generally kept these secrets to himself, lest some other adventurous spirit would reach the spoils before him.

Still, I managed to get into Dave's confidence, and many a time I wrote passes for him, signed by great colonels and generals (in a horn), and assisted him in passing the grounds and pickets, and thus earned a share of the booty. I found it pleasant and profitable to stand in with Dave. As I was at head-quarters most of the time, doing writing for the officers which they were not competent to do for themselves, I had many a chance to purloin tobacco, cigars, ham, potatoes, and occasionally a bottle of whisky, of which Dave was almost if not quite as fond as they were, and would smuggle a good part of them out to Dave when his business was dull, and his stealing chances slim. These good offices made an excellent impression on Dave, and he never failed to reciprocate when he returned laden with the rich spoils of war after his long midnight excursions beyond the camp—always provided that I stayed up, and watched him before he had a chance to hide his plunder, eat it up, or drink it up, and lie out of it. For, just as sure as he got in without me seeing him, he come around the next morning with the gravest and most honest of faces, and swear on a stack of Bibles he got nothing. He would bear watching, and I gave him the full benefit of it. If out on the edge of camp, well on toward morning, I happened to divine correctly the road of his return, and met him loaded to the guards with honey, whisky, soft bread, headless chickens and the like, and looking for all the world like a walking market-house, or a perambulating hennery, it was indeed hard for him to look me in the face and swear, as he was ready to do on the slightest provocation, "that he had n't got a —— thing."

I used to steal the officers' coats, epaulets and all, and send my brave out on his errands of plunder as grand as any officer. You ought to have seen him, with his false whiskers, his password, and his blazing uniform, sneaking out of the lines on horseback, attended by three or four orderlies, galloping behind, no better than himself; but if their departure was imposing, imagine, if you can, how anxious I awaited their return in the solitude of the mountains, not knowing when my gay cavaliers would return, or whether they would not end their careers at the hands of some cowardly bushwhackers. But had I not written their passes with a gay flourish, ruled grandly in red ink, put them in stunning envelopes and bound them in their belts, for not a soul of the mess could read or write but myself. I might have put their death warrant there with perfect impunity, for all they would ever have known.

Thus, with carmine ink for blood, and steel pens for swords and bayonets, did I bear my part, like the generals, in the great war for the Union.

I was a private general—a sort of unknown commander of parts, enjoyed the joke there all to myself, and now am trying to get the whole world to enjoy it with me. I kept it to myself these one and twenty years, but now that the generals are cracking their jokes, spinning their yarns out of their fancy, why may not I be permitted, at least, to write the bald-headed and wrinkled truth of the war? I fought it through with pen and pencil once, as the generals did, and in some way like them. I go over the same ground again. I have seen whole regiments, divisions, and corps wither away under the consuming fires of the lead pencil, much as I have seen the same havoc wrought in the romantic pages of the Century by the like instrumentality wielded by generals whose swords returned bloodless as turnips from the dread carnage of war!

I hope the discriminating and appreciative reader will not confound the truth of the details of history with any ill-natured sarcasm, or railing, for I have not forgotten, nor has he, that whole corps did sometimes melt to the ground under the blazing and merciless fire of the guns of the rank and file of the Union army, to whom belongs the credit or the blame, whichever he please, for filling every rebel grave (not one excepted) from the Potomac to Texas.

But, to return to a more congenial theme, the narrative of Dave's exploits, as well as those of the few choice spirits whom he and I selected to execute our most difficult enterprises, or rather, to be more exact, to bring into camp booty too large and numerous for one man to capture and carry.

Dave used to play dead. He tried all manner of tricks to keep me out of my equitable share of the stuff. He would at times prove too smart for any thing to detect him. He could lie like a general, and with as solemn a face. Separating himself from the rest in the dark, in some dark mountain recess, he would fire off a carbine or pistol, then raise an unearthly yell and gallop toward his companions, who would give their horses the spur, drop their chickens and other truck, or any thing that impeded their flight, and return to me with ashen cheeks and ghostly whispers, to tell how poor Dave had at last passed in his checks and fallen a victim to bushwhackers. I would pretend to be terribly cut up over it, get their coats and carbines that I had stolen, and, cautioning them on their lives not to say a word about Dave, or they would all be bucked and gagged, they would turn their horses loose to find their owners the best they could, and sneak off to their dog-tents, as if nothing had happened. A half hour later, Dave would come in drunk as a lord and hard to repress, with oceans of whisky and enough poultry and other provisions to last us and the general a week.

When the officers got their proportionate share of the whisky, well watered, and a like amount of the toughest and oldest of the chickens, they asked Dave and me no questions.

But you ought to have seen the other fellows next day,
as they passed our tent and saw Dave and me at a quiet
game of poker, both full as geese, and each with the
same canteens they had dropped swung around our
necks! That was the way you had to keep your canteen
in those days if you wanted an eye-opener yourself. It
would not do to lay it down, or it would be dryer than
a powder-horn in two minutes. We laughed. They
swore like our army of West Virginia only could swear.
It looked blood-thirsty for a minute, but, as there were
but three or four of them, we made our peace by giving
them each a snifter at the canteen, and off they went,
singing,

"We've drank from the same canteen,"

and that was the last of it.

Next time we planned extensive excursions they were
left out. We had no use for people of such intelligence,
and chose fresh victims, in turn to be duped and dis-
carded like these. Discipline was very loose in those
days. When not on picket duty, the boys did about as
they pleased, and these intrigues were more easily managed than when Phil Sheridan took command after, and,
enforcing strict military rules, had many a poor fellow
bucked and gagged, and some even shot, for ten times
less than we were accustomed to do almost every week.
Death was announced as the penalty for straggling or
pillaging beyond our lines when little Phil started up the
valley a year or so after these events, and well do I remember that, during the prevalence of that order, how
carefully and frequently Dave and I pursued our old
pastime. But we were a little more sly about it. Still,

the added danger of such movements somehow only made
them the more relishable to Dave, and, besides, habit
had become a second nature to him now, and he could no
more keep from robbing hen-roosts and stealing whisky
than a general can, nowadays, abstain from a little innocent lying in the magazines. "Thus does use breed a
habit in a man." But to go back to our story.

I do not know why it is that I keep running off into
these episodes, parallels, and moral reflections, except
that it may be, in this renaissance of war literature, in
using the wild and entertaining memoirs, annals, histories, and sketches with which our periodical literature
abounds, I may have all unconsciously, certainly unin-
tentionally, acquired the habit, so manifest in all these
forays of the fancy yclept war history, of magnifying foreign details on purpose to obscure the real facts of the case.

I shall avoid all such excursions of the fancy hereafter, and religiously stick to details of the utmost moment to a true development of the military history of
my country, and what comes much to the same thing, of
myself. It is hard to separate U. S.!

I hope no one will smile. Writing history is serious
business.

> "To smile were want of goodness and grace,
>   Tho' to be grave is beyond the power of face,"

in reading much of it.

*   *   *   *   *   *

These stars indicate a complete revolution of style and
subject-matter—a sort of jumping-off station, to let me
down to complete the sketch with which I began, and
now I return with great pomp and circumstance, and be-
coming gravity withal, to Dave, and never forgetting

myself, which, indeed, in all military narrative with which I am conversant, is the Alpha and Omega of history. Dave got ahead of me at last. Sigel was *on* his famous retreat from Woodstock, June, 1864 (indeed, he was seldom *off* a retreat). Dave and I were not behind. The truth of history compels me to state that we were about a mile ahead of the retreating column—at the heels of Sigel and his generals, making good time, that hot afternoon, in the direction of Cedar Creek, with the rebels firing *far behind us*. Not the most powerful gun in the Confederacy could have reached Dave, me, or the general who lead that *Sigclopædia!* We got tired of the main road, and in the confusion and disorder of the mad, and senseless, and uttery causeless retreat from a foe not the third of our number, now was our chance to resume our old operations against hen-roosts, distilleries, and things. This was more to our taste.

So we ciphered off into the country a mile from the line of retreat, far in advance of the flying fugitives and their doughty general.

We were hungry. We had been running toward the enemy three hours and from him nine, and had not had a morsel to eat. Our commissary was far in the rear, perhaps in the hands of the rebels. Before it could reach us we would starve, sure. So, after due deliberation in that council of war, for which we were always ready, Dave and I highly resolved to hunt up a negro and cook or torture him until he told us where we might find food to appease our military hunger, and drink to quench our military thirst. Those were military days. So on we trudged across the fields, through the woods, away off the Winchester road. Every house near the

road was already looted, and we could neither beg, buy,
nor steal a morsel to eat or a drop stronger than water.
Any one less skilled in the predatory art of war would
have been discouraged at the disappointments that met
us at every house. The women and children were fam-
ishing. As I look back to it now it makes me shudder
to think what might have occurred if we had found a
loaf of bread, or even a chicken. We might have taken
them, and been filled with everlasting remorse and re-
pentance, all in vain after the bread was eaten, and
the last limb of the fowl picked to the bone. Our conscience was spared this mortal offense. We had some
conscience, though a hungry stomach speaks in such
tones of thunder, under such circumstances, that nothing
less than the failure to find prevents the overt act, and
leaves the soul without the stain of larceny, however
petit. On we went, discussing the situation, until, just
as we emerged from the wood again into the open fields,
we came upon an antiquated darkey, viewing the retreating army from the hill tops. When he saw the color of
our coats, he knew we were friendly to his race, and he
fairly grinned and bowed with delight.

Our parley with Sambo was short, sharp, and decisive.
We told him we would shoot, hang, burn, and destroy
him from the face of the earth, if he did not instantly
pilot us to where we could get provender. He looked
solemn, and, with the instinct of his poor, down-trodden
race, using the last and only defense of servitude and
subjection, lied in his throat, and swore, "Fore God,
massa, don't know where you can get a bite." We
quickly assured him this would not do, and, fixing bay-

onets (Dave and I were matches for any unarmed, crip-
pled old negro in the Confederacy), bade him trot ahead
and show us our desired food or he would soon be welter-
ing ankle deep in his own gore. This was all put on.
We never killed negroes or any one else. Oh, no! not
a bit more than if we had been generals.

But we were acting upon military necessity, and he was
contraband of war, and by the rules of our council Dave
and I had solemnly resolved to devote him, life, limb,
and honor, to the service of our country—that is,
of us.

He dodged on ahead, and wanted to be garrulous, but
we checked him into reticence by a few light prods of
our bayonets, which made him scream with real terror,
and promised us all we desired. After leading us across
a mountain gorge, over a creek, up a steep wooded hill,
and a mile or so further on, he brought up at the garden
fence of a cozy little log hut, near which a cow was graz-
ing in the pasture. Here was the land of milk—if not
of honey at least, the Canaan for which, footsore, weary,
sweating, and swearing, I regret to pause to remark, we
had been bending our steps these two hours or more.

The poor old fellow told us we should find what we
wanted, and we let him go, for after we were gone it
would be death to him, sure, if what he had done should
be discovered. A solitary woman and baby kept the
hut. She manifested little surprise or concern at our
rude entrance. Years of war in that region of hostil-
ities had familiarized her with such visits, though being
so far off the main road her retirement was more seldom invaded than if her dwelling had been nearer the
great highway. We had been paid off a few days be-

fore, and had no chance to spend our money, so we had plenty. We were not the men to rob a lonely woman. So we bought three canteens of milk, and two loaves of bread, the only eatables she had about the premises, and gave her a five-dollar greenback out of my pocket-book, and went on our way rejoicing. It was the first time the sagacious Dave had ever beaten me. It was not the last. Striking across the country, on our return to the main road, we took a drink of the milk, but concluded to save two canteens of the milk and bread for our supper in camp, wherever the infernal crowd should stop. Loose as discipline was there, yet we must be in camp that night—I to write general orders, and Dave to lie to the boys, with less red tape about his fabrications than I should wind around mine.

Dave was stronger than I. I never saw him so kind and considerate before, as we leaped and stumbled along toward camp, which turned out to be Cedar Creek. The sun was setting as we fell in with the retreating forces, mingled with them, and were lost in them, as pebbles drop into the sea and are seen no more.

Dave had kindly, in consideration of my weakness and exhaustion, taken it upon himself to roll the bread into his haversack and string both canteens about his neck !

Confound his kindness !

Every man has his moments of weakness, when he is easily duped. One had better be on the alert if he has a Dave near by. This was the cause of my disaster: We had run, walked, trudged, stumbled, or climbed thirty miles that day, spent two or three weary, monotonous hours in the battle of Newmarket, and here we were at

Cedar Creek for the night, with nothing to show for all the toils of the war but two loaves of bread and two small canteens of milk, which we were to furtively stew or boil for supper down some lonely ravine as soon as we could conveniently meet.

I reported at head-quarters, wrote orders and dispatches for an hour, and slipped out to find Dave, the milk, and the bread. I asked the men of his company. No one had seen him since the battle—few had seen him then. He had a magic way of keeping himself invisible in the smoke of war. So had I.

Maybe that is why we were such familiar friends, and on such terms with our generals. But if you have a familiar friend don't trust him out of sight with the milk and bread when he is hungry—no matter how hungry you are. I ran this way and that, down among the mules, among the ambulances, where over three hundred and more poor wounded fellows writhed in agony in the dark and alone. One poor fellow shot in the abdomen— a stranger to me—called piteously for water. I filled my cup hastily in the creek and raised it to his lips. He drank eagerly, rolled over, shuddered, and died before I got out of the ambulance.

Then I ran on. There were no rations in camp. I was starving. I actually chewed mouthfuls of grass and pennyroyal, as thousands had done before. We had put off eating our bread to have a royal feast of bread and milk boiled together. Where was Dave? Doubtless down in some secluded cave or dell, dingle or thicket, eating my bread and milk.

I could not find him. I laid down on the wet grass, supperless and swearing. I preserved no record of the

words I said, as I now saw how stupidly I had permitted
Dave to steal my supper right out from under my eyes.
He kept out of my way for a week, and then one day
came grinning around with some toothsome chicken and
whisky, and in five minutes we both were singing

"We won't go home till morning."

II.—Not all Fun in the Army.

Christmas day was not the merry, rollicking affair it
used to be at home. As we old soldiers try to recall the
experiences of our camp life, we always endeavor to
keep the best, at least the gayest and most thoughtless,
side out. But if any one supposes the human heart is
other in war than in peace, he is much mistaken. It had
its moods there as elsewhere. It was not all sunshine.
Shadows chased each other there as here. We are accustomed to speak of it lightly, robe it with romance,
picture it in poetry, and overarch it all with laughter and
song and playful pranks; but oh, me! At times, floods
of sadness, deep, dark, and abiding, full of gloomy
sadness that no pen can portray, swept over the hearts
that throbbed and sighed in their blouses of blue. Oh,
the weariness of the long and lonely vigils on the picket
line, who shall ever describe it? On some lonely mountain top, pacing his solitary beat, among the tall, dark
pines, all the hours of the night, sleepless and shivering
with cold, in the fierce blasts of winter, the picket boy
had many a sad and serious thought that no historian or
poet has ever yet described, for ere the relief came and
the first gray streaks of dawn began to light the crags

and cliffs that frowned above, the soldier had met his
fate and lay stiff and stark in death at his perilous post
of duty. And then, when the relief reported and found
him there, however young and thoughtless they might
seem, as they tenderly lifted his lifeless corpse and
buried it hastily in the frozen earth near by, who shall
try to record the sad thoughts that swept through their
souls? No merriment there. No, glee, no joke, or
prank, or song—an awful burial scene; a lonely and unmarked grave below and weeping eyes above. These
were seasons of despondency and gloom, when even hope
itself was clouded and yielded not a single ray to illum-
inate the darkness of the hour. Oh, the weary waiting
for the "cruel war" to cease! The sad letters from
home and the sad replies that went back in response,
until every chord that united severed hearts vibrated
deepest woe. The ministry of mirth, at times, it is true,
was evoked to chase away these shadows from the heart,
and many a time the lips thrilled with songs and cheers
and cheerful discourse when the harp of a thousand strings
within wailed and trembled only with notes of sadness,
melancholy, and despair. Much of the glee of camp
was put on to exorcise the magic spell of sorrow, and
much more to cheer the friends of freedom, and more
still to intimidate the enemies of our country's honor. If
the great, bleeding heart of the army in times of gloom
and misery had been laid open to the gaze of friend and
foe, and not covered over with a halo of merriment and
glee, as it truly was, our friends at home would have
been discouraged beyond distraction and despair, and
the insolent foe, whose greatest fear was the unbroken
spirit of the great army of freedom, would have hailed it

as the death-knell of the Union, and saluted it with defiant yells of mockery.

And so it was that thoughtless observers of the army then, and still more thoughtless historians of it since, have kept in the background all the melancholy reflections of the soldier in the field, and recorded nothing scarcely but the lighter and more joyous phases of that eventful period. And now, if any one shall suppose—I mean any one of the young people born since the war, or any one who was too old or too cowardly to enlist then—shall suppose all was joy and merrymaking in the soldier's life, and that no serious or solemn thought ever possessed his breast, then their estimate of the soldier will be fearfully amiss.

We had our jokes and games, and have them yet, " to make the bitter draught of life go down." We had our songs and merry pranks, and many an amusement besides as innocent and guileless for the most part as any that holy altars or firesides here shall have at Christmas time. We could not sit down and mope and sigh like so many melancholy Jacques! We could not hang our harps in the chapperel and mourn like the dove, or chatter like the sparrow. We could not sit in the ashes with Job or stare and sigh with Democritus. We were charged with weighty duties and felt the responsibility like men, though in the weary waiting hours of camp life we acted and spoke often like boys. Serious? Did you ever know congregation or assembly at any shrine or altar more serious than we, less playful, less frolicsome, less given to folly, when we dropped the mask of jollity and good-fellowship, and leaving the boy all behind, in a moment became men of iron and steel in the stern face

of battle? Oh, we can crack our jokes and spin our
yarns now to the utmost verge of exaggeration for the
amusement of the generation born since the war, but let
it never be forgotten that the army that could laugh at
pain, and cold, privation, and distress, and for the moment affect the hey-day gayety and sprightliness of youth,
seemingly without a care or thought of the morrow, or a
memory of yesterday, was the same army that, with
blood and smoke-begrimed faces, with steady step and
clenched teeth, stormed the heights of Mission Ridge,
forced the gates of Vicksburg, opened the Father of
Waters to the sea, and unfurled its flags of victory at
Appomattox over the broken battalions of Lee, and ended
the war in a blaze of glory. No boy's sport, that. No
child's play, let me say. These were earnest men in no
holiday sport. I tell you now, and so whenever you
think of these men at their plays and sports in camp,
let it forever be remembered to their credit, that they
could fight as well as pray or play either.

Fitz Daber was a lieutenant of cavalry in our brigade,
which was the First of the Second Division, Eighth Army
Corps, Department of West Virginia. Short, wiry, mer-
curial little fellow, with flaming red beard and hair, a
real, wild, flying little Dutchman, never still for a moment, dashing about on a sorrel nag with a glass eye,
and about as nervous and gingery as he was himself: of
course every body knew Fitz Daber, of the New York
Cavalry. He was always in a towering passion, sweating, swearing, and swaggering—a real little Lilliputian
bully on horseback. He and his fiery horse were one,
and a chicken with its head cut off—a favorite figure
with me, as the reader observes—was composure and

dignity in comparison with the furious little Dutchman. He had been a beer-slinger in a low down saloon in New York until he got his commission and big brass buttons and shoulder straps, and now was beside himself with ridiculous vanity. The military reader will remember many like him. "Some are born great, some achieve greatness, and some have greatness thrust upon them," says the old brochure, but few like Fitz Daber attain it all at once by all three of these routes. One morning he became famous. He had his little company of cavalry out on a drill. Forming them in double file, as if on dress parade, Fitz dashed his spurs in his peppery steed, his flowing whiskers streamed out like fire-brands back over his shoulders, as with drawn sword he galloped directly away from his command for three hundred yards. Then, wheeling madly about, he rode as furiously back toward them, while they wondered what the hades he was up to, or whether he was not gone mad sure enough, since he was so near crazy at best. When within thirty paces of the front line of men on horseback, he reined up his cranky steed so savagely and suddenly as to throw the latter back on his haunches, and nearly pitched Fitz out of the saddle. Recovering his seat he halted, while the men, able to hold in no longer, laughed and cheered in his face.

This was too much for Fitz. He fairly frothed with rage, and waved his sword defiantly at them, which made them laugh the more. Frantic with passion, and struggling to command the most expressive English that his broken tongue could manage, he bawled out: "Attinshin, battaly-on! Look fierce! Not look so tem like von cafs! Not like von sheeps! Look like hil! Look

like me!"   Again he brandished his flaming sword and
wild red whiskers, while his eyes fairly rained fire, and
the boys on horseback screamed with laughter that
could not be suppressed.   The parade was dismissed
and the drill ended for the day.   It spread all over the
valley.

For days and days, at all hours of the day or night,
whenever Fitz appeared, he heard nothing but his own
warlike words.   It rang up and down the lines, and became a by-word in all our camps, whenever any fool of
any sort put on airs or pretended to be extremely brave.
"Look like hil!"   "Look like me!"   And its moral
effect has continued even to this day.

III.—The Stomachs of the Boys in Blue.

Stomach!   I guess we had.   It was copper-bottomed
and lined with something akin to boiler iron.   Turned?
Not often.   It was hard to turn.   Talk about the ostrich's
power of digestion.   It was nothing to ours.   The pos-
sibilities of human digestion is a curious subject, patho-
logically or physiologically considered, but plain as noonday compared with the tangled labyrinths of philosophy
in which one is plunged on attempting to describe the
same under military environments and necessities.   No
man who never was a soldier can possibly fancy to himself the strains and pressure the digestive apparatus will
bear under the hard trials of war.

It takes a tremendous, almost incalculable force from
within to turn a good locomotive boiler inside out, but
the military gastronomic engine will bear a thousand
times more pressure than that and never budge an inch,

or even a hair-breadth, from the right line of its perpendicular.

If wheezy young dyspeptics, who are dieting themselves to death, and afraid of every thing offered in the whole cook book, would take a morning walk of thirty miles over mountains and rivers, wading and swimming the latter in all kinds of weather, and then proceed without a change of linen, sleep out in the open air on the mountain side, supperless and hungry, get up with the earliest streak of dawn and march till noon, still hungry and fatigued, and then smell a cup of coffee! What would follow? The drug stores and doctors would go into bankruptcy, the lunatic asylums close for repairs, and the undertakers lose their occupation, except for nonogenarians occasionally, or a good crop of centenarians every centennial day.

That's what's the matter with the American stomach, poetry, and politics; stuffed like a goose, three times a day, with all manner of meats, when the poor thing cries "*peccavi*," and refuses to entertain the mess without frequent ructions, much whisky, bad temper, and divorce suits. It is the prime cause of atheism and anarchy, for who can believe in God or man with a pain in his stomach? If it hadn't been for the war, I would never have found out I had a stomach, or have to treat it. But then it asserted itself, and was never in better humor with itself and the man who respected it. If you ever knew a soldier who had dyspepsia, you need not examine his person for the scars of rebel bullets. He wasn't there! Hanging about Washington, bumming at the rear, loafing out of the range of lead, he may have acquired this peculiarly domestic disease that lingers about

the hearthstones of "sweet home," but he never acquired
it scouring the mountains with Milroy, pushing up the
valley with little Phil, or plunging through Georgia to
the sea with Sherman. 1 wish I knew how, in polite and
decorous language, which would offend nobody but a
dyspeptic, to relate an extreme and somewhat delicate
illustration of the foregoing remarks.

I guess I will risk it. So brace up, and be prepared
for rather a realistic and graphic delineation of the power
of a well-ordered stomach to resist the influences that
would prove too powerful altogether for one that fared
sumptuously every day, and two or three times more so
on Sunday. I was with a detachment of General
Suthorn's forces at Stevenson's Station, near Winchester,
Va., in January, 1864, a few days after the First Virginia Cavalry had had a sharp little fight with Imboden's
guerrillas, and it was our lot to encamp near that field
for the night. As was too often the case, our wagons
were behind, and we had no provisions, not a bite, and
had appetites like circular saw mills or politicians' aspirations, that yearned after almost any thing or every
thing. We would not have quarreled with any cook or
cookery that night, as we lay down and looked up at the
stars and tried to fancy they were good to eat, but too
far off, like our good commissary. Hungry all night.
You don't need to be called three or four times for
breakfast, and then turn over on the wet grass and wish
the breakfast and the cook both at the devil. Oh, no!

You could eat every thing—the cook not excepted—
and rise with the lark and out-sing him in your native
lay, so to speak, poetically. We rose with something
less poetic—the pig.

Do you know the pig is an early riser? Go to the pig—at Stevenson's Station—thou dyspeptic sluggard, and learn to be wise. In fact, he must have been up and abroad all night, to be dressed so early as I saw him dressed that morning.

A pig dressed—it is a fact. I saw him dressed, and helped dress him myself, and he looked quite charming dressed so. A pig dressed? I guess so. Else how would he be a fit companion for gentlemen soldiers such as we? I have seen pigs since that—nay, more, hogs, of all genders, admitted to the best circles on his or her dress alone—hast not thou, gentle reader? But never a pig like this! But, to return to our pork—our dressed pig, to adhere to the figure of speech more exactly still. And our pig had something more to admit him than his swinish dress, something more substantial for the thousands of empty stomachs that ached to receive him. He got a warm reception.

I heard the guns go pop. I smelled something—not a rat, not a pig—what was it? Were we attacked? Following my heroic impulses, I led, as usual, on the retreat which I imagined to be forming—our daily occupation in those strategic days—and ran plump over a dead horse and a—a—a—what do you think it was? Could mortal man believe it? A live hog, fat as butter, a real hog, in the Shenandoah Valley, stripped, as I supposed it was, as clean of every thing movable as the White House is by our retiring Presidents! An instant and I resumed my natural heroism, and shot the poor swine—no, the fat hog—dead on the spot. A swarm of fellows ran up, and in a jiffy slices were cut, hair and all, from the dead porker, spitted on bayonets, and roasting before he had given his expiring grunt. In fact, I thought I heard the first half cooked piece I swallowed grunt audibly in my gastronomic cavity. It was all cavity—all void, an aching void—that it seemed could never be filled. I did not look at the defunct horse, out of which the pig had popped! Now, go and read Charles Lamb's Roast Pig, with its rich, delicious flavor, and tempting juices, and imagine us hungry fellows swallowing the mess as if we were feasting at Delmonico's, and you will have some idea of the powers of endurance of a first-class military stomach, well disciplined in the school of exercise and starvation.

IV.—THE FORCED MARCH TO MOOREFIELD, W. VA.

"*Dido et dux*," sang the divine Mantuan, but we didn't —it was chickens. Our natural fondness for poultry was not so discriminating, mind you, that we should have eschewed duck if we had to choose our chews. We were ready to go upon a fowl fare, any thing fair or fowl, and would have picked a duck as quickly as a chicken, provided, always, we could have found the duck. But our armies had ravaged West Virginia a full year before our regiment commenced its bloody work—on the hen-roosts of that disloyal region.

We were encamped at New Creek, W. Va., in the winter of 1862-3 for a short time. There was quite an army there—for what purpose, or what fool sent it there and kept it there during the beautiful weather of the late autumn of 1862, I do not know, but the world will no doubt ring with his fame when he publishes his memoirs. He must be a very modest man to have so long withheld his name from the glowing annals of his country's military romances, at the weight whereof the shelves of the people, not to say the poor people themselves, are now groaning.

I have noticed that the titled gentlemen who planned most of the masterly inactivities, and were responsible for most of the disastrous campaigns and battles of the war, are disinclined to claim any credit for the preliminaries that led up to such tremendous results as well nigh destroyed the nation; but, marry! how they come in on the home-stretch in the magazines to claim the credit of successes due partly to accident, or others due more to the spontaneous fighting of the clumsy rank and file, who, of course, are left out of the story with all the propriety of the omission of Hamlet from the play that bears his name!

But to my chicken story, and here it is. It was early in December that an order came signed, or scrawled rather, by some official, or officious fool, ordering our army to march to Moorefield at once. The hurry and bustle of preparing, on ten minutes' notice, for a forced march of forty miles into the mountains, packing knapsacks, loading wagons, striking tents, and all that confusion and shouting and swearing attendant upon such occasions were made doubly interesting by the noteworthy fact that a blinding snow-storm, the first of the season, prevailed, and winter was on us suddenly in all its fury. The week before the weather had been fine and the roads superb, and the rebels were at Moorefield, as we all well knew, and that in force; now they were gone, but a crisis was on the country, and it was ours not to reason why this idiotic move was necessary in a blinding snow-

8

storm. It could be justified by only that stretch of charity which covered all the blunders of the war—a million or so—under the precious name of strategy. That campaign, however, was not without incident. There was but one incident which occurred, and that solitary and melancholy result the muse of history now proceeds to record, for she would not have posterity stop here and conclude that nothing resulted from a forced march of forty miles to Moorefield and forty back, with two regiments of cavalry, a full battery of artillery, and five thousand picked infantry. (I was one of the latter, and you will see I was picked worse than any chicken before this solemn recital closes!) We went trudging along, knee-deep in snow, carrying great big knapsacks and forty rounds of cartridges in each cartridge-box, and that at almost a double-quick. The grotesque spectacle was only relieved from utter and most convulsively laughable absurdity, a veritable repetition of the ancient charge of the windmills made by the Knight of La Mancha himself, an ancestor, as I have often been told, of the general who planned this tremendous campaign, we should have all rolled in the snow, filled our mouths full of it, choked, and died laughing, had it not been for one splendid knightly figure, mounted on a black charger, and dashing on before the glorious, gallant Mulligan, in his green shirt-sleeves—for he disdained to wear a uniform—as kingly a man as ever rode at the head of an army, simply obeying the orders of some fool.

I found it monotonous to march with the rest in the road, and so deployed into the fields as a skirmisher for chickens. A goodly number of loyal spirits followed me, and on we went, marching on a line parallel to the army for many a weary mile—but no chicken. Cabin after cabin was passed, but the keenest and most searching investigation I could bestow, with all my vast store of experiences on the subject, failed to disclose a chicken. On, on we went. It was late in the afternoon. We had actually waddled, and waddled, and walked, run, stumbled, and shambled over streams, along mountain slopes, up hill and along ravines, full twenty miles, but not a chicken was yet discovered by any of us.

I grew desperate. I struck out further into the country, and fancied I was alone. Alas! how often the criminal deems that no eye sees him, as he presses on, intent only on the commission of desperate deeds, when, in sober truth, the two great eyes of justice, all unbandaged, are fixed upon him, and her swift feet are flying at his very heels, while her nimble fingers are ready to pick his pockets legally! And so it was with me. Soon I saw a little cabin down in a ravine below, and on this I marched with all speed and rapidity, and without fear, except that it might be chickenless, always a terrible thought to me. As I passed around the corner of the wretched hut, with its chimney on the outside, as such habitations are constructed, imagine, if you can, my surprise and gratification on seeing the head of a live hen protruding from a coop on the angle of the chimney and hut. A little dog ran out and barked, but not before I had seized the hen, put her, squalling for dear life, under my old blue overcoat, and was off at a run. Two old women came out with their night-caps on, raised their glasses, and gave a scream like a pair of demented locomotives. Their scream was a wail of terror that, I

doubt not, echoes among those mountains yet. But I
ran on. I was drilling and practicing for retreat—a
hundred or more of which my memoirs will record before my charcoal gives out. I had a hen. Heaven was
won. I had gained a prize that at that moment I should
not have exchanged for a full membership in the French
Academy of Science or a Harvard degree of LL.D. On
I went, over fences and ditches, toward our army. But,
on looking back, hang me if those two old termagants
were not following me, screaming like mad, yelling, as
Lord Ullin cried for his daughter: "Darn you, bring
back that ar hen. Oo! Oo! Whooh—oooo!" I believe that was what Mr. Ullin said. Surrender that hen!
No, never; and so, with increased speed, accelerated by
a wholesome fear of the two old she-devils, one armed
with a big long-handled fire shovel and the other with a
hand-spike, on I ran, until I was in hearing distance of
the head of our passing columns. Like a flash, an
officer, mounted on a good horse, came galloping down
upon me, and ordered me to halt. This order I obeyed.
He drew his sword violently on me, and swore a terrible
oath that he would cleave my thick skull in twain if I
did not release the chicken which the old Amazons, with
their stentorian voices, had told him I had stolen. With
downcast countenance, I released the hen. She gave a
squawk, and a flop of rejoicing, and darted away toward
the brush. In a moment, more than forty men were after
her, for the great man on horseback, now in his natural
element, and carried away by his first and last great
military movement, in delivering a hen from captivity
and death, ordered the boys to catch the old women's
hen.

She was caught, delivered with great pomp to the old creatures, and they knelt, with the hen in their mutual arms, at the feet of the officer's horse, and prayed " God to bless him." Vain enough before, this fulsome adulation and homage made him ten times more vain, and, raising his hat to the beldames and bowing grandly, he put spurs to his horse and dashed off to where I was, as he supposed, to arrest me. But, during the splendid ceremony, I had quietly dropped my overcoat (knowing I could easily steal another that night), and quickly throwing my cap in my knapsack, that I had as quickly unslung for the purpose, snatched out and donned an old slouch hat, in which even Dave Sheppard himself would not have recognized me. He looked through the ranks, but didn't recognize me muchly. That officer is looking for me yet! I passed him where he was breaking stone on a thirty days' contract for the state since, but he did not speak to me, even then! But my hen was gone. Not far. A fellow belonging to our mess had grabbed her from the old pair the moment the officer had disappeared, and he and I made merry over that chicken at a private banquet of our own, away out in the woods near Burlington, where we camped that night. This was the great event of that memorable march, and whenever hereafter it is named, that hen alone will be remembered.

V.—The First Death in the One Hundred and Sixteenth Ohio.

Jim Stoneking was a tall, broad-chested, robust young man, as he marched out with us to the war for the flag.

I remember well that he was by common consent regarded as the strongest and most active man in the entire One Hundred and Sixteenth Ohio; a concession, mind you, not made in those days until demonstrated fully after many a vigorous contest of a friendly, but nevertheless earnest and determined, character. The championship was not yielded to the first one who came along to claim it without putting it to the proof.

Jim was as modest as he was strong and athletic, and never was known to boast of his strength. He was of gigantic build, but in his manners gentle and kind as a girl. He was in our mess, and we were all proud of Jim. He had no enemies there or anywhere that I ever knew of. Handsome, intelligent, generous to a fault, as strong in his affections as he was in his muscles, he might have stood model for the god of war, or Hercules stripped for his seven labors, or for Apollo tuning his lyre. He constantly wore a smile, and his well-chiseled features were always radiant with the resplendent light of youth and manly beauty. I never saw his peer before or since. With a thousand such picked men—if, indeed, the continent might have yielded so many of such magnificent proportions and warlike vigor—Mr. Seward's ninety days' prophecy, perhaps, might have been fulfilled. In the midst of so many pale and attenuated school boys, and green and half-grown striplings, who later were to develop into robust veterans, Jim Stoneking passed for a prodigy of every military equipment physically and mentally—a born leader and master among men. He was only nineteen, and carried a musket yet: but in the bloom of his enlistment, and the prestige of his striking personal presence, he gave promise of official distinction ere the war should close.

We were in camp at New Creek, and had been mustered in then but three months. We were drilling yet, in squads, in the regiment, and by brigades, going through the tedious and toilsome preliminary school of arms, and had never yet smelt gunpowder or even seen a rebel. The weary days of camp life slowly rolled away. We longed for the day when we might be ready for the field and get into active service. Jim was assiduous in his study and practice of all that is taught in the Manual of Arms and the School of the Soldier, and his musket was but a plaything in his hands, which he could handle with all the skill and grace and ease of the trained veteran of many battles. But this idle, monotonous camp life was not to his taste. He longed for something more than the mimic charge on imaginary foes, something more inspiring than the merry reveille or the solemn taps. And so the weary days of discipline—all too few, as we found later on—wore away, and the autumn leaves were falling. One day Jim said to me: "I hate this schoolboy life. I did not enlist to practice the manual of arms forever, but to fight the enemies of the flag. I long for the day when we shall meet the foe in deadly battle. I can not bear this much longer. I am sick of it. I know our superior officers are right in insisting that we shall be well drilled and disciplined before we go to the field; but look at the three months' men, who are famous already and have fought many hard battles, yet no longer in the service than we have been. I know we are ready, and for my part. I want to see if I can stand fire coolly and do my duty like a man, don't you?"

Jim was right, and our officers agreed with him then, though we knew nothing of it. Even while he was uttering his complaint and longing for the real contest, marching orders were preparing in Washington, and ten days later the army moved to the scene of conflict. But Jim Stoncking was not with us. He was striken with typhoid fever, sank rapidly away, and died within a week.

He was the first man in the One Hundred and Sixteenth Ohio Volunteer Infantry to die—the first dead soldier my eyes ever beheld! As his noble form wasted quickly away, and at last lay stark in death, then amidst the playmates of his youth, we who survived mourned him with a bitterness of bereavement and regret that I should in vain try to describe. O, what a wreck of youthful hopes! O, what a calamity of woe! O, what ruin of heroic ambition and manly strength lay silent and motionless there in that rough pine box, buried under the shadows of the motionless mountains now, and covered with the pitiless snows of winter. As I look back now at the interval of a quarter of a century to that humble mound, and then recall the stalwart form of my noble friend, and remember the hopes and dreams of ambition that he cherished, so ruthlessly ruined by the hand of a most untimely and inglorious death, my eyes again swim in tears. If Jim Stoncking could have fallen with Reese Williams, and with him gathered up the folds of the flag in his dying grasp, and kissed them with his expiring breath on a field of battle and victory, I know he would have sunk to rest without a single sigh or regret. But it was not to be so. And yet why not I never shall know. But in the record of the brave and true who devoted their lives for the flag, let us never forget those humbler heroes who, like Jim Stoneking, felt death's destroying wound, not in the heat of battle, but in the quiet hospital of agony.

Henry T. Johnson was our color-bearer after Reese Williams was shot down at Piedmont. The colors, stained with the blood—O God, no! not stained, but sanctified, with the blood fresh from the pure and gallant heart of the standard-bearer, had dropped almost to the ground, but the icy fingers of that brave young hero closed in a grip of patriotic death about the flagstaff still when Henry T. Johnson sprang forward, seized the staff in his strong hands, and carried it on in the thickest of the fight. Shells were exploding and bullets raining thickly around him, but on he went, in advance of the charging columns who followed close in lines of flashing muskets and glittering bayonets.

It was no holiday sport. It was no parade rest. It was no sport or pastime now. The boys who had yesterday been so frolicsome and gay, now wore the serious aspect of thoughtful and determined veterans, every man resolved to conquer on that field or leave his body there cold and bloody in death.

The battle of Piedmont under Hunter was short, hot, and one of the most brilliant victories of the war. Rebel lead flew through the flag, and still it streamed on. It was the target of traitors who hated its every stripe and star. At every wound the flag received vengeance rose in every breast, and then and there took fresh courage for the deadly fray. I had read of treason and traitors and of rebellion, but I never understood it at all

9

until I saw them shoot at that flag. When John A. Dix
said, "If any man attempts to tear down the American
flag, shoot him on the spot," he only gave expression to
the sentiment that actuated the boys in blue. No Union
soldier ever felt the blood run hot in his veins and ar-
teries, and fairly cry for vengeance on the traitors, until
he saw the rebels fire on that flag. The war is over now
these two and twenty years almost, and yet I dare say
there is not a city, village, or hamlet in all the North, at
least, if indeed in the South, now, as I would fain believe, where any man could fire on that flag and live
another minute. I asked Henry T. Johnson but this
very day what was the uppermost thought in his mind at
the moment he took up our flag from the dead color-
bearer at Piedmont, twenty-two years ago and more.

What do you suppose was his reply? "Thoughts! I
had no thoughts, Jim, not one. I had the flag in my
hands. Who could think there with that old banner
waving over him in the center of the battle? But I had
feelings, Jim, no thoughts, not a single one. I was
sorry for poor Reese. I was angry as h—l at the men
who shot him down, but ten times more so at the damnable traitors who fired on our flag and shot it to tatters
with their guns of treason. Jim Dalzell, before God, I
tell you now I would send them all to hell for it yet if it
were in my power. Talk of unpardonable sins—firing
on that flag must not, shall not, be forgiven in this world
nor the next, let sentimentalists and Mugwumps who
were not where I stood say what they may."

Henry T. Johnson was wounded badly; had an arm
shattered before that battle ended, but on he went, and
refused to yield his flag to any one. That arm hangs

limp and helpless by his side now, but let us say of him as the Spartan mother of her wounded son: " Every time he looks at the wound, it will make him remember his valor with pride." Though he had but one sound hand, he held it aloft at Appomattox by divine right of heroism on many a fiery field.

I shall never forget that first day he carried it at Piedmont. I was alarmed at his reckless daring—for a thousand guns were leveled at that flag and its heroic bearer. He rushed on with his face to the foe with an utter abandonment of fear which bespoke but little less than a madman. Under a galling fire once our line reeled, staggered, and almost broke and fled, but Johnson pushed on until Colonel Wildes, as brave and true a man as ever commanded a regiment, feared color-bearer and flag both should fall into the enemy's hands. Waving his sword on his horse, the Colonel called to Henry, " Come back to the regiment!" I see Johnson's transfigured face yet with the battle-seared and riddled banner streaming over his bare head, and the blood pouring down his blouse sleeve and over his pantaloons, as he yelled back with rage in every fine feature of his beardless, blood-stained, and begrimed face, " Bring your regiment to the colors, Colonel Wildes, for I'll be —— if this flag retreats while I carry it," and he flourished the flag in a tempest of bullets.

Every man *saw*, though few heard the brave response in the thunder of the conflict. In a flash Colonel Wildes dashed forward on his coal-black steed, and we followed with a yell. The rebels fell back, the day was ours, and the old flag, the only flag that can wave on this side of the Atlantic, did it all, and won new glories there that shall shine forever in its eternal stars.

VI.—HOW THE PRIVATE AND BEN TILDEN ENJOYED A BUGGY RIDE.

I enlisted as a private soldier in Company H, One Hundred and Sixteenth Ohio Infantry, and expected to do my marching on foot, of course; but even the proudest private in the world will sometimes condescend to ride a horse, a mule, or even a buggy. This is my apology for the exploit I am about to relate. I neglected to take my buggy with me to war, but we all got buggy enough before long. I had to trust to the chances of war to throw one in my way. It would not stand in my way long. We had marched about from Clarksburg, Buckhannon, the chief mountain region, to Romney and Moorefield, and every-where throughout West Virginia, over its snowy ranges of mountains, up and down its valleys, the whole winter of 1862–63.

I was tired of following those fool generals around for no wise purpose in the world that I could see with my naked eyes, and so I determined to lead the expedition myself, and have some fun at the risk of a court-martial and the Rip-Raps, or Dry Tortugas. We had been marching, marching constantly for weeks, and never saw a rebel of the male gender, except some old chaps about as old as old Methusaleh, who, with their specks on, picked off our men occasionally in the night, and sat grunting with affected servility in the chimney corner at home all day long.

A West Virginian never dies, never grows too old to

bushwhack. In the spring of 1863, we set off on a forced march from Romney to "Winchestertown," and this is how I achieved the distinction of which I am about to inform a gaping and admiring world.

Ben Tilden, my old messmate and companion in all manner of deviltry, was a thirsty soul. He always carried more canteens than any other man in the regiment. They were thirsty, too, and as the hare pants for the water brook, they did not. They panted with Ben for apple-jack. So did I, if the truth of history must at this late day blazon the annals of my country.

So that morning Ben and I started out alone, a mile or two in advance of the army, in search of the delicious apple-jack, chickens, corn-bread, or other prosaic objects of sense. We had grown weary of water and hardtack. It was only sheer luck that we both did not fall a prey to the rebels that day, as we marched along hastily far in advance of Milroy's great army. The only explanation that I ever could find for our miraculous escape was that there were no rebels there.

This would often explain a great many of the hair-breadth escapes so graphically delineated in the magazines and the dime novels. But it would spoil the symmetry and attraction of the Munchausen yarns, and so is wisely left out. About noon we invaded a rickety old hut where an old woman and a few young negroes lived, and found good store of solids and liquids, and resumed our march with cuisine and canteen much replenished. A few draughts from the same canteen and a few more from the other canteen too, and we were merry as larks, brave as a pair of uncaged lions, and ready for deeds of daring that would make your hair stand on end to think of for a moment.

As we sauntered along, not caring if it snowed oats, we saw an old, one-eyed, hip-shot horse hitched by the roadside to a dilapidated buggy of the G. Washington era. Said I, "Ben, let's take a buggy ride." No sooner said than done, so quickly did one soldier respond to the wildest suggestion of another. Indeed, if I had suggested to Ben to eat the old nag he would have tried it, or choked on the harness.

In we jumped, reined the old Rosinante around into road, and off we went, tearing over the road, on "to Winchester, twenty miles away." The horse heaved and groaned, limped and stumbled, but we plied the whip, and as he warmed up he made better time. Whoop, hurrah, away we go! A merrier, jollier pair of young scapegraces never made the wild woods of Virginia ring with such cheers, laughter, and songs before. Wasn't this glorious? We despised foot soldiers. We wished we had enlisted in buggies. We had lost so much valuable time hoofing it in the mud, that we determined now to make up for it all in a ride that should go down to history, hand in hand with the wildest one ever accomplished by the Knight of La Mancha himself. Before this, we had thought three years a long term to serve in the army. Now, we began to discuss the brevity of the time until we must be mustered out of the army—or the buggy. The vehicle creaked and clashed with age, and surged and jolted, and threated to go to pieces, like the Confederacy. But, like the Confederacy, its time had not come yet. As the horse warmed up with the apple-jack and the whip which Ben constantly applied, as I drove like Jehu, he became nimble and fleet of foot, and whirled us along, I know not how many knots an hour. Still on we went. We saw nobody except a few frightened women and grinning negroes staring at us from the cabins along the road, at long intervals. From the noise the antiquated buggy made, and the din we raised ourselves, they evidently thought us crazy—possibly two armies were coming upon them to destroy them.

I said Ben applied the applejack and the whip. He applied only one of those to the horse, the other he applied to himself. Gentle reader, thou knowest which the poor horse got, and which Ben and I !

But, alas, all things, even buggy rides in the army, end all too soon, and so must this John Gilpin chase and this military memoir of mine.

Long before we reached Winchester we heard the clatter of horses' hoofs, "nearer, clearer, deadlier" still, the clank of sabers, and the wild shouts of the cavalry in pursuit of us. We had been reported to the general, and a body of cavalry were in pursuit of us. Rounding a bend in the road, we quietly dropped out of the buggy, and let the horse run on with it.

Just across the road, and in plain view, was an old-fashioned Virginia brick mansion. Concealing ourselves until the cavalry detachment galloped by in pursuit of the buggy, we quietly slipped over to the house, awaiting developments to cover up our identity and prevent detection. We knew that, as soon as the infantry came up, crowds of bummers would break ranks and rush for the house in great numbers for forage. We had not to wait long. In a few minutes in they came like bees ; no one saw us, each was so intent ransacking cellar, garret,

and cupboard, for any thing and every thing eatable,
that no one took any account of us. We mingled with
them, joined them in ransacking the house with loud
shouts as any one in the general confusion, and when the
house was completely looted, left with the rest and returned to the ranks, looking as innocent and non-com-
mittal as the general who had marched us all over
Virginia for nothing. Then it was we heard of the exploit in the buggy. It was on every lip, and the boys
were in no good humor over it either. The scouts had
spied two men in a buggy, evidently rebel officers of
high rank. They had driven off like mad at the ap-
proach of the advance guard. That meant business.
Certes, the rebel army was near. All this was reported
to General Milroy, who ordered the whole army to advance and attack the rebels. And so the entire Union
army had been double-quicked after us for four miles,
and were nearly exhausted. We could not but smile as
we heard all the stories, but never mentioned our connection with it. It would spoil the general's report to
Washington then, and a nice article about that gallant
reconnoissance now. Oh, no! We listened demurely,
as if we knew no more about it than the rest.

VII.—A High Private at Rich Mountain

Doubtless my readers are all familiar with the history
of Rosecrans' victory on the very summit of Rich Mountain in 1861, and how an humble guide led him up by a
circuitous route in the rear of the rebel army, though history has utterly failed to transmit even the name of that

MY WAR SKETCHES, ETC.

humble guide, to whom the victory was more justly due than to Rosecrans.

But there was another army led up that long and steep mountain side, by the ordinary route, and now for the first time posterity is to be furnished with his name.

It was I.

The results in the two cases were very dissimilar, indeed, and though the struggle on the rugged and stony top of that historic acclivity was attended with bloody consequences in the former case, yet I hasten to assure my sympathetic and gentle reader that in the charge I led nothing followed more serious than laughter and cheers, the echo of which, it is said, lingers in those mountain fastnesses even yet.

It was a cold, clear morning in the early winter of 1862 when Milroy's army broke camp at Buchanan and made the famous three days' forced march to Cheat Mountain, ending in nothing, for there was not a rebel force of the size of one of our companies within twenty miles of there, and had not been for months.

This was some of the strategy of the war concerning which you do not read as much now as we musket-bearers actually witnessed from the ranks. It does not read pretty in the magazines. It is too like the truth, and they mind the old Biblical injunction to "buy the truth and sell it not." It is not salable. They keep their truth in pickle, and set out the fictitious as more palatable to the public. But as these articles run along, all written out in charcoal, without the help of maps and plans prepared in Washington in 1886 by young men who were not born at the date of my historic ascent of Rich

Mountain, the reader will be apt to conclude before I am done that I dabble in the truth by way of variety.

It is tempting, indeed, and I have half a notion one of these days to take a small flag, climb on the top of Rich Mountain, and, giving play to imagination, fill it with rebels firing big cannons, have myself capturing six or eight cannons that never existed in the smoke of their discharge.

But, alas! *descensus averni facilis!* It was not cannon—it was slapjacks, delicious slapjacks, rolled in butter and honey, hot from the griddle, and washed down with generous potations of West Virginia applejack that I captured Rich Mountain with without the loss of a single man or gun, and with no more serious loss than that of an appetite that erstwhile hungered for any solid or fluid except water.

Inadvertently I have anticipated the climax of my story, for, but for the slapjacks and applejack, this story had never seen the light, and this achievement had never blazoned the history of our great civil war.

Lieutenant Spriggs, as thirsty a soul as ever drank from the same canteen with me, set out in the gray of early morning from our encampment, ten miles west of Rich Mountain, and together we wended our weary way a mile or two in advance of the army, in search of corn-bread, chickens, and mountain dew. Hunger and thirst are great virtues in war, and achieve wonderful exploits.

By the kind assistance of a contraband. away beyond camp, we found the applejack in copious quantity, sampled it in true army style, and then faced the mountain with light steps and heroic hearts, making music as we went.

If the entire army of Lee had been posted on that mount, Spriggs and I would have walked up and routed it, for we were thrice armed with canteens, revolvers, and my grand old musket, which never sat so lightly on my shoulder before. After going up a mile or so by the circuitous mountain road, we sat down to smoke and view the landscape o'er. Bonaparte crossing the Alps was not a circumstance to the spectacle we presented, and there were two of us—only one of him.

We could look down, it seemed, on half of the world, and as we saw the army below commencing its toilsome ascent we could imagine ourselves the two bright particular heroes who were destined to end the war and ride into the White House on the wave of popularity that should roll at our feet as the result of our heroic exploits. How small and contemptible that army seemed! We yearned for a million men, and then three hundred thousand; yea, six hundred thousand more. As the faint notes of the bugle and the soft strains of the bands swept up the mountain sides and saluted our eager ears, our hearts fairly danced and throbbed with enthusiasm for a moment, until a more practical and realistic suggestion from our stomachs promptly dispelled the illusion and urged us on to find a dinner before the hungry horde below should have time to reach it. So on we went, shouting, "Excelsior," at every bounding step. No hart ever scaled a mountain with steadier or lighter tread.

The summit was reached. A lovely cabin stood there, all bullet-riddled from the sanguinary conflict of the

year before. In we go, without ceremony, and find the
family, an old weatherbeaten crone and her melancholy
daughter of the mountain, at her elbow eating—how
shall I express it? Slapjacks rolled in honey! The
gods and goddesses on Olympus never feasted as we did
then. But, hark! it is the tramp of armed men. I
should smile. In they rush, and soon the house is full of
Yanks. The skillet was still hot on the hearth, but
Spriggs had despoiled it of the last of its charms.
There was no more batter. We wept like Alexander
that there was no more batter for our battery. [This is a
feeble attempt at humor for the diversion of the reader
of this veracious bit of dry military history. I believe
the harsh outlines of military narrative are sometimes
softened and subdued, if you please, by a graceful and
gentle touch of wit and humor, though most histories of
the war are as destitute of the delicate accompaniment
as they are of truth. Of the latter they have very little.] We popped out of the house as they went in, and
dodged off into the brush behind the big rocks that
grew up there to the size of a church. We chuckled
with delight and applejack over our adventure. The
main part of the army was still struggling painfully in
column at close distances up the rugged mountain side.

I fired my gun!

"H—ll!" shouted my lieutenant close at my side.
"What did you do that for? Now there will be h—l to
pay." And there was pretty soon.

At least it looked like it, sounded like it, and smelt
suspiciously so in the next five minutes.

I quietly dropped in among the hustling, jostling, mot-
ley crew of unknown bummers, and looked as innocent

as "Mary's little lamb.' "Who fired that gun?" shouted men right and left. No one knew. No one ever knew or could discover. The boys did not tell on each other, and poor Lieutenant Spriggs would have lost his right hand, yea more, three canteens of applejack, before he would have told.

Up dashed orderlies and officers, field and staff, blazing in new uniforms and mighty shoulder-straps, with swords drawn, and the whole army on the double-quick at their heels, madly rushing, as they sincerely felt,

> "Into the jaws of death,
> Into the mouth of hell."

My old colonel (heaven bless him now in his old age at Madison, Wis., brave, true Colonel Washburne, of the One Hundred and Sixteenth Ohio), with his teeth set and his spurs buried in the sides of his foaming old horse, rode up, exclaiming loudly: "Show me the d—d fool that fired that gun!"

I did not answer to that name, and he rode on. Soon the whole army was on the top of the rocky mountain, all talking at once, all swearing and sweating, and Babel itself was a deaf and dumb institution compared to that excited and noisy army. Still, whenever I could get a chance, I piped in with the rest, "Who fired that gun?" No one could tell me, and so I had my laugh all alone.

VIII.—Another Story of the Old Flag.

Milton James was a member of the Sixty-second Ohio, which, with the Sixty-seventh, was consolidated with the One Hundred and Sixteenth Ohio shortly before the surrender of Lee, three regiments, having, from first to last, on their muster-rolls 4,974 soldiers, officers and men; yet the day the three gallant old battle-scarred regiments as one charged Fort Gregg, we had present and fit for duty, all told, 300 men! Not one man more.

Less than 200 of these survived the five days' race after Lee, and were able to stand with us at his formal surrender. Some idea of the losses of all sorts which the veteran regiments sustained in that four years' terrible struggle may be gathered from a brief statement like this; but when it is added that I saw the Twenty-fifth Ohio come out of the battle of Gettysburg with seven men, and three of these badly wounded, and on the morning of Grant's final encounter with Lee, near Appomattox Court-house, there were present with us, including Milton James, precisely twenty-four men of the gallant Sixty-second Ohio, the reader who was not with us will begin to have some faint and feeble comprehension of the havoc wrought by the fearful war.

An idea strikes me: If every soldier who was with Grant at Appomattox would give the actual count of men—and all who were there easily can—in their respective regiments, it would correct many gross errors in history.

Sheridan's men, dismounted and contesting every inch of ground with a bravery never excelled before by that gallant command, were falling back, when the Second, Fifth, Sixth, and Twenty-fourth Corps emerged from the woods and went in with a yell on the morning of Lee's surrender.

The half has never been told. As General Crook rode up he recognized brave old Captain Robert Davidson (now of Caldwell, O.) and his twenty-three men, all that was left of what had once been a regiment of 1,800 men. It was getting hot. The boys were wading into the dismayed and surrounded Johnnies. Captain Davidson's men had been fighting and falling all morning. The tears came to the glorious old Crook's eyes as he said, " Hold, boys of the Sixty-second, you have done your share. You need not go in unless you want to. Go where you please. Do as you please." Every cap was thrown up, and with a cheer the Sixty-second, a mere handful of one of the best regiments I ever saw, fell in on the right flank of the Sixth Corps, and with a yell joined in the final charge—the last charge of the Rebellion, with the cold, merciless steel. Milton James was there. He is now the American Express agent at Caldwell, Ohio, in peace, as in war, one of the best of men. When the charge was made on Fort Gregg a few days before, Milton James was there, then but seventeen years of age, and a veteran soldier of thirty-one battles. He had never missed a battle or a march that his regiment encountered, and carried with him a charmed life, always in danger but never to be harmed. He never was wounded or even scratched. When a fearful charge was made on Fort Gregg, the One Hundredth New York on the left was preparing to advance. It was said that regiment had once shown the white feather. It was about to advance under the terrible fire of the fort. " That regiment shall never go ahead of the Sixty-second," shouted Milton James, and sprang forward with the tattered flag in his hands, and the rest followed with a yell. A few feet from the ditch, which was broad and deep, the withering fire of the fort became too hot for even the most desperate men, and the whole column recoiled and fell back, but James, with the colors, leaped into the ditch with only Joseph Willis with him. The leap of Curtius was not more reckless. Now James with the few strings, ribbons, and tatters of the old Sixty-second banner, and Willis were alone in the ditch, directly under the parapet fifteen feet high, and right under the booming guns of the fort. The rebels knew it. They dared not bend over the fort and fire down on the two devoted young heroes, for that would be but to court instant death from our sharpshooters. So they began to throw single-trees, old muskets, stones, and every missile they could reach down after the boys in hope of crushing them. They hugged the walls closely and dodged every falling object, and it kept them busy. They scrambled about in water waist deep, for it had been raining many days, and the ditch was half full of water. Still the flag of the Sixty-second flew in triumph and derision almost within reach of the enemy. The fire was desperate on both sides, and the chances were a thousand to one that the two young dare-devils would be killed by our own shells exploding in the ditch. They fell thick and fast, but the poor boys were neither hurt nor scared but held their ground! What else could they do? If they left the ditch and started back to reach the Twenty-fourth Army Corps, now under the gallant Gibbon, advancing in close column at half distance, they would fall an easy prey to the rebel sharpshooters, once they were out of cover of the fort. A shout rang along the line of blue; the Twenty-fourth Corps advanced to double-quick on the blazing parapets of Fort Gregg. Their losses as they swept across the open field up to the fort were

fearful. As they rushed into the ditch with fixed bayonets a new danger menaced the two boys. They had
hard work to make the first who leaped into the ditch
understand who they were, for the smoke was dense, and
they could not see the flag. Fortunately, just in time to
save their lives, they convinced their friends who they
were, and up they all started, climbing the parapet, as
I have before tried to describe in a former letter. Captain Davidson, with that Thompsom whom I mention elsewhere, clambered up the steep walls on the shoulders of
their men. As Davidson reached the top he stuck his
sword to the hilt in the earthwork, and by the handle
was raising himself up when the rebels began to batter
his hands with their muskets, and though they succeeded
in crippling him for life, he held on, drew his body to
the top, and sword in hand leaped into the fort! He is
pensioned and was promoted for it. So there can be no
dispute of this—nor can there be of any fact I give—for
I was there and saw it all! I don't care what books may
say I know better than they do who wrote them. They
have their papers based largely upon hearsay—I base
mine upon what my eyes and those of a thousand others
saw there and then. Poor Willis ascended the human
ladder only to receive his death shot at the top. But
where was Milt James? Right beside his noble captain
now in command of what was left of the Spartan frag-
ment of the Sixty-second Ohio, of course, for where else
should the flag be? Henry T. Johnson, with our flag,
was there, shattered arm and all. As James climbed
upon the parapet, a half-dozen rebels reached for his flag
and snatched it out of his hands. The brave boy rose
to his full height, and though a wall of cold steel con-

10

fronted him, he jumped down ten feet right among the
rebels and seized his beloved banner. "I should have
jumped into hell after that flag without hesitating," said
he to me to-day. Joe Jerls, Captain Davidson, and a
dozen more of our boys rushed in and soon James stood
there while the most fearful hand to hand fight Grant
ever saw—so say his memoirs—went on, and the Sixty-
second's flag floated over the scene of carnage and confusion, and James was happy, unharmed, unscathed, un-
wounded, and unfrightened as he will ever be in heaven
where before long he is going, as he held it up and
waved its blood-stained tatters in the storm of battle
once more. The day was ours! The flag once more
had won the battle!

IX.—How the Valorous Private Stampeded One
Army and Led Another.

The serious and serio-comic sides of the war for the
Union have been written all to tatters with "damnable
iteration," as one said of Lord Brougham's speeches.
Yet, as another said, "much remains to be said on every
great subject" without repetition. History has been
written and repeated o'er and o'er, a thousand times
o'er, in the vain effort to reproduce the great civil war
on paper for the delectation of a generation that never
heard the gun of Sumter echoing round the world. After
so much had been said, and so well said, it was a long
time before I concluded to take up my pen and sketch
that war roughly in charcoal. My heart sank within me
in the presence of Grant's memoirs, Sherman's memoirs,
and Badeau's thrilling romances.

But with Montesquieu, reciting the words of Corregio, as he contemplated the masterpieces of the great artists, I exclaimed, "I, also, am a painter," and so flinging my modesty to the winds, I began my contributions to history, of which this is neither the first nor the worst. Did you ever see a stampede? Not a stampede like that of Bull Run, where there was good cause for it in rattling musketry, fierce rebel yells, black-horse cavalry, and all that "thunder in the index" with which the chivalry of the South set out to eat up "the ragged and cowardly Yankees." No, not at all that sort of affair, but a stampede—I mean without cause, reason, or sense; causeless as a final cause, and senseless as a political speech—that is the sort of stampede I allude to, a regular skedaddle for nothing. Didn't ever see one? Well, here is one of that sort which I caused myself. You must have certain conditions before you can have a fire—fuel and combustion, for instance—and so of stampedes. The nerves of the men must be unstrung, a general feeling of weakness and helplessness in the presence of a superior foe must exist, or you can't stampede or skedaddle an army; and the danger, real or apparent, it makes no difference which, must descend suddenly and unexpectedly, like a thunderbolt from a clear sky, like a meteor shooting down at noonday. Precisely such were the conditions with which Milroy's brave little army of 7,000 men were surrounded on the clear, frosty night of January 1, 1863, near Petersburg. W. Va. (not old Petersburg). We had had our first fight at Moorefield the day before, a sharp little affair with Jones' cavalry, that ended in nothing but a big scare and a long retreat through the

mountains the coldest night that I was ever out of doors.
We hastily piled our stuff, quartermaster's and commissary stores, in the brick church at Petersburg, and set it
on fire and ran off in the blaze. This was strategy.

Our wagon train—you remember every regiment had
ten wagons in those fool days—started off, and we with
it, mules, men, and horses, possessed of a horrible fear,
without reason or sense. Our generals saw to it that
our knapsacks were empty. We had not tasted ham all
winter, yet we burnt up forty wagon loads of hams and
shoulders, and went off on this wild goose chase toward
Burlington and Cedar Creek, forty miles, freezing, hungry, and without a bit of bread or meat. So the orders
ran! So the war was conducted for years, as if the idiot
asylums of the whole land had been robbed to get our
commanders.

After going thus pell-mell ten miles our forces halted,
for what reason I never learned, about 10 o'clock that
night in a narrow ravine in the mountains, parked the
wagons, built our fires, and sat down around them like a
pack of fools, hungry and with half-frozen feet. It was
a sight for your faithful historian. But he was not going
to sit there long, you bet. A bright idea struck me. I
got a couple of old chums to join me, and we soon had
mounted three stolen horses, and were scampering away
over the light snow toward a farm-house, a mile or two
away. We took three or four canteens with us, and as
we had been there before we knew where to go. Dis-
mounting at the gate, we were soon in the old Virginia
mansion, sitting by a great fire talking with the rebel
girls. Applejack, yes, it was, that filled our canteens,

and corn-bread our haversacks, and after an hour's chat, and paying our bill, we remounted to ride back.

The stars fairly glittered in the cold blue vault above, and the snow sparkled like diamonds about us as the horses galloped over it. It was not deep, a mere rift of snow, dry and light as feathers and the flying hoofs rattled on the hard frozen road like volleys of pistols. A merrier set never returned to camp, as cheering and singing, and laughing we rode back that night. As we drew near the place were we supposed the camp was when we left, there was a sharp curve in the road, and as we rounded it on the gallop, digging the spurs into our horses, and cheering like Comanches, suddenly, quick as thought, we saw a line of men six rods in front, muskets aimed, and the clear beams of the stars shining on every barrel. Fourteen men ready to fire. "Halt!" cried one, but we could not stop. Flash, bang, went every barrel, and so close that the balls went over our heads, and the smoke of the discharge into our eyes, before we could turn our horses in their mad career; but in a jiffy we reined them about and were on the retreat. Our camp had been captured. We had been fired upon by rebels, of course; what else could it be, and so we retreated for all there was in it, but without the loss of a single canteen, and not one of us wounded. As we rushed along like Jehus, time came for second thought. We could hear shouts in all directions, like bedlam let loose. Wagons drawn by mules, and without drivers, came rushing madly behind us, and soon we were forced to take to the woods to avoid being run over. Pandemonium reigned. Guns went off in every direction, and the shouting continued from all points of the compass. After a hasty consultation, as we galloped along through the brush, we all burst out laughing together as the true situation at length dawned upon us. It was our own men and not rebels who had fired on us. The army had broken camp while we were off on our frolic, and resumed its march without our knowledge, and we had been fired upon by the advance-guard of our own army. So, as soon as we reached this conclusion, we dismounted on a high bluff overlooking the road, and, holding our horses' reins, sat down in a council of war, as many a great general has done, to contemplate the disaster that we had so innocently precipitated upon an army frightened out of its wits. We enjoyed the racket hugely. Teams came thundering along, banging wagon against wagon, and riderless horses rushed by, but no men; they had taken to the woods at the first fire. Reader, would you believe that these were the very men who but a little more than a year and a half after that scaled the heights of Cedar Creek, and gained the greatest and grandest victory for the Union army accomplished during the war? But a year and a half later they did that, not under incompetents, but under gallant Phil. Sheridan.

*　　　*　　　*　　　*　　　*　　　*

But we had not long to wait. Soon along came a detachment of the brave and dashing First Virginia Cavalry. The foremost man fairly raised in his saddle as he spied us three woe-begone, panic-stricken fellows sitting on the cold top-rail of that fence in the edge of the woods. He leveled his carbine, but I shouted before he could fire: "Don't shoot your own men; we belong to Milroy." He took down his piece, and began to laugh and swear. "I knowed it all the time. It was our own d—d fools that caused all this racket. Why, they said that 13,000 rebel cavalry dashed into our camp, and killed all the vanguard but that one poor devil that got his leg broke by a panic-stricken mule, and set us on your trail. We arrest you on the spot." Glad to be arrested, we crouched back humbly onto our nags, and fell in between two files of cavalry to be marched back to head-quarters.

We marched back in solemn procession like three mounted culprits going back to be shot by a drum-head court-martial. We knew what we would catch. We let go of all hope, every thing but our canteens. They stood us in good hand. We lavished our hospitality on our captors, and pressed them to drink from the same canteen. There was probably not a man in the crowd over twenty-one years of age, most of us eighteen. So you can imagine how generous they soon became. In five minutes they were all so bamboozled with the good old applejack that they were hugging us on our horses, and singing, "We won't (hic) go home till (hic) morning (hic)." It was grand strategy. Those were days of strategy, and the generals didn't have all of the strategy to themselves.

Before we had gone a quarter of a mile we came across a sutler wagon that had been upset, cheese, tobacco, cigars, bologna-sausage, canned fruits, and all scattered about. We dismounted to gather things up, the horses got away somehow, and we, too, and, mingling with the crowd of poor frightened creatures now, no one ever knew who it was caused all the devilment until this appeared.

X.—THE CAPTURE OF FORT GREGG.

I had heard of many an ancient river, from Alph, the sacred, to the dusky torrent of Styx, but to me the Appomattox River was a stream wholly unknown until, in the wake of Sheridan's magnificent cavalry, with the Twenty-fourth Army Corps, I crossed it on the night of March 26, 1865, in the rain and mud. From along the swamps of the Chickahominy to the west side of the James and across the Appomattox, we had marched under continuous fire. Wading through swamps, half starved, harassed by the desperate enemy, now fighting in his last ditch, day and night without rest or sleep, on we went, little dreaming as we crossed the ignoble and sluggish Appomattox, that its tepid waters should soon be resplendent with a victory that should class it with immortal rivers, and catalogue it for eternity with the Euphrates, the Granicus, and the Delaware. It runs through and along bluffs covered at intervals with small trees; while back of it, and west as far as the eye could reach the country was clear, level, and open. It is white oak timber land, and stunted shrubs of that species grew like vegetation, gnarled, knotted, ugly, and possessed of the devil, along its banks. We were south-west of Petersburg, and near Hatcher's Run. Ours was the second division, commanded by General Turner, as gallant an officer as ever led a charge. All this on the Appomattox River; and yet who ever heard or read about the Appomattox River before?

Oh, what a sweep the Union line made from the Appomattox west, away to the north beyond Petersburg, thirty miles or more, and fire along the line by day and night. To our right was the Sixth Corps; north and west of us were the Second and Fifth, with Sheridan's cavalry to the east of that, a half moon, inclosing to that extent the doomed city of Petersburg. Clouds of smoke by day, flashes of fire by night, the earth trembling with the mighty final contest. I have never felt large, but I never felt my individual insignificance more than in this titanic contest. To me, with little stretch of the imagination, it seemed all the world was in arms and Armageddon was before me in all its glory and terror. One man was a mere speck on a horizon of gray and blue like that. It was my humble task merely to wield the ignoble pen in that final struggle, while the very table on which I wrote rocked in the tremendous concussion of mighty cannon, and the tremendous messengers of death frequently fell near our tent, wherever we pitched it, by day or night. Rest there was none for man or dumb beast.

On the 28th—so runs my diary—we moved to the extreme left of the rebel line, at Hatcher's Run, soon to turn crimson with some of the best blood America ever shed.

We were under heavy artillery fire at close range, and cutting timber as we could, advanced our lines at night under cover of it carried forward. The boys would push it ahead at night, and skip over lightly with spades and shovels, and creep and dig up as best they could on the rebel works. The young pines six inches in diameter and less were cut off, and looked like masts. It was a swampy place, and our progress was slow under the galling fire of the enemy, which we returned with interest.

11

Corduroy roads were made, and our artillery drawn forward until, by its magnificent management on the night of the 29th, the enemy's batteries were at last silenced forever at Hatcher's Run.

Over and through their *chevaux de frise*—and I never saw such a network of timber and iron before or since, it seemed impassable—yet on went our pioneers with their axes, under the brave Captain Jim Mann, of my regiment, cutting it away, while General Turner, with our corps (the Twenty-fourth) massed in close column, half distance, by regiments, advanced with a yell, and charged the works, when up went their white flag just as the day dawned, and Hatcher's Run was ours. The One Hundred and Twenty-third Ohio took charge, while we swept on. It had rained for three days and nights steadily, but the morning of the 30th the sun rose clear, as if it rejoiced with us in our great victory.

Fort Gregg was before us, with its frowning parapet, fifteen feet high, hitherto unapproached by any foe except to be hurled back in disaster and dismay. On Sunday, April 2, we moved to the right of the Sixth Corps, and assaulted Fort Gregg. Unlike that at Hatcher's Run, here we had a clear field. Our column advanced in splendid order under a raking fire, not only from Fort Gregg itself, but from all the earth-works of the rebels, clear along from the Appomattox to the north of Petersburg. Here occurred the most desperate fighting that was seen at any time under Grant in the East. So he says in his Memoirs. The contest did not last fifty minutes. In a tempest of grape and canister our heroes pushed forward, firing and cheering as they went, until they reached the deep ditch under the walls; but how to get over them, that was the question. A moment's pause, and Corporal F. C. Thompson, with thirteen other soldiers whose names history will cherish forever, clambered up the parapet. Almost at the top one was shot down and fell back into the ditch. Thompson was struck with a musket and fell, too, with several ribs broken, but in a moment climbed on a comrade's shoulder and was up again, fighting on the parapet against fearful odds. Close beside him were Clay Mountens and Joe Smith, of my company, until Clay's foot was shot off, and Joe shot clear through the neck, and both tumbled back into the ditch. Comrade on comrade's shoulders, up they climbed, fighting like demons. Some below loaded guns while the blood poured from wounds, and up they handed these muskets to Thompson and the rest who struggled on the parapet above, and soon the whole army swept in, and the fort was ours. They used each other as ladders to climb to the top, until the day was won. Congress voted the first gallant thirteen medals of honor for their bravery, and I saw Thompson's to-day. He is marshal of the town of Caldwell. These were delivered to the survivors in the presence of the army and General Grant.

It was the greatest feat of personal heroism recorded in the history of the war, grandly recognized in an august presence.

I copy the order under which the medal was bestowed:

WAR DEPARTMENT, ADJT. GENERAL'S OFFICE, }
WASHINGTON, *May* 9, 1865. }

CORPORAL F. C. THOMPSON, CO. F, 116TH OHIO:

Herewith I inclose a medal of honor to be presented

you under resolution of Congress for distinguished service at Fort Gregg.

By order of the Secretary of War.

Very respectfully,

E. D. TOWNSEND, A. A. G.

I have never yet seen any account of the transportation of the rebel flags at Washington. Here is the true story in brief, for my space is limited.

The surviving ones of the gallant thirteen common soldiers at Fort Gregg had the honor of carrying these flags to Washington, and F. C. Thompson and Color Bearer Van Meter, of my regiment, were two of that number. The rebel flags were all placed in one box of huge proportions—the colossal coffin of the Lost Cause. It was twelve or fourteen feet long, for I remember we piled them in, flag staff and banners, closely furled, and nailed the lid down tight and strong. On the morning of April 28, the following order was promulgated:

HEADQUARTERS ONE HUNDRED AND SIXTEENTH
OHIO VOLUNTEER INFANTRY,
RICHMOND, VA., *April* 28, 1865.

ADJUTANT-GENERAL, TWENTY-FOURTH ARMY CORPS:

Sir:—The bearers, Corporal Freeman C. Thompson and Private Joseph Van Meter, color bearer, are the enlisted men selected from the One Hundred and Sixteenth Ohio to accompany General Gibbon, corps commander of the Twenty-fourth Army Corps, to Washington City to present flags received at the surrender of General Lee, in obedience to the personal order of General Grant.

I am, very respectfully,   W. B. TETERS,

Colonel Commanding 116th Ohio.

Thompson and his heroic comrades, with the great box, under command of General Gibbon, proceeded to Washington by special steamer, and were received by Secretary Stanton with great ceremony. Out in front of the war office, Thompson and his comrades stood holding up the doomed banners of treason until they were photographed, and these pictures together with the accursed of God rags of disloyalty, were buried forever in the archives of the Department of War.

Secretary Stanton took each of these heroic men by the hand, and thanked them in words of heartfelt gratitude for the service they had done their country.

Thompson* is a poor man, but to-day I saw his great beautiful medal voted him by congress for loyal service, and I copied from the originals the orders conferring these distinguished honors, and I said then and I say now that not all the gold of a Vanderbilt or a Jay Gould can equal wealth like his, as all the gold on the globe piled in one mighty mountain would have availed but little in the day of battle, but for hearts so godlike and heroic as his.

XI.—ADDRESS OF WELCOME AT SOLDIERS' NATIONAL REUNION, SEPTEMBER 1, 1875.

MY FRIENDS.—The delicate duty of welcoming you to these ample and hospitable shades falls to my lot once more, and I owe the Committee of Arrangements many thanks for the honor which their appointment of me to this place upon their programme implies and confers. I could only wish that I had the knowledge and wisdom

---

* Thompson died since the above was put in type.

and eloquence requisite to the proper and graceful discharge of this important and honorable trust. But you will bear with me while I vainly seek to adequately express the welcome that struggles within our hearts to-day, to find fitting utterance at my lips. You have come from near and from far, and from many distant States of our Federal Union to celebrate this joyous holiday. You come not as enemies, but as friends, neighbors, and fellow-citizens. You have drawn around your camp a magic circle, which discords and contention may not enter, and within which the camp fires of patriotic good will in constant luster burn.

This reunion is National in its importance, and attracts the thoughtful attention of patriotic people in every quarter of the Republic. To-morrow the report of your proceedings, carried on the wings of the lightning, will be spread out in the columns of every important American newspaper and read by millions of your fellow-citizens. To-day representatives of the press from many parts of the state honor us with their presence, and we miss our hope and prediction much, if they do not find in these reunion ceremonies, and this meeting of old comrades, materials from which to compose correspondence of unusual interest for their respective journals. Brave soldiers, separated for many years, dwelling in distant parts of the country, to-day clasp hands again under the folds of the star spangled banner, and at these reunion altars, again together lift their hands to Heaven and swear that "this government of the people, by the people, and for the people can not perish from the earth." [Loud applause.] To-day, fellow-citizens, you take respite from the strife of partisan contention, three days of armistice in this war of politics, and here, in this beautiful city of leaves, make the forest resound with your patriotic glee. The East forgets for a time her commerce and manufactures, and trips gayly into our camp. The West reverses the course of her car of hire, and rushes to meet her fair sister of the East. The South, beautiful as a dark eye in woman, and garlanded with magnolias, sweeps in like a queen, and sits down between the East and West, and their kisses warm their mutual lips, while the tear of reconciliation and peace wets their glorious cheeks. The voice of Heaven makes music among the sheltering branches above us, and the whole camp is wafted on the wings of harmony and peace. The South throws aside the crimson mantle, and in her beautiful right hand holds a gleaming sword. The West and the East rise up, and the South gracefully redeems her pledge of honorable submission and reconcilement by surrendering the sword to the West. And the West, true to her pledge of peace, takes the sword from her sister of the South and sends it ringing home to its scabbard, there to remain until the honor and safety of the three reunited sisters may call it out again for their mutual defense. [Applause.] Well might the angels themselves stoop from the skies to witness this grand closing scene in the great drama of the civil war.

My comrades, you have come here to celebrate the anniversary of great contests and great achievements in which you were all participants. The old comrade feeling is as warm within your hearts to-day as ever, and can only die with the last spark of mortal life. Words can not express the welcome our hearts are dictating toward you to-day. These annual meetings are the brightest links in the golden chain of our existence, and we shall keep them up until the last comrade lies down in the grave.

Welcome! welcome, all! My friends, some of you, with streaming eyes and fluttering hearts, watched that fearful conflict from afar, and many of you have trod the bloody plains of battle and received the fiery baptism of war that baptism which Napoleon declared made all soldiers equal. But we make no distinctions here to-day. While for the old comrades we must entertain and express a tender attachment and devotion, shared by no others on earth, yet, to day, we meet as friends and fellow-citizens, and the canopy of our camp is the outspread wings of the white dove of peace. We darken not the fair avenues of our camp with sectional lines, to-day, but welcome all alike.

Whatever your politics, complexion, language, or nationality, you are welcome, welcome all, to this reunion, and we want to hear your every voice sounding out the chorus of peace on earth and good will among all the people that inhabit our common fatherland. [Cheering.]

In the name of our common constitution, made for the protection of us all by the power of all; in the name of our starry banner, equally dear to all as it is the symbol of the power of all; in the name of the great American Union, the home of us all; and in the name of the God of Peace, our refuge and defense, we bid you welcome here to-day. [Applause.] Be this our aspiration ever more, and be it written in letters of gold across every fold of our Union banner, as the prayer of freemen and the motto of a reunited nation, "Peace be within thy walls, and prosperity within thy palaces." "How beautiful upon the mountain are the feet of him that bringeth glad tidings and publisheth peace." Let us all become heralds of peace, and each take our station on the lofty places of the nation, and proclaim to each other and to the world that "peace has come, and, thank God, it has come to stay."

> " Then the night shall be filled with music,
> And the cares that infest the day
> Shall fold their tents like the Arab,
> And as silently steal away."

In all the four long years of march and bivouac and battle, the rosy walls of memory are being touched by a magic brush, whose gorgeous impress can not fade or perish. Every day and every night the mysterious artist was at work in every soldier heart, transforming its crimson walls into galleries of imperishable beauty, and even in the hours of sleep penetrating the drapery of dreams, to daguerreotype visions of beauty and loveliness on the weary sleeper's soul. Those pictures to-day rise before the eye of recollection, and in the subdued and somber light of fleeting years, they seem like glorious groups surrounding the emerald gates of heaven. The memories of these strange, wild, eventful years rise in grandeur far surpassing all that painters ever traced or poets ever dreamed. Pluck from the soldier's soul all the memories of those distant years, and you rob him of a treasure which he values more than all the wealth of Ormus or of Ind. The recollection of his marches, sieges, battles, the lonely prison pen, the nights of social glee with comrades departed long ago—these constitute the soldier's reward, and he would part with life sooner than part with them.

And so the dear dead faces look down on us to-day. I see them now as I have often seen them in days that are gone. Strong, fair, beautiful, and young. They rise to-day from their beds of glory, and gaze into our eyes again.

"They came in dim procession led,
The brave, the faithful, and the dead,
Each hand as warm, each brow as gay,
As though we parted yesterday."

And here, amid these joyous rites, let us not forget our dead comrades, though our best tribute to their memory be silence and tears.

" On fame's eternal camping-ground,
Their silent tents are spread,
And glory guards with solemn round,
The bivouac of the dead.

" O, it is a beautiful belief,
That ever round our heads
Are hovering on angel wings
The spirits of the dead."

It may be that from some flowery eminence of Paradise our departed comrades look down on this reunion, while every harp of heaven hangs in silence, and the music of our reunion reveille sweeps across the river of death and rises to the skies like cathedral chimes.

"The world will little note nor long remember what we say here; but it never can forget what they did here." The muse of history bends reverently forever above their holy dust, while the genius of liberty guards their graves with tender care, and lays her myrtle and her amaranth upon the mural tablets that mark the martyr's tomb.

They can not be forgotten until the skies be rolled together as a scroll, and the earth shall flee away. Their memory is safe, while there is left the sweet voice of woman to tenderly proclaim it to little groups of children gathering at her knee, or a poet left to commemorate their glorious deeds in immortal song, or a sculptor to carve it in enduring marble, or a painter to depict it on the speaking canvas, or a grateful Nation of brave men and lovely women left to adore the starry banner that was made our heroes' winding sheet. That peace which to-day covers our land as with a mantle of snowy whiteness cost mountains of treasure, rivers of tears, oceans of blood. Our national security did not drop from the skies or spring from the ground, the child of chance and change. It was born of the heroic throes of patriotism and heroism. How often have we all repeated this, yet how seldom realized its solemn significance! You saw your young men go forth in grander legions than ever Napoleon or Charlemagne or Cæsar led to battle, and how anxiously you watched and waited for their return. When the war was over, and peace had come, and come to stay, there was one dead in every house; in every house was a vacant chair. The unreturning braves were numberless, and O how sadly you missed them then and miss them yet, and you must miss them still till you shall join them beyond the dark river. They were the flower and pride of the Nation, and, crowned as they are with the undying laurels of patriotic martyrdom, they seem to me to-day, as they always seemed, the best men the world ever knew.

Those who came back from the war bearing in their hands the tattered and bloody standards of battle were no longer young and smiling and fair. They had gone out boys, with the morn and liquid dew of youth on their cheeks and in their flashing eyes. They returned bronzed and bearded men, with the light of battle reflected from their faces. They were no longer the boys whom mothers and sisters had kissed at the little gate, when the moon was low, and bid " return with your shield or upon it." Oh, what changes in this fragile human form of clay can four years in the field effect! When men take to the tented field, and dwell for years under the rain, and sun, and storms, and stars, the relentless elements of nature so transform them that their dearest friends would hardly know them. The reapers in this harvest of death grew prematurely old, and bent, and wrinkled, and gray. Once in a while, now, I, myself, scarcely thirty-six, meet an old comrade, trudging along, pale and weary, a premature old man, and hardly recognize in him the boy who, ten short years ago, marched at my side in the ranks of the Union army, in the full pride, and strength, and beauty of his young manhood.

You can never estimate the cost of that long and wasteful war. I have no patience with those flat-headed , and flint-hearted creatures who always reckon the cost of that war in dollars and cents. Was the blood of American citizens nothing but dishwater, that its priceless value is never to be included in the cost of the war?

Not a man fell before Richmond or Atlanta but was

worth more to some mother, wife, or sister, than all the
gold on the globe. Not a life was poured out on the tide
of battle but was worth more to its heroic possessor
than all the gold and silver that ever rolled from the
American mints. The young men of the Nation, heaps
upon heaps, lying dead upon the field of battle, this is
all the war cost us, a price to which all else is nothing!

Look upon the hecatombs of slain, hear the widow's
moan, and the orphans' cry from a million dwellings,
and suffering, sorrow, and desolation, on the plains of
war, in the wretched homestead, and in the ghastly hospital wards—walk, if you please, with me back through
these scenes of sorrow again, and then talk about the
dollars that war cost!

The dollars are as nothing! Nor can the Nation ever
forget the price it paid for its redemption. After such
great sacrifices, brethren of the North and South, let us
determine to protect, and defend, and cherish our blood-
bought inheritance forever and forever. And in this
bright centennial year, when all ears are attentive to the
solemn words of the fathers of the Republic, the beautiful prophecy of Lincoln becomes crystallized in fulfill-
ment: "The mystic chords of memory, stretching from
every battle-field and every patriot's grave, to every
heart and hearthstone in this broad land of ours, are
vibrating the sweetest music of the Union, now that they
are touched again by the better angels of our nature."

This precious treasure of national peace was purchased
as well for Texas as for Massachusetts; as well for
Louisiana as for Ohio; as well for those who lifted up
their hands against the Federal Union as for those who
bared their breasts in its defense. Christ on the cross

taught the great lesson of malice toward none—charity to all; and this great Christian Nation, following in its Founder's footsteps, taught the South and the world a lesson of charity and forbearance which the history of all ages before had failed to exhibit. This is the marvel of the century, the wonder of the Nations, and the glory of America; that the same mighty hand that hurled our enemy to the earth, and there disarmed him, was reached promptly forth to lift him up again and place his feet securely on the rock of full and equal citizenship. The past is forgiven, no revenge has been taken, no punishment executed, and the whole sisterhood of states to-day clasp loving hands and trip gracefully along, keeping step to the music of the Union.

This address was delivered at the second one OF MY SOLDIERS' REUNIONS, held in 1875. I claim to be the originator of all such reunions. I called the first reunion of this kind ever held. They have since been held in all parts of the United States. Mine was *the first*. At the National Reunion of 1875, Senator Cockrell, a Confederate, was my guest.

Senator Cockrell, United States Senator from Missouri, was present as a guest of the camp, and spoke in substance as follows, in reply to me:

Ladies, Soldiers, my Fellow-citizens:—It gives me great pleasure to appear before you to-day. Soldiers, probably I have met many of you before to-day, and under far different auspices. I was invited to come here if I was willing to meet you half way, and I am here. I always tried to meet you half way on the battle field, and I am willing to go further than that now. I allow no man to go further than myself in my love for my country and a wish for her prosperity. What I say to-day are the real sentiments of my heart. I am glad that I am here, for I feel it will be good for all of us to be here. Humanity is the same in all ages of the world, and we can not divest ourselves of our humanity, even if we would. We can not always control ourselves when laboring under great passion, and I do not want you to hold me responsible for all I have said and done under circumstances incident to a cruel and fratricidal war. But I am willing to ask your forgiveness for any real wrong I have done. I like to talk to soldiers, for we have met on the march, in battle, and in prison. You well remember, those of you who were before Vicksburg, what jolly times our pickets had under improvised flags of truce, how they dispassionately discussed the situation. Now, I verily believe that if it could have been so arranged, our private soldiers of both armies could have settled our late trouble amicably six months after the war closed; but that is over now, and we won't " cry over spilt milk." We have had a few men in the South of a class I suppose you in the North have, who were like what the brave Mulligan said of his troops, " invincible in peace and invisible in war." Now, I hope you will not hold the good people of the South responsible for the idle babblings of these doughty warriors. I hope to meet you to-morrow."

The speaker was heartily applauded.

———

The following confirmation of my claim to be the author of soldiers' reunions is from the pen of my noble

friend, Hon. J. Medill, and appeared editorially in the
Tribune of August 20, 1881 :

In a note of invitation to the editor of THE TRIBUNE
to attend the soldiers' reunion which is to take place at
Caldwell, O., September 9, Private Dalzell writes in an
interesting way of the origin, object, and character of
these remarkable meetings. The letter was not in-
tended for publication, but we take the liberty of giving a part of it to the public. Mr. Dalzell writes as
follows :

" Here upon this ground, many years ago, a few of us
who carried muskets in defense of the old flag undertook
to organize a society of soldiers regardless of rank.
While the army societies saw fit to exclude the rank and
file on *caste* principles, we invited officers and men alike
on the same plane of perfect citizen equality; for the
war is over, with its odious distinctions and discrimina-
tions of rank. Right or wrong, this has been the commanding feature of this reunion, on which a thousand
just as good in all the North have since been organized.
General Sherman gave it his hearty indorsement, and
presided at its first meeting in this town, in 1874. It
has met with the heartiest indorsement possible in all
quarters, and so far diffused its republican ideas that,
even in the regular meetings of the Army of the Tennessee, more than once an effort has been made to make
its terms of admission to membership the same as ours—
an honorable record in the Union army, irrespective of
rank. General Sherman has repeatedly urged it, and
only the young upstarts of the regular army have sneered
at the proposition and voted it down, for they are, of

course, the majority, and by surrendering their rank distinction they would surrender about all they possess. Until what we set out to accomplish is done, this reunion will be kept up. Hundreds of officers who, like Garfield, Hayes, Kilpatrick, Wallace, Leggett, Warner, etc., have something of manhood over and above their rank, have attended its meetings here on the spot of its birth, and fully indorsed its simple and solitary principle of equality of comradeship and citizenship.

" Men of many states, who indorse and approve its distinctive feature, come to its meetings every year in large numbers, and so it goes on increasing in numbers and interest. Other reunions on this plan have sprung up and are held in all the North—the more the better for our idea.

" Only in one respect does it acknowledge itself a failure. At first, and for five successive years, a most cordial invitation was extended to the Boys in Gray as well as the Boys in Blue. I regret to say that every effort utterly failed to induce them to come. Letters were sent them, with passes, etc., and the press of the South year after year teemed with the most pressing and courteous invitations. Many of the prominent men South promised to come. But, when the time drew on, they failed to be here, except only Major Jones of Alabama, General Key, of President Hayes' cabinet, and Senator Cockrell, of Missouri. In all the five or six years of the early history of our reunion, we were able to induce no others to come. And so that feature, two or three years ago, was dropped as a failure, an utter failure, after a full and fair trial."

Dalzell's zeal in behalf of the private soldiers, and

12

,their inalienable right to hold reunions and be recognized
as having done something for the country, has caused
him to be laughed at a good deal, but there is sound sense
at the bottom of it. The people may remember that no
battles in the late war were won by the officers alone.
There was no prouder title in our volunteer army than
that of the private soldier. Private Dalzell is right
about it.

XII.—How the Private Went After but Didn't Get a Christmas Turkey.

Joe Purkey and I were not the soldiers to lie down
supinely and wish we had turkeys, chickens, apples, potatoes, and other good cheer, like the folks at home,
Christmas, 1863. Not we! if the court knew herself,
and the court was of opinion that she did. We were in
the wild mountainous region of Petersburg, W. Va. It was
cold and dreary, and with the exception of an occasional
bushwhacker caught or shot while plying his cowardly
vocation in the bushes, we seldom saw a rebel. But the
country was filled with roving and sneaking gangs of
guerrillas, who, like Arabaces in the play, were liable to
turn up where they were least expected and least wanted.
So it came to pass, now and then, that some one of our
more adventurous spirits who ventured beyond the lines
fell victims to these lurking foes who watched about our
camps and picket posts for just such unsuspecting game.

I had a holy horror of them. So had Joe. Therefore,
when Milroy issued his order forbidding soldiers to go
beyond our picket posts, it found ready and willing
obedience. But to all rules there are exceptions, and if

ever an exception should be made, or, at least, would be, whether it should be or not, for our logic and ethics were not over nice—it would crop out about Christmas. What, stay in camp Christmas and New Year's, in that miserable wooded ravine in the valley, and eat hardtack and abdominal pork, while our companions at home were fairly luxuriating and reveling in wine and wassail—not we! At all hazards, we determined to pass beyond our lines and "cabbage," "confiscate," "gobble up," "press into service," purchase, or *steal* some of the good things with which, in the earlier and better days of the Republic, we had been wont to regale ourselves "in the old house at home."

And this is how we put our plan into execution. Common soldiers could not pass the pickets, but officers might. So, stealing a pair of officers' coats, big brass straps and all, which we easily accomplished the night before, and getting passwords and countersigns from a drunken lieutenant, whom we bribed, and whose soul could have been purchased for the promise of a dram of "mountain dew," which he was sure to get on our return, we climbed on a pair of stolen mules, and rode leisurely down the highway leading to the outposts. Our gorgeous coats we did not display, for our great blue overcoats covered them, straps and all, until we had passed beyond the camp and into the woods near the picket post. Hiding behind a hillock there, the change was quickly made by pulling off our overcoats, and presto! there sat two as gallant and ferocious-looking young officers as ever straddled a mule since Sancho Panza first threw a leg over the renowned dapple. Riding up with a haughty

and overbearing air, full of contempt and scorn for the
half-dozen pickets who stood shivering with cold about
the fire, we barely touched our caps as they (all strangers
to us and members of an Indiana regiment) gave us the
military salute of present arms, and as we gave the password correctly no questions were ventured, and we were
soon beyond the lines, and galloping away for the wild
hills beyond. We had performed our part so well that
the simple-minded pickets saw no difference between our
hauteur, nonchalance, and insolence and that of the
genuine officers who galloped by them every day on
their debauchs and amours outside the lines, an honor of
war denied usually to the rank and file, unless, like us,
they donned the paraphernalia and insolence of office,
and, with lofty airs of superiority and impudence, galloped by the sentinels without so much as saying, " by
your leave."

Joe and I were younger then than we are now, and as
we galloped over the frozen road through the keen, biting,
frosty air, our glee and merriment were unbounded, and
found expression in frequent peals of laughter which
echoed through the pine and laurels at the very risk of
our lives; for we knew not how soon we should hear the
crack of a bushwhacker's gun, and be called to bite the
frosty roadside. But there were " two souls with but a
single thought" possessed; " two hearts that beat as
one "—for turkey, chickens, and sich! We thought of
nothing else. So completely was the country stripped
that we did not think worth while to invade any of the
cabins or barn-yards that we passed at long intervals in
the hills, until we had gone five miles from camp. Suddenly, as we dashed around a sharp curve in the road,

we came upon an old negro bawling one of the songs with which his oppressed race had been used to beguile the weariness of slavery, and solace themselves during two hundred years of bondage.

The old fellow jerked off his ragged possum-skin cap, salaamed full low in his ragged clothes, and grinned from ear to ear, as he exclaimed: "Fore God, Massa Linkum's men, sho!" "Where can we find some turkeys and whisky, Sambo?" I inquired. The creature, who was old, gray, and wrinkled, drew his face down to uncommon length, and solemnly protested he did not know. "That is too thin," said Joe in a voice of thunder that made the old man jump up and look scared. "Now, you see here, old man. Tote along ahead, and no more back talk or foolishness. You must find some chickens, turkeys, and whisky, or I will blow your head off your shoulders." And, suiting the action to the word, Joe leveled his navy at the frightened contraband, who threw up his hands, and, while his eyes rolled with fright, cried out: "Don't pint that are at me so. I'll show you directly what you want, boss." And so Joe put up the pistol, and the old man trotted ahead a mile or so until we came in sight of a fine old Virginia mansion—first house not made of logs we had seen that morning. He solemnly assured us that we should find all we wanted at Massa Seymour's, as he told us the owner's name was, and, giving him permission to retire, the poor old soul trotted off, and was soon out of sight. It would have cost him his life had it transpired when we were gone that he had acted as our cicerone. We soon reached the plantation, hitched our mules, and entered. A beautiful young lady met us at the door. These were no days of ceremony, so, our errand being quickly made known, with apparent alacrity, she sent a colored woman for the whisky, who soon came beaming and grinning with a big bottle and some glasses on a silver salver. We embraced the bottle lovingly, and frequently, and, seeing a piano in the room, asked the young lady to play. She courteously took her seat at the piano and played "My Maryland" and other rebel airs, accompanying them with a voice of bewitching sweetness. As she sang we had time enough to look around. An old man, her decrepit father, the haughty lord of Seymour mansion, came limping in, and sat down beside us, eyeing us coldly enough. He was a haughty, gray-haired gentleman of the old school. In answer to our questions he simply said: "Certainly, when you gentlemen command it is ours to obey. You are irresistible—to old men and children. You shall have a turkey and some chickens. I shall send my servants for them this minute. Make yourselves at home." And so saying he stepped quietly into the hall, and we never saw nor thought any more of him, but kept regaling ourselves with the music and the bottle. The young lady played on as if she was playing for a wager—and she was! I wondered that she did not grow weary and stop to be coaxed to continue, as is common with ladies at the piano. Not a bit of it. It seemed to delight her to entertain us, and she would have played on, it seemed, forever. She was playing more than a tune. Once or twice a young lady, whose complexion and lineaments plainly showed she was not of the family, flitted nervously through the hall, and as she did so she glanced uneasily at us and was gone. This she kept up for some time, until at last, pausing for an instant, she motioned me to come out. As I did so, where the piano fury could not see me, she slipped a feather in my hand, which I quickly slid into my pocket unseen, and she simply whispered to me, "Fly," and was gone. I never saw her again. Her air and manner spoke volumes. The warning was not unheeded nor a moment too soon. I called to Joe to come out quickly, for in those days one did not have to speak twice to be understood; and, communicating my alarm to him in a look, for I dare not speak, we started to leave—the bottle, the girl, and the Christmas turkey, without any tender leave-taking—much as it might surprise the lady at the piano!

Miss Seymour, noticing our movements, rose quickly, and said : " Gentlemen, do not be so hasty. Father has sent out for your Christmas—." But we heard no more and made no reply, but in a jiffy were on our mules and dashing down the lane. Not a moment too soon. Thanks to the warning of the unknown girl; for out from behind the barn came a number of rebels, and we could hear their shouts: " Halt! you Yankee —," and a volley of bullets whizzed over our heads, harmless as the words they uttered. We were lucky that they were not mounted, and soon were out of reach of their guns, and on our way back to camp, turkeyless and chickenless, but full as fiddlers ! Next day was Christmas, and we feasted on conjectures as to who our deliverer was, but never a turkey or chicken for us that Christmas day. Our expedition was as utter a failure as if we had been brigadier-generals.

XIII.—DECORATION DAY ADDRESS IN WHEELING, 1883.

Soldiers and Citizens:—Invited on behalf of the committee having in charge the arrangements for the dedication of this monument, I am here to-day to speak such words as may seem to befit the occasion. This monument to the memory of the dead soldiers of West Virginia is an eloquent witness of the veneration in which you hold them every one. It is a credit to Wheeling. It is a credit to West Virginia. It speaks well for your patriotic gratitude. To suffer the speechless dead to lie forgotten of those who have so largely benefited as you have by their services on the fields of mortal combat, in defense of your homes and firesides, and in defense of your country, as well as theirs, would be base ingratitude indeed. This monument is not reared for them. It rises up as a testimonial of yours to their children and yours, to bear witness that you are not unmindful of their heroic lives and deaths, and that those who died for the perpetuation of the American Union are of " the few, the immortal names, that can not die."

They sleep the dreamless sleep. Unmindful of these august ceremonies, deaf to your words of praise, they rest dreamless and alone, each in his sepulcher of glory. On fields of war where they fell; in the quietude of the country churchyard at home; in the crowded cemeteries of your cities; by the wayside; in the depths of mountain solitude, in the rivers, and in the sounding seas; hard by prison pens that realized an earthly hell; in swamps and fens and everglades; and some, alas! unburied still, whose uncoffined bones lie bleaching in the

sun, your heroes rest, peacefully and still. Your songs
of praise, your eulogies, they shall never hear. It is all
one to them whether you uncover your heads and shed
your tears above their graves of glory. Your flowers
shall fall, your words of praise shall sound unheeded;
they are dead to you and dead to me, and nothing shall
awaken them from their dreamless and eternal sleep;
nothing shall raise them from these slumbers in the dust,
this dumb resting after days and nights of toil and labor
and daring, nothing ever but the thunder call of God.

You pause in abstract contemplation, to-day, attentive
by their graves, expectant, almost, as the flowers drop
upon their graves from the hands of Beauty and Love,
to hear a response of gratitude that shall never come.
Little children, in the auroral blush and bloom of childish innocence and glee, gambol about these sacred
shrines. The old soldier's heart is cold, and his eye is
blind, and his ear is deaf. Their merry footsteps he can
not hear; their warm and open hands he can not clasp.
Mother and father, sister and brother, have laden these
sacred graves with tears, and lament the loss no time can
wholly heal; and yet the soldier heeds it not. He is
wedded to the dust. The worms are his father and his
mother and his sister. In vain, all in vain, you call his
cherished name, he shall never answer back; and his
footsteps, once so familiar to your ear, shall never more
sound upon this planet. It is hard to realize, even yet,
they are gone, and gone forever. Somehow they were
so young, so beautiful and brave and true, that we
thought them only sleeping, and that they would soon be
back.

But they come again to us only in our dreams, and
13

vanish from our sight the moment we awake. We shall all go to them, but they shall never come again to us. Never. Then why build these monuments or strew these memorial flowers and speak these words of praise? If they to whom we dedicate this day can not with us enjoy the solemn rites, why observe them still from year to year? God knows we would reach them if we could. God knows with what fervor and gratitude we should kiss their lips and embrace their forms, and with what lavish gratitude we should pour words of praise into their ears if we could. We strain every nerve, every living power and emotion we have, and it is hard to realize that they who did so much for us can never know how grateful we are to them for their unselfishness, their devotion. The Christian believer addresses Christ in thanksgiving and praise for what he did for him by his life and death. Calvary is on his lips. He falls at the foot of the cross. He addresses a dead but living Christ, conscious that Christ hears every word of praise, and that though dead he still lives. The devoted Christian sings the praises — the praises not of a dead, but of a risen and living Christ.

But these saviors of us, of our homes, our country, have had no resurrection yet. They can not hear us, they can not know but that they are forgotten of us all. This to me is the saddest of it all. This calamity of the war might be borne without much pain or regret, if at the shrines we have we might find, living and intelligent still, the loving objects of our devotion. If, when we weep, they could only smile back to us: if, when we sing their praises, a voice could only rise from the tomb to tell us that its occupant had heard the songs; if, when the words of praise and eulogy were pronounced, an answering voice from the eternal shadows could only come, these solemn rites and ceremonies would have other potency and significancy than now they have. But they are dead and silent in their graves. We may speak, they will not reply. We may call, they can not hear. Decoration may come and go, and in due time be pretermitted and observed no longer, and yet these heroes of ours shall never complain.

Selfish and cold as it seems, and as it appears ought not to be, in justice to these noble, heroic dead of ours, this Decoration Day is not for them—it is for us, and for our children's children, forever and forever more. Not for the dead, but for the living, are we come here to-day. This grand column of remembrance and gratitude does not rise for them — it is for us, and for our children forever. It is to emphasize with eternal record, so far as poor human art may go, the lesson of fidelity to the flag, of faith in the American Union, and patriotic devotion to the cause of human liberty. This is the lesson this shaft shall teach when you and I are dead. Our children and our children's children shall read it in its crumbling and decay. And when it is leveled with the earth, and we and our poor transient ceremonies are forgotten quite, still the faithful pen of history will proclaim that the men who died for their native land, "who gave the last full measure of their devotion for it," were not forgotten in their graves, nor neglected by those who enjoyed the fruits of their victories.

It is for this that these fair ladies, these sweet children, and these earnest men are here to-day. It is that one day may be consecrated and set up to the memory of those who fell in defense of the American Union. It is that their gratitude to their brave defenders may be voiced in this monument, and by it proclaimed to posterity. A hundred Decoration Days yet to come, when you and I and all this vast multitude shall have passed away, this monument shall be our orator, to speak for us what we can no longer say for ourselves, and with its silent eloquence proclaim the Nation's gratitude to its brave defenders. This Nation has made a great mistake —one that it must in time repair, and which even now it is not too late for it to remember. While it is well that at more than eighty National cemeteries to-day ceremonies of decoration are observed, and the heroic dead are not forgotten quite, yet no truly National monument has yet been erected by the Congress of the United States, the servant of the people, to commemorate the valor and devotion of the Union army, the heroism and self-sacrifice of half a million men who died for their country.

It is time this act of justice were done, creditable alike to the art, the genius, the civilization, the patriotism, and the gratitude of a nation.

Future times and people, reading the story of that conflict, shall look for a monument truly national; disappointed, and with no good opinion of the present age if they do not find it somewhere in our vast domain. States have performed this sacred duty. Many of them, West Virginia among the first, and others are yet to build monuments of this kind. But the Union, the whole Union, joining as one man in the grand, sacred task, has yet remaining to it the great duty of building one really national; vast in proportions, grand in design, and with the permanency of the pyramids stamped upon it. The Nation need not be ashamed of the colossal task. It need apologize to no one for the undertaking. It owes it to itself. It need give no offense, and woe to him or them by whom offense cometh, if the Nation in recording its gratitude in granite or marble columns to its brave defenders, exceeds any monument hitherto raised in the history of the world.

National exequial observances are not peculiar to our country and age. Decoration Day was first instituted on the motion of Aristides in the Athenian Senate just after the battle of Plataea. The exequy was annually pronounced by the great orators of Greece precisely as it is in these latter days in America. Thucydides gives us a full report of a decoration address delivered by Pericles more than two thousand years ago. The ceremony of strewing the graves of the heroes of Plataea, Marathon, and Salamis was observed precisely as it is now, centuries before Christ.

All Greece assembled on these great occasions annually, and Plutarch himself was an eye witness six hundred years after the first burial rite was first instituted. He says that, for at least six hundred years in succession, it has never been neglected for a single year. Verily there is nothing new under the sun. It was a great part of the religion of the Greeks to bury their heroes with solemn pomp and ceremony, mark their tombs with special care, and annually strew them over with beautiful flowers at the expense of the nation. So much stress did they place upon the duty of victorious generals to carefully bury their dead on the field of battle, that Xenophon tells us that, after the ten commanders who had won the naval fight of Arginusæ returned to Athens, they were tried, and eight of them condemned to death and executed on the spot, upon the single charge that they had not buried their dead! Pericles has furnished posterity with the best model of a decoration address. Hear him, as he pronounces these words over the graves of those who fell in the Samian war:

"They are become immortal like the gods, for the gods themselves are not visible to us. Only for the honors they receive, and the happiness they enjoy, we conclude they are invisible, and such should these brave men be who die for their country."

The whole oration will richly repay perusal, but I have room here for but that single sentence.

In the Italian wars of the middle ages, it is a fact that there were few graves and nothing to decorate in the shape of heroes' tombs. It may seem a grave joke, indeed, but it is the truth of history, that these wars furnished nothing to decorate, and had it not been for the invention of gunpowder, the art of constructing impenetrable armor would by this time have done away with Decoration Day! Those wars cost no lives. At the battle of Zogonora, in 1423, according to Machiavelli, but three lives were lost, and these were suffocated in the mud, where they were held down by their heavy armor.

That is the worst case of stuck in the mud I ever heard of. But that battle was not less destructive of life than the one which occurred sixty-three years afterward between the Neapolitan and Papal troops, for in that battle, though it raged fiercely all day, from sunrise till long after dark, according to Ammarato, not a soldier was either killed or wounded. There were no graves to decorate there, and many an energetic young woman was disappointed in not being made a widow. War in those days was much less hazardous than a snow-balling match is now. With their massive plates of metallic armor, two armies would whack away at each other with ax and spear from morning till night, with no other cost than to pile up big blacksmith bills for repairs! War had become a screaming farce, in which nobody was frightened and nobody hurt. No one could put on airs over his fellow-soldier and claim that he, more than others, bore about with him, like Cambyses, Cyrus, Cæsar, Napoleon, and Grant, a charmed life. They did not have on them even the one vulnerable spot which the Grecian hero had. From the crowns of their heads to the soles of their feet, they were all over invulnerable, until, at the close of the fifteenth century, gunpowder was discovered and shattered their armor to atoms, and war again became that terrible thing it had been of old.

> " Deadly as Kuli's sword;
> The purple testament of blood and death,
> Fields of slaughter and red with gore."

There is a graveyard somewhere that I should love to see decorated with flowers. It is of those 90,000 little children, commanded by a child, who, carried away by the wild fanaticism of the Dark ages, marched to the rescue of the sepulcher of Jesus, dispersed and murdered by the Saracens—all but 3,000 of them! Grander than the monuments on the field of Marathon should be the cenotaph that should mark the resting place of those de-voted children of the 13th century who sacrificed their beautiful young lives upon the altar of religion; and O that Jesus himself might stoop from the skies, as doubtless by his creative power he has literally done, and strew their graves with flowers. Let not the chilling breath of modern rationalism scornfully sneer at devotion like this, however much it may have been mistaken, for their sentiment for which they died is immortal as the souls that conceived it, and wreaths their graves with everlasting glory. Contrast with such a tomb as that of Sardanapalus, the Assyrian prince, noted only for his effeminacy, luxury, and cowardice, ordering his grave to be marked with these words:

"*Haec habeo quae edi, quaeque exsaturata libido hausit; et illa jacet multa, et praeclara selicta.*"

"An epitaph," says Aristotle, "fit for a hog."

There is nothing new in our decoration custom. It was suggested by the passage I have referred to from Grecian history. It is well that we annually observe the beautiful custom recently revived of strewing the graves of our soldiers with flowers, and commemorating their gallant deeds by the triple and mystic power of painting, poetry, and oratory. It does the dead no good, but it educates the living, and instils into the hearts of the young the patriotism and manly virtues of their heroic ancestors. The martial glory of Greece made its classic literature possible, by giving it something worthy of an imperishable record, and much more by exalting and refining every true and honorable sentiment and passion that can adorn and beautify human nature. Recalling the example of Cato, as he looked back on the field where Pompey and Caesar had just fought a terrible battle, and as he saw the bleeding bodies of a thousand Romans he covered his face and retired weeping, exclaiming, "Though they were enemies they were my countrymen;" so we may stand at the graves, not only of our comrades but of our enemies, and drop the tear of pity, for they were misguided countrymen. O, let us pray for the coming day when wars will cease, when wars and discord shall be banished from the world, and when the dream of the ancient philosophers shall be realized in one full diapason of harmony, and "the bugles of God," of which Charles Sumner wrote so beautifully, shall sound the harps of peace.

XIV.—The Effect of the Old Flag Upon Young Patriots at Enlistment.

I know no more of the manual of arms than did my field and staff officers, though quite as much as officers of the line did—and that was precisely nothing. I shall never forget them—those halcyon hours of blissful ignorance, when I lifted my hand under the folds of the starry flag and swore to defend it and the constitution, and laws thrown in for good measure, for three years, or during the war. The flag rippled out in graceful folds in the morning breeze, and couldn't hold itself for laughing, as it floated proudly over us, as we green, raw boys, fresh from college, rallied under its streaming pennons and took that great oath of loyal service for its defense. As I look up at it now it seems wreathed in smiles and convulsed with laughter at the grotesque display we made.

It fairly flapped and rolled in great and glorious billows of merriment and glee. It seemed younger then than it does now. Age and battle have written fiery

scars on its folds since then. It is, indeed, the old flag
now, a quarter of a century older than it was when we
first fell in behind it, and it streamed on before. Then
it was the morning of our lives—nothing had aged, our
wrinkles and scars were yet unrecorded on the fair scrolls
of our hopes and ambitions. A gun—I knew no more
about war than it knew about me. Yet we had all sworn
to take up muskets and shoot rebels dead, dead, dead,
or oftener if need be. No wonder the flag laughed, and
only we were solemn, all ignorant of coming events, yet
innocent of premonitory shadow, for there were no shadows anywhere yet, curtained as we were then in the
armored blush of youth. We stood with our bright
young faces there in the sunlight of early day, and, as
we faced the future, it stood out all blank before us.
But behind that awful shadow "God kept watch above
his own." And so a pair of fair young hands firmly
seized the staff from which the flag floated, and the old
banner looked lovingly down ; its stars glittered as they
gleamed at us from their fields of blue, and their alter-
nate stripes of red and white swayed in the morning
air with a beauty no tongue can ever express. It—
the old flag—the young flag, the bright, new flag, seemed
to whisper a promise of coming strength and glory, and
in the undersong of its soft rustling above, a voice
seemed to come out and down from its silken waves, as
if from the very skies, sweet and solemn as matin chimes
summoning every heart to adoration, praise, and prayer.
The charm of the flag on the heart of youth—how shall
I describe it? It was at once spiritual and serene, commanding every heart and knee to worship it, and by its
mystic beauty and power converted plain young men to

heroes as it floated on before. Who doubts the fire and cloudy pillar of old were carried on before in the unseen hand of God, and that every devout pilgrim's eye read in their mystic procession much more than material flame and shadow? What power the fire and cloud, as pictured in the presence of Deity, had to the Israelitish hosts of old, our starry banner symbolized to us as it swept on before.

Our first drill-master, therefore, and our best, was the bright new flag that the ladies at home had intrusted to our care as we marched down from the village on the hill the day we took the oath of service. It was our leader. It was our visible presence of the Lord and the Republic. It was all there—all of heaven, all of earth, all of home, all of memory, all of hope, and there was no place left on all its ample and restless billows to find a place for fear or make a mask of shame. It went on before, an inspiration and a guide, bearing more authority and power of command in its robes of beauty than ever belonged to the divinity of kings.

Some might question the right of this or that general to command—none ever dreamed of questioning the supremacy of the stars and stripes. Some might hesitate to follow where ardent and impetuous soldiers might dare to go—none ever hesitated for a moment to go where the flag flew!

"Our flag is there" ended all question; it had marked the path of duty with its flowing folds, and to quail at any danger, or feel the touch of any fear in that majestic presence was to distrust the good providence of God and to incur his wrath and curse forever. And so we stood, looking up at the deep mysteries of the new flag that first morning of our soldier life. I do not say we deciphered aright all its mysterious meaning, or read fully and accurately the secret of its power, but there was that about it anyhow, there and then, in the first hour, year, the first second of our soldier life, that thrilled every heart to the core, and filled every bright young eye with tears.

We had not put on our uniform of blue. We had not seen a musket yet. We had only just been sworn in. Young, raw recruits, every face innocent of a razor, and every eye flashing with "the morn and liquid dew of youth." At the altar of our country there we stood willing to sacrifice our young lives, with all their bright young chapters in the lexicon of hope, in defense of that star-spangled banner, and all of the future that it represented. All of the future? Nay, more. All of the past, too, for since it was first flung to the breeze at Princeton what glories had it gathered on many a bloody field and wave, and these, as by enchantment, now were pictured on its folds. It was Washington's own flag. It had the light of battle all over its tri-colored form, and the sweet and sacred charm of victory hung about it as a revelation of its power. It bore the glory of three famous wars for our country. It had streamed over the very cradle when liberty was born. It had sheltered liberty in its youth, and under its effulgent beams liberty had grown to her full stature and beauty, and now that she was threatened with ignominy and death its mystic presence was about her still. Liberty stood there majestic in her woes and tears. At the apparition of the flag that had ever been her protecting angel, we, the sons of liberty, gathered from the East and the West at the talismanic call of the flag, and there behind the glorious ensign we beheld the colossal form of liberty, and her great white hands were stretched above our youthful heads in benediction.

And so, as we gazed with beating hearts and tearful eyes on the dear old flag, we raised our hands all together, and, with lips quivering and voices choking with emotion we vainly tried to suppress, we repeated the solemn oath of service and devotion.

It was the accolade of the flag! It had transformed us in a moment, in the twinkling of an eye, from boys into soldiers. Henceforth the bright rubicon of youthful gayety, frolic, and hilarity was to be behind us, and we were committed to the task of saving our country, or dying for it—no boy's play, indeed, was that to be! Many men, indeed, worthily some, unworthily more, commanded us, ere our task was done. Some were obeyed and some were scorned. But one commander there ever was that never failed nor faltered, and whose influence daily grew upon us until the closing gun was fired, and that was the star spangled banner. It was the greatest of all the generals—the commander-in-chief par excellence. It fought and won more battles than all the generals put together. It never got sick. It was never relieved for failure to do its duty. It was never folded away on furlough. It never disobeyed orders. It never faltered under any fire, though entering mouths of hell. Its sentinel stars never closed their eyes in slumber on even the darkest night. Riddled with bullets, shattered with shell, it often fell, and always when the fight was the hottest. But it was soon up and on again—an inspiration to its followers, a holy terror to

its enemies. It was borne sometimes in visible and
sometimes in unseen hands, but it floated on always and
every-where—the beauty of the battle.

Would you know how to answer this riddle military—
three days on long marches of many miles, and every
night in the same bed? If you belonged to the First
Brigade, Second Division, Eighth Army Corps, and Milroy's command on the Shenandoah in the spring of 1863,
you can read my riddle at a glance; otherwise, it will
probably stump you. It was military strategy peculiar
to the times I write about, and, as there was no reason
in the world for it then, none has come along since, unless twenty-three years of hard study has taught some
of our generals who were there, and led on this wild
goose-chase after nothing, that it was nicely planned and
executed according to the approved science of war.
Give them twenty or thirty years more, and they will
have proved that the battle of Bull Run was a glorious
victory! We were nearly all green young soldiers, enlisted the year before, and knew no more of war then, at
the time of said W. G. chase, than McClellan on the Pe-
ninsula. Not a bit more. So we just went it blind—
the blind leading the blind—and off we started on a
scout, with a battery, the First West Virginia Cavalry,
the Thirteenth and Fourteenth Pennsylvania Cavalry,
One Hundred and Tenth, One Hundred and Sixteenth,
One Hundred and Twenty-second, One Hundred and
Twenty-third Ohio, Eighteenth Connecticut, and the
Fifty-fourth Massachusetts, and a host of citizen scouts
always attached in great numbers to Elliott's division of
Milroy's command. General Elliott had charge of our
expedition in person, leaving Milroy with the remainder

of his army in the garrison and fortifications at Winchester.

It was a bright May morning when we started out of Winchester, flags flying and bands playing, going—the Lord knows where and what for—because I never knew, and no one else ever did. It was a great piece of strategy to keep such things quiet, so quiet that nobody, not even the generals in charge, knew what they were doing until the thing was done, and they have been writing it up into a big thing ever since, though then it seemed a fizzle and a failure. It is wonderful what a fine effect such things produce in history, when set off with maps and charts prepared at great expense, and without any regard to the facts, twenty years after the war. It was a parade march, that long, hot day, thirty-three miles to Wardensville, where we camped that night in the open fields. A more tired and weary army never rested their bones in the green, dewy fields. We threw out our pickets in the brush along the skirts of the mountain, and two of them, I remember well, were shot dead by the cowardly, skulking bushwhackers that night.

The bushwhacker, the cowardly stay-at-home, prowling on the mountain slopes, following along after our armies, was the meanest and most dangerous foe we ever encountered in West Virginia. Next day, bright and early, we broke camp and marched seven miles south to Lost River. It was a raging torrent, hugged in closely in a narrow ravine in the mountains, and at the time impassable. Just a few rods below the ford, for there was no bridge, the impetuous torrent rushed fairly against the mountain, down under its base, and was lost to sight. That is why it is called Lost River. I never knew where its floods debouch from the mountain, or if indeed they emerge at all. Doubtless some of our generals who have been engaged upon the geography and topography of that region for the last twenty years, in order to prove the wisdom of the expedition, and to explain why General Elliott, his staff, and his corps of engineers should march an army full upon an impassable torrent before discovering that its passage was impracticable, have prepared maps and charts which will make all these difficulties to disappear, much as has been done in the case of the surprise at Shiloh or the failure at Bull Run.

After a council of war, it was ordered that we occupy our old camp, until the pontooners and engineers could bridge the stream.

It was then learned for the first time that a body of rebels, some two thousand strong, were encamped but a few miles south, under the command of General Jones, and General Elliott was anxious to get at them with his army of 8,000 or 10,000 well armed and well equipped soldiers.

So we worked back to our old camp at Wardensville, and slept a secure night right on the same spot.

Meantime the bushwhackers and scouts who hovered about us constantly had twenty-four hours' notice to give General Jones of our advance, and he folded his tents like the Arab, as history tells, and never waited a bit for us to come and eat him up! This was some more strategy, but it was *all* on the rebel side, as usual.

On the morning of the third day we resumed our march, crossed Lost River on the new bridge constructed the night before, and off we went, at a double-quick almost, after General Jones, who was now probably laugh-

ing at our strategy thirty miles away. About noon our
scouts returned with a message to General Elliott that
the rebs had vanished, and so we counter-marched fifteen
miles, and slept the third night in our former beds, on
the green grass at Wardensville. Since the days of Don
Quixote, I do not think such wonderful movements have
been accomplished, unless it may be in other parts of our
army, of which other soldiers may tell.

XV. — EXTRACT FROM SPEECH AT SPRINGFIELD, OHIO, AUGUST 20, 1879.

Mr. Speaker. — [Here the Speaker pointed to the
clock on the wall, and said: " The five minutes of the
Honorable member from Noble begins at 3 P. M. He
will please take notice of that."

As Mr. Dalzell arose he had the attention of the entire House. Mr. Dalzell, bowing low to the Speaker,
continued: I thank Mr. Speaker Neal for the kindly
admonition, that the clock, like the world, moves, and
that " while we take no note of time," it marks our
progress in the great and mighty work of codifying the
laws of Ohio. I thank the Speaker for this pregnant
and suggestive text: Look at the clock! It marks
three—pretty late in the afternoon—pretty late, I say,
for this legislature to be fooling away its time on reorganizing the board of public works. Thus, day by day,
are the Democrats wasting the time of this house, while
outside Democrats lie and lie to the people about codification detaining us here. We have codified nothing
yet but O'Connor, Jeff Davis, and the public institutions
of Ohio. This legislature, fitly named for O'Connor,

14

wastes all the golden hours of May in defending Jeff Davis and reorganizing the board of public works, and attempting to reorganize Dayton. Thus have we spent the last five days, at a cost of $5,000 to Ohio.

I have watched the Democratic party policy, as a member here, two years. From the past, I am authorized to suppose we shall stay here till dog days in the great Democratic work of "codifying" the cities of Ohio. I don't wonder the Speaker points me to the clock. I point him and his party to that clock on the wall. Its upper dial marks three o'clock. Its lower dial marks May 14. Still you linger here disgracing Ohio with Democratic tricks and schemes to organize our cities in the interests of the Democratic party, the devil, and Jefferson Davis. It is that alone that has kept us here, and nothing else. All this talk of "codification" is bosh. It is a lie. Not a word of codification have I or you heard here lo! these many days. Not one word. No wonder the Speaker points to the clock on the wall.

It is high time, this 14th of May, when all the people of Ohio are begging us to adjourn and go home, when we have stayed here longer and spent more money by thousands than any legislature ever did in Ohio, that we consult the clock on the wall. Where are the codifying bills? No man knows. No man cares. They are lost sight of. We never hear a word of them. Not one word. Yet the people of Ohio are to be stuffed with the lie that we have remained here two hundred and fifty-seven days, at a cost of $257,000, to codify, ye gods! the laws!

We have not spent over twenty full days at that.

Our whole time has been spent defending O'Connor, your leader, Jeff Davis, and the Democratic party, the devil, and gerrymandering Ohio, overturning, degrading, disgracing, polluting, destroying, prostituting, aye, burning our public institutions. It is time to consult the clock on the wall. You have, by your legislation, degraded some of our public institutions to houses of ill-fame and prostitution. If that clock is not run down yet, it is certain that the patience of the people is well nigh run down. Yes, I look with the Speaker and the House and the people at the clock on the wall, while we linger here to make offices for hungry and thieving Democrats, and for no other purpose, while the codification of the laws is wholly, every day neglected. It is high time our last hour had struck; but we have not so much consulted the clock on the wall as the interests of the Democratic party. This Legislature drew its first breath in reorganizing schemes and infamy; it has dragged out all its long expensive days reorganizing, and now its last fetid breath is slowly going out in reorganizing Republican cities into Democratic hands. It is that which keeps us here, while the dial plate on the clock marks 3 o'clock, May 14. We are codifying the laws! What an infamous lie. No, sir; we are codifying O'Connor, Jeff Davis, the devil, and the Democratic party. We are at this moment codifying Democrats in and Republicans out, while the pendulum swings in the clock on the wall. Yes, sir; we are codifying Cincinnati, while the clock on the wall marks the hour when we should go home.

If that old clock there could speak, what a story it

could tell of two hundred and fifty-seven days of a
Democratic Legislature! I do not wonder the Speaker
points me to the clock on the wall, while every eye in
Ohio marks the swinging of its pendulum and the revolution of its hours, hourly praying that the next may be
the hour of the departure of the O'Connor Legislature.
And behind that clock on the wall, Mr. Speaker, behold
the handwriting of the people on the wall. It is before
all our eyes. Patience is ceasing to be a virtue. An
organized political caucus may sit forever and concoct
all manner of partisan schemes, and the people only
smile if it costs the public nothing. But if it costs
$1,000 a day, and purposes to itself no other object than
to "codify" Democrats in and "codify" Republicans
out, the people can not and will not endure the expense
of such a caucus. This Legislature is such a caucus.
Behold the clock on the wall, and the handwriting of
wrath of 3,000,000 of angry people. Behold—[Here
the gavel of the Speaker fell, Mr. Dalzell's five minutes
having expired.]

XVI.—EXTRACT FROM ADDRESS OF PRIVATE DALZELL,
FIRST GRAND ARMY DAY, CINCINNATI, OCTOBER 27,
1887.

*Mr. Chairman, Dear Old Comrades, Ladies, and Fellow-
Citizens:*

The old Greeks had a beautiful legend that the stars
as they circle in the heavens make music as they go, and
that the reason why we can not hear the symphony of the
starry spheres is because of the grossness of our senses,
and for no other reason. So it was that the great master

of human passions, Shakespeare, put the same idea into
the lips of the devoted lover, addressed to his girl :

> "Sit, Jessica: see how the floor of heaven
> Is thick inlaid with patines of bright gold;
> There's not a single star which thou behold'st,
> But in its motion like an angel sings,
> Still choiring to the young-eyed cherubim."

So, my friends, I have sometimes thought on occasions
like these we are lifted up into an atmosphere out of ourselves until we can hear the divine harmony of the
spheres.

It was a famous saying of the lamented Garfield that
our unconscious things are our best things. And so it
comes to pass when we least expect it. When we devote
ourselves, as the Commander of the Department of Ohio
said to-night, to the good of others, it is then that we best
serve ourselves. So that it might be stated thus, that
they who serve others best, serve themselves best; and
that the highest self-service is others' service, or service
of others.

But, my friends, I am not to forget, for the brief time
allotted to me, the purpose for which I have been called
to this platform. I am here to-night to take up and
repeat words so eloquently expressed by your distinguished Mayor of Cincinnati when he said—and it was a
most impressive remark—that he never felt his weakness
more than when he stood in the presence of the veterans
of the Union, the scarred warriors of Grant, and of
Sheridan, and of Sherman. I don't wonder that he
should feel so, or that any man should feel so, or that I,
my old comrades, should feel so to-night.

I was summoned here to deliver an address, only on Monday morning last, and I have not prepared one, and I would do as Frederick Douglass used to say to his audience, I will try to give you back, ladies and gentlemen, as good as you give, and if I get something good from you, I will send it back to you, and if I do not, I won't. I am relying largely on the inspiration of the occasion, the inspiration of the subject, for what I may have to submit to-night on the theme allotted to me, the Grand Army; and, comrades, is n't that a grand theme to which I have been called? It is one for which I feel wholly unworthy—wholly unworthy, I say; and someone else could have been found to fill this place much better than I.

In briefly alluding to the subject to-night, I shall only touch upon the hem of the garment of this argument. The subject is too large.

The subject, then, assigned to me is " The Grand Army of the Republic " — its organization, the purpose for which it is organized, its present objects and aims.

Why, my friends, I am reminded, Mr. Chairman, right at this point here, of a very fast young man, who had just emerged from college, and who took it into his head he would deliver a lecture, if he could only get somebody fool enough to listen to him, and so he announced his subject, " Women, Napoleon, and the Devil." That was the theme upon which he was going to speak, and he never got through with the women. That was more than he could handle.

The subject is entirely too large for a single evening, even to someone much better acquainted with the subject than I pretend to be.

The Grand Army of the Republic — what a great
theme it is! It is an aggregation of all the men who
bore a more or less distinguished part in putting down
the most infamous and wicked rebellion the world ever
saw. I am not one of those who are willing to weep
over the loss of the lost cause. I am one of those who
believe that the lost cause is lost, justly lost, and lost
forever, beyond all redemption, and beyond all reser-
vation.

I know there are good people within the sound, perhaps, of my poor voice here to-night, who may say, and
who may think, just at this point here, that we have
politics in the Grand Army of the Republic. When we
cross the threshold of the Post room, we are simply
comrades. When General Sherman comes into the room,
he is comrade Sherman; and when Corporal Tanner
comes into the room, he is comrade Tanner. We are all
equal there.

Why, I am sometimes reminded of what is told in this
regard of Clovis, after his campaigns in the Middle
Ages, when he brought his mailed warriors about him,
and brought out the rich spoils that he had gathered
from a hundred cities, and among the rest the old vase
that was brought, sparkling with diamonds, rubies, and
brilliants, from the old church at Rheims. And he set
out the vase, and said he would take that vase to himself,
because he was commander of the army, when a sturdy
soldier strode from the battle ranks, and said: "When
you have fought your battles alone, and not till then,
you will have earned all of the reward;" and, raising
his battle-ax, suiting the word to the action, he smote the
precious vase to atoms, and dashed it down. Now, we

have nothing of that kind in the Grand Army of the Republic: you and I, dear comrades, never have done anything like that. There is glory enough for all—glory enough for the private, glory enough for the lieutenant-general, glory enough for the general, glory enough for the corporal, and glory enough for all the army, and we have no quarrels about it. We are all equal, every man who worthily wore the blue, and did his duty as God enabled him to do his duty; in the Grand Army of the Republic, he is equal to every other man.

It is worth that marks the grades of manhood; it is character that is the supreme consideration after all, not brilliant abilities; but character, and solid manhood, and worth, they count for as much in the Grand Army of the Republic as elsewhere.

Now, my friends, you and I came down out of that war, and when the birds began to prepare to fill their nests in the mouths of our yet smoking cannon, and when the broken battalions of Lee had surrendered their arms to the victorious legions of Grant—I say, when you and I came down from the army, and you went off to your home, and I went off to mine, and met our sisters, and our mothers, and our wives, that were to be at the gate, and kissed them with pride—after a while you began to feel a longing to hear from old Joe, and old Bill, and old Tom, and the rest of the boys. So we began to feel we would like to meet them again, and we had reunions in the little towns and larger ones all over the country. But this was found not to be enough, and so somehow, in some way, the Grand Army of the Republic sprang up like Topsy—it "just growed, it just growed up."

Why, I remember, as one of the most interesting passages in the historian Hallam's work, that he tries to find the origin of the common law. He tries to find the origin of the constitution of England, and then, after having made fruitless search for it, makes a remark something like this: that to find the origin of these things is like searching for the sources (then unknown) of the Nile.

The Grand Army of the Republic was born in the hearts of the drummer boys, the privates, the general, the colonels, and sprang up as Decoration Day.

I noticed a little pamphlet they had around tells us it was the idea of an old soldier; we won't rob him of the honor—a blessed old soldier in Iowa thinks he invented the Grand Army of the Republic. He might as well say he invented the sun as it shines in its course; he might as well think he invented and put in their places the sparkling patines that shine in the ethereal blue above.

It was born in the hearts of the soldiers. It was born of tears, and of love, and of kindness, and of friendship, and of holy memories that we never, never can forget. There the Grand Army of the Republic was born.

Now, then, we had to have principles in this Grand Army of the Republic. Why, we did n't have to have many of them. At first they were hardly formulated on paper. They are few, and they are so simple that the little boy who walks down the aisle at this moment could understand them if he wanted to.

Why, what are they? Our worthy Commanders for the Departments of Kentucky and Indiana have already gone over these things, and I shall only touch them lightly.

The Grand Army of the Republic proposes brother-

15

hood, fraternity—brotherhood among us all, and that we should be "brothers by the baptism of the banner—battle-scarred but glorious banner; no church, no creed, no race, no nation can divide us, and whatsoever fate betide us, brothers let us ever be" (Miles O'Reilly).

Wherever we meet a man who worthily wore the blue, and who was honorably discharged from service, he is our brother, meet him where we may.

To-day I noticed that you had a number of intelligent and beautiful ladies here, representing the States, and I noticed them upon the platform here and was pleased to see that too, and certainly was pleased to see also the manifestations with which Cincinnati to-day has done herself great honor in honoring the Nation's defenders. I was glad to see all these things; I was glad to see the Department Commanders of various States, and the dear old comrades from different places. But, my dear comrades, we only come from one State. I don't care whether it it is the Department Commander from Indiana, Kentucky, or Ohio, whether it is the comrade from Tennessee, from New York, or from California, we all belong to one State. We didn't fight for Ohio. We fought as much for South Carolina and for Georgia and Kentucky, for Mississippi and Alabama and Louisiana, as we did for Massachusetts, New York, Pennsylvania or Ohio. We made the Union one and inseparable, now and forever.

As Daniel Webster once voiced it in an address he was making to the young men at Albany: "Now," said he, "young gentlemen, good evening, and may you all live forever and may the Constitution and the Union outlive you all."

We have no North, we have no South, we have no East, we have no West. But we fought for the Union, and that is the reason why the Government of the United States ought to assume the burden of taking care of these wrecks of humanity, the broken down soldier, broken by wounds and broken by disease. It is a shame, a crying abuse to have a lot of miserable politicians mouthing up and down the country about a surplus. I tell these Democrats and Republicans and Prohibitionists and Laboring men—I will tell them what to do with that surplus. We saved— the Grand Army men saved the Nation from destruction. Who put that money there? The soldier. Not a single dollar is there in this Nation to-day, in the pockets of anybody in the whole North or in the whole South, not a dollar of it on the streets of Turin or London or other foreign cities in the pockets of American travelers, but was saved to them by the sacrifices of the defenders of the Union. Who found that money and who made it good? It was the best blood of America.

Talk of the politicians making the money good. It was the blood, the sacred blood of the boys in blue who died that the credit of the Nation might be good and that we might have a Nation at all.

Talk about your surplus. Shame, shame that the old broken veteran to-night, in his patches and rags, and in his cabin and poverty, with blind eye, with broken health, and even as poor Garfield once said, with a broken mind —think of it, my friends. What would you take for a finger; what would you take for a limb; but oh my God, what would you take for your mind? One hundred and seventy-five thousand men incarcerated in rebel prisons came out wrecks physically, wrecks mentally many of them.

And now, then, we go about and talk about these things and try to make party questions. There is no party question in it. Distribute your surplus among the soldiers!

There is only one party in this country and that is the party of loyal men and loyal women. Not Democrats or Republicans; we won't have any other party in the United States than a party that will swear, by the eternal, the Union must and shall be preserved.

I have no tears to shed, as I said before, over the lost cause. There has been a great deal of maudlin sentiment expended upon it. When I was younger I used to dream of a reconciliation so perfect as to be embodied in a figure something like this: I saw a tall and stately maiden, with plaited hair and with blue eyes, and her fair jeweled fingers were held out, and I saw another dark-eyed maiden standing looking to the North, and moving her footsteps Northward, and stretching her jeweled hands, and I saw them meet and clasp each other around the neck and wet each other's cheeks with tears, and they covered each other's cheeks with their mutual kisses.

But it is all fudge. I have not seen any thing of that kind happen.

That is what we want. The Grand Army of the Republic has no hatred to the South. Our motto is, "With charity for all and malice toward none, doing the right as God gives us to see the right," compromising all questions, leaving every miserable little, wretched, dirty, offensive partisan question out of our little post room, too sacred for politics, leaving them all out of there, compromising on every thing except one thing, the American Union, now and forever, in the room or out of it.

Why, somebody said to me, not in this room, but elsewhere, why this is all sentiment. It is. You are here to-night to honor a sentiment. This day, this Grand Army day was so grandly and fittingly inaugurated by the good ladies and gentlemen, the soldiers, and even the little children of Cincinnati to-day, as it will be remembered for a hundred years to come as one of the brightest days that the Queen City of the West ever saw, in honor of its sentiments.

Sentiment rules the world to-day. Sentiment built every church that you can find on the face of the globe. Sentiment brought the pilgrim fathers to these shores. Your flags sprang out of a beautiful sentiment. Your Union grew up out of a beautiful sentiment. Wasn't it a magnificent, wasn't it a sublime, a soul-stirring sentiment with which the young Ellsworth ran up the stairs, and pulled down the flag of treason, and trampled it under his foot, and baptized his love for the old flag with his blood? I say it was a grand sentiment. Some cool, calculating fellow would have said, how much money will I get for going up those stairs and pulling down Jackson's flag, or what will be the risk to me?

Sentiment rules the world. Some believe physical force rules the world. It does not. It has its place, but sentiment in its power is omnipotent and transcends all.

In a moment, in the flash of an eye, as quick as the lightning from the dark sky above to the earth, in a moment the whole loyal American people were aflame for a sentiment, and they said—By the eternal, this government must become all one thing or all the other. It must be-

come all slaves or all free, and that sentiment went on
and triumphed, and in the fires of war the shackles were
loosed from the limbs of these dusky millions, and they
sprang up in the sunlight of freedom and stand there en-
enfranchised and free to-night. The soldiers did it; the
soldiers did it all, by the help of loyal women and loyal
men of the North standing at their backs.

I take no stock at all in any mourning over the lost
cause. If I ever rear a monument to it it shall be one
sulphurous and dark. I save my tears, not for the lost
cause, but for the three hundred thousand brave young
men, the brightest and most beautiful men of my generation, who went down in the red fire of war, that the government of the people and by the people, and for the
people, might not perish from the earth.

I save my tears for these. I save my tears for the
widow in her weeds, in her loneliness and despair, whose
husband, broken down by suffering in rebel prisons or on
fields of battle, wounded, pined and died, and left her
there alone with the little ones and poverty and misery.
I save my tears for you. I have no tears for the lost
cause.

I save my tears for the old one-legged and one-armed
veteran, who goes about the world the wreck of the man
that he ought to be, and would have been, but for the
war. I save my tears for these.

I save my tears for those who have been struggling
vainly for years, and are glad to find a rest at last in the
soldier's home, or in the green tent in the silent valley.
I save my tears for these. I have no tears to shed for
the lost cause.

It is a sickly sentimentality. It is illogical and unreasonable. It is unpatriotic and untrue. We have nothing to mourn for the lost cause. When the lost cause from the brimstone depths of eternal hell is dug up and lifted, I can only hold my nose. I have no veneration for the lost cause, or for any man who supports it.

The people in this country must be taught that there is a difference between politics and loyalty. That a man can be very loyal and love his flag, and love his constitution devotedly, and keep true faith and allegiance to the laws and constitution of the land, and respect the President of the United States, and yet hate treason and traitors.

Show me an unshriven traitor and he is my deadly enemy to-day. Show me a repentent rebel and he is my friend, and I will shake hands with him, not across "a bloody chasm," but across my own hearth-stone, and will welcome him to it.

Those I understand to be some of the principles of the Grand Army of the Republic, and how do you like them? Are not those pretty good principles?

One of the purposes of the Grand Army of the Republic is for us to meet and strike hands, and, as boys would say, have a good time, and shake hands under the shadow of the old flag, baptized with the blood of the best men the world ever saw. Oh, was n't that a beautiful thought of Goethe, speaking of Schiller, when he said he loved to always think of Schiller as having died in his youth, fair and young, and beautiful forever.

And now they stand, the three millions of those who went to that war, and there they stand, the three hundred thousand who never returned—some who died in their bloody shirts, and some who found their deaths at the mouths of merciless bloodhounds and still more merciless men, and some who died and passed away in a single flash of glory on fields of war. There they stand. I see their beardless faces before me, young and beautiful, crowned in the hallowed love of everlasting fame and immortality. I can think of nothing more beautiful, more endearing than this.

By these sacred shades, we say, to-night: If any man attempts to tear down the American flag, we will shoot him on the spot.

Why, do you not know this, my old comrades—some of these comrades know it better than I can tell—that no man that ever stood under the stars and bars can ever enter a Grand Army Post—never. Before he can get in there, a soldier must swear that he was never a traitor. Why, I knew one man, a noble fellow, and I could cry for him to-night if it would do any good, that fellow was one of the best rebels I ever saw. But he was wrong, always wrong—as every rebel was wrong, you know—and he could never enter a Grand Army post.

There never was any rebel right. Every rebel was wrong. Every pulsation of the fiendish, dastardly, cowardly, traitorous heart of Jeff. Davis, from beginning to end, was wrong, and it is wrong to-night.

Do you know what that rebel flag means, old friends, you who were not in the army? Ask these boys in blue, whose hair is turning gray with the frosts of the coming winter, whose eyes are turning dark with the shadows soon to be; ask them what this rebel flag means. They will tell you that one morning in the sunlight, after they themselves had received the accolade for the dear old flag, the star-spangled banner, they looked across the hills, and there, behind the frowning cannon and long lines of men in gray, they saw the cross of St. George, the hated stars and bars, the standard of the lost cause. They hated it then and they hate it now. If our continent was ten thousand times as big as it is, we would not tolerate any flag upon it but that one.

Every one of its silver stars shines in the blue throne above to represent a State in the American Union, not one out, not a single one. That is our flag; that is the flag of the Grand Army of the Republic; that is the flag that was baptized in the blood of the best men the world ever saw.

Oh, comrade, bear with me a moment. I want to say to you and to these gentlemen present, something I have never forgotten to say and never will until this breath shall fail me forever. You are not as good men as they were, and I am not. The man does not live that is as good as the men who died for the flag. Is that saying too much? You risked your life, it is true, but mark what Lincoln said. He drew the line right; he drew it philosophically; he drew it correctly. They gave the last full measure of their devotion that " the government of the people, by the people and for the people," might not perish from the earth. And in dying they wrested these rebel flags from rebel hands, and, by the eternal, the sunlight shall never see them.

That ain't politics, is it? That ain't politics. Now, that is what the Grand Army of the Republic teaches us. I would like to see some fool bring a rebel flag into one of our Post rooms, or even in a camp of the Sons of Veterans. The boys wouldn't hurt anybody, but they would take the thing and put it in the fire, to say the least of it.

I have sometimes wondered why men could love the lost cause. Why, I would let it go down, down, down, until it sunk into its native hell, and is covered up and forgotten forever and forever.

We want no lost cause reverenced in this country, we Grand Army boys, and we will have none of it.

Where did they get that standard of treason? Why, I have sometimes thought, when I read Milton's pictured battle in heaven, that, when the contest was had in the battlements of heaven between the fallen angels and the Almighty and his host, that the standard that Satan carried there was hurled with him from those battlements when he was finally overcome and cast to hell, and that the rebels picked it up; and I have sometimes thought that that was where the banner of the lost cause came from.

Now, if that is strong doctrine, I can't help it. That is what these Grand Army boys have been teaching me for the last twenty-five years, anyhow. And if that ain't Grand Army truth, I don't know Grand Army truth.

Now, we have charity. "Oh, ho!" my friend of the lost cause, if he was here, would say, "charity, and yet you talk so ugly about the rebels?" No, sir; we have not an angry word to say, not an angry feeling, but all we want them to do is to keep their contract, made when we whipped them—for they swore that they would submit, or we would not have let them up. We want them to abide by the settlement that they made under the apple-tree at Appomatox, and, by the Eternal, they shall do it. That is another principle and purpose of the Grand Army of the Republic.

Why, we want to perpetuate this nation. We old fellows are soon to fold our arms, and lay ourselves in the dust, but these young fellows are coming on. and when we hand this flag of ours to them, and this great and growing country of ours to them, we want them to remember what it cost to save their country and to save their flag, and we want them to keep it flying forever.

As Bishop Simpson said once for the young ladies, on their presenting a flag to a regiment just going to the war, " Now," said he, " boys in blue, take that flag, nail it just below the cross—that is high enough—and keep it there, and never take it down."

Was n't that a beautiful sentiment? That is the sentiment of the Grand Army of the Republic. I know it is often said, " This is all sentimental." It is sentimental, and, as I said before, this sentiment rules the world. Why, ask some of these veterans here, and they will say their love is nothing but sentiment, and their wives rule them; and is n't that sentiment ruling, too? I can prove it that way without going very far away from home.

Now, my friends, I have talked about long enough, but I want to say a word about charity. That is one of the principles of the Grand Army of the Republic.

Charity toward each other. Where is there a man without a fault? If you can find one, let him cast the first stone; and he will be the first man that ever did cast one of that kind. We have to have charity with each other and toward others, and so the Grand Army of the Republic inculcates charity; it inculcates loyalty and devotion to our country and our country's cause.

My friends, God bless you! I thank you for the

welcome you have given me to-night. I ask you, old comrades, to increase your ranks; bring in every soldier in Hamilton county who is not a member of the Grand Army of the Republic; bring him in, and keep him there; stand by the flags and the principles of your order; encourage the Ladies' Relief Corps, and they will encourage you; encourage the Sons of Veterans, and they will help you; and, by and by, old boys, when the day is done, when our tasks are finished, we shall lie down, not, like fallen slaves, cursed to our rest, but " sustained and soothed by an unfaltering trust" in the dear old banner and in the dear old cause, " And the night shall be filled with music, and the cares that infest the day shall fold their tents, like the Arabs, and shall silently steal away."

[The speaker then closed by calling for three cheers from the soldiers present for the Grand Army of the Republic, the dear old flags, and for the loyal ladies of Cincinnati, which were given standing.]

XVII.—PRIVATE DALZELL'S SOLDIER CIRCULAR.

CALDWELL, OHIO, *December* 16, 1887.

Comrade:—Some days ago I published an account of the Ohio legislation in favor of soldiers, in the *New York Tribune*, and in our own great organ, *The National Tribune*, which has been extensively copied and commented upon by the American newspaper press, and reproduced already in England, France, and Germany, as I happen to know. It has aroused a profound interest among the dear comrades all over the North, and elicited from them so many letters of inquiry that I am compelled to take this method to reply. I could not possibly respond to all with the pen.

The laws of Ohio simply provide for the levying of a tax of three-tenths of a mill on the dollar on all the property in the state, to raise a fund for the relief of indigent soldiers and their families. This goes into the county treasuries, and is drawn out by commissioners in each county, appointed by the court, two of whom are soldiers, and paid directly to the soldier or his family, in all cases of distress. No papers are employed; all is done orally; no delay is possible; no attorney is permitted to have any thing to do with it, and no expense is incurred. Could any thing be more simple or beautiful? This law I desire to see enacted in every state this winter. It is late in the day, but better late than never. Dying time has nearly come to most of us. We are mostly poor. The general public has an idea of the amount of suffering, privation, and distress which the soldiers and their families are now called upon to endure, and which they bear so silently and patiently that no one except themselves knows that it exists. They are not noisy anarchists or fanatics, but as brave to suffer as they were to dare and to do. This alarming state of things is daily on the increase—ten-fold worse in 1887–1888 than in any previous years, for diseases multiply and increase in violence, and wounds grow more disabling every year, and have nearly reached their climax of death.

Now, my object in all I have done and am doing—a poor, broken-down old soldier myself, illy able to bear the labor and expense thus voluntarily assumed by myself—is to prevail, if possible, upon the comrades in all the states to move at once upon their legislatures and newspapers, and give them no rest until every state, from sea to sea, shall have laws on its statute books as patriotic and generous as those of Ohio, which, here let me say once for all, are not half what they ought to be, but better than none! They are susceptible of many amendments yet.

Divided, we can do nothing. United, we are omnipotent in American politics. We hold the balance of power in every state, county, township, and municipality.

Let us exercise it for once, and touch elbows, and charge all along the line—no stragglers, no deserters, no coffee coolers, no sneaks, but all as *one man*. We number a million, though that will not long be true. We are melting away like melting snow.

It is now or never.

But we must *combine*, COMBINE, COMBINE.

That done, all is done.

The politicians then must obey us, or step down and out of office. To this end, therefore, I submit a form of oath which I have taken, and which I abjure every comrade to register in heaven for himself before the first day of January, 1888, *and keep it*, as I shall keep it, even as we all kept the oath of service, the solemn sacrament of the flag! "I do solemnly swear, in presence of Almighty God, that I will never, directly or indirectly, give political support to any candidate for office who this winter, in any legislative body, state or national, as a member thereof, or as executive, shall fail to support any bill or measure granting pensions, relief, bounty, or repealing limitations, or in anywise benefiting honorably discharged Union soldiers or their families. So help me God"

Print thousands and thousands of these oaths, and scatter them in all the states. At the same time, I counsel you to forward these oaths as fast as signed to your senators, members of Congress, state legislators, governors, and the President.

These will be more potent and significant than a thousand petitions, to be read, laughed at, referred, and pitched ignominiously into the waste-basket, never again to be thought of. When you lifted your hands before, and took the oath that " the government of the people, by the people, and for the people, should not perish from the earth," that oath you solemnly and religiously observed until it was redeemed, and the Nation's life saved by your courage and self-sacrifice. Keep this oath now, comrades, and forget it not when you stand at the polls with your all-powerful million votes in your hands. Forget it not.

The politicians, instead of laughing at it, will turn pale and tremble before it, for it is clothed with the power of the thunders and lightnings of heaven. After recording that oath on earth and registering it in heaven, have no further concern about legislation. It will come as naturally and as surely as the summer rain follows the lightning's flash! It is simply idiotic to send up any petitions. Send your *commands*, not prayers!

We have tried turf long enough.

Let us imitate the old farmer, who, at length, was forced to resort to stones. Away with petitions to Congress and the legislatures! Faugh! They would only laugh at them. Let them deride or disregard this fearful oath if they dare. No party cry will save the candidate who scorns and disregards this significant appeal. Ask your newspapers to publish this and your comment thereon.

Only those editors who were not soldiers, and those who are, and always were, your enemies, will refuse a respectful request for space for this patriotic purpose. All others will publish it with editorial comments. To be frank, this is our only hope. Unless the press co-operates with us, the legislatures and Congress, and even the President, will not heed our appeals.

They have the Ohio soldier laws in all their libraries, and will reproduce them in their newspapers. Do this, do it at once, republish this circular, add to it, change it in any way you please, and move in a solid phalanx, as you did at Gettysburg, Atlanta, and Appomattox, and before the springtime returns we shall procure all needed legislation.　　　Your comrade,

PRIVATE DALZELL.

XVIII.—POEMS.

THE BLUE AND THE GRAY.

You may sing of the Blue and the Gray,
　And mingle their hues in your rhyme,
But the Blue that we wore in the fray
　Is covered with glory sublime.
　　So, no more let us hear of the Gray,
　　The symbol of treason and shame—
　　We pierced it with bullets—away!
　　Or we'll pierce it with bullets again.
Then up with the Blue and down with the Gray,
And hurrah for the Blue that won us the day!

Of the rebels who sleep in the Gray,
    Our silence is fitting alone;
We can not afford them a bay,
    A sorrow, a tear, or a moan.
        Let oblivion seal up their graves
            Of treason, disgrace, and defeat;
        Had they triumphed, the Blue had been slaves,
            And the Union been lost in retreat.
Then up with the Blue and down with the Gray,
And hurrah for the Blue that won us the day!

Of the rebels whom our mercy still spares
    To boast of the traitorous fray,
No boy in the Blue thinks or cares,
    For the struggle is ended to-day.
        Let them come as they promised to come,
            Under Union and Loyalty too;
        And we'll hail them with fife and with drum,
            And forget that they fired on the Blue.
Then up with the Blue and down with the Gray,
And hurrah for the Blue that won us the day!

As they carried your flag through the fray,
    Ye Northmen, ye promised the Blue
That ye'd never disgrace with the Gray
    The colors so gallant and true.
        Will ye trace on the leaves of your souls
            The Blue and the Gray in one line,
        And mingle their hues on the scrolls
            Which glorify Victory's shrine,
And cheer for the false, and hiss at the true,
And up with the Gray and down with the Blue?

Let the traitors all go if you may,
    (Your heroes would punish the head,)
But never confound with the Gray
    The Blue, whether living or dead.

16

Oh! remember the price that was paid—
　　The blood of the brave and the true—
And you can never suffer to fade
　　The laurels that cover the Blue.
Then up with the Blue and down with the Gray,
And hurrah for the Blue that won us the day!

———

INTROSPECTA.

Two pair of eyes to see,
　　One pair without, and one
To scan the world within,
　　By man are seldom won.

The ox has eyes to see
　　The straw on which he tramps,
But in that mammoth bulk
　　There burn no spirit lamps.

Man alone has power to gaze—
　　And few men even this—
On Beauty's charms, and feel
　　Electric romance, bliss!

This is the cyne I love,
　　The power to look within,
To fill the empty air
　　With visions bright akin

To the higher forms and molds
　　So transubstantial broad
The glowing bust divine
　　Of Beauty, Music, God.

To hear anthems pealing
　　The spirit aisles all through,
Till the heart quakes with joy,
　　Stirring, sublime, and true.

I see the shapes in the night
　　No other eyes can see;
I hear strange voices ring
　　In accents full of glee.

And pale groups of ghosts
　　Around my pillow flit,
And I wake from ghostly dreams
　　"To many a musing fit."

I feel the touch of hands
　　No other mortals feel;
And fight, with demon arms,
　　Hosts mailed in more than steel.

I talk familiar with
　　The spirit of Perfect Life,
And see her footsteps strike
　　From earth its toil and strife.

The dusty toil and drag
　　Of a weary life, and poor,
I would not lengthen out a day,
　　Compelled to live a boor.

But sometimes it seems to me
　　'Twere better I were dead,
Than drink at founts of joy
　　By the heart's red current fed.

For these passion lamps must drink
　　The being's ripest oil,
And end its flickerings all
　　With life of aimless toil.

Burn on, ye lamps within, burn
　　Till ye burn the spirits down;
Then ashes fly in Fate's cold face,
　　And tell her I was not a clown!

Come, ye cold eternal winds,
    And flap your wings into my face,
For sooner shall it cool not
    In time's tempestuous chase!

———

EVAN F. DARDINE.*

A painter of scenes, of crimson-stained scenes,
Of the hills of Virginia, her camps and her streams,
A right royal soul, and a kindred one too,
An artist, a soldier, in Abraham's blue;
Let me rhyme of thy genius and courage, and tell
What I pray all the muses to aid me do well,
Inscribing these lines from the depth of my heart
To the young imitator of nature and art.

I honor the skill of your pencil and brush;
From the morning's first dawn to the evening's last flush,
Your sketches of camp-life and battle-death too,
Are tinged with devotion to " Red, White, and Blue;"
For the lightning of war is often thy lamp,
While the thunder of battle resounds through the camp,
And a seat on a mountain while bombs burst around,
Is the place where the Artist must often be found.

An honor, a blessing through all these sad wars,
Is the pencil baptized in the temple of Mars,
And the drawings of forts, of sieges and camps,
Will glow in the future like magical lamps,
That poets, historians, and statesmen may see
The scenes that transpire in "the land of the free;"
Thy pictures reflecting this era of strife,
All glowing, immortal, and real as life.

—— ——

*My old comrade, of whom I wrote the above a quarter of a century ago
nearly, now lives in honor in Wheeling, W. Va.

The mother and sister, with love's anxious eye,
Still tearful and sad as when bidding "good-bye,"
Are gazing with pride on these pictures of war,
As a maiden would gaze on some sweet chosen star.
This, this is a recompense due to thy name,
A life full of honor, and glory, and fame,
A place on America's glorious scroll,
Which ages shall treasure as onward they roll.

MOTHER'S PRAYER FOR HER SOLDIER BOYS.

An old man sits in his easy chair
His eyes grown dim with years,
And the frosts of age are on his hair;
His cheeks are wet with tears.

The old man sits in his lonely chair,
His wife is long since dead;
His heart is full of an echoing prayer,
The last on earth she said!

"My two brave boys in thy mercy spare,
God, if it be thy will;
Wherever they may be to-night, there
Thy goodness guard them still."

Her spirit fled to the far sweet land—
Her boys had gone before;
Up from the battle reaching a hand
To greet her on that shore.

The old man sits in his lonely chair,
His wife is long since dead;
His heart is full as it echoes the prayer
The dying mother said.

John Gray

PART III.

John Gray, of Mount Vernon,

THE LAST SOLDIER OF THE REVOLUTION.

Born near Mt. Vernon, Va., January 6, 1764.
Died at Hiramsburg, Ohio, March 29, 1868.

AGED 104 YEARS.

DEDICATION.

To the Old Dominion, the birth-place of John Gray, and to Ohio, where his sacred ashes rest, and to the American people, whom he loved, and for whom he fought, this memorial of the last soldier of the revolution is respectfully dedicated by

JAMES M. DALZELL,

CALDWELL, OHIO, *May* 1, 1888.   *The Author.*

(190)

A POEM.

One by one the several links have started,
  Bonds that bound us to the sacred past;
One by one our patriot sires departed,
  Time has brought us to behold the last;
Last of all who won our early glory,
  Lonely traveler of the weary way,
Poor, unknown, unnamed in song or story,
  In his western cabin lives John Gray.

Deign to stoop to rural shade, sweet Clio!
  Sing the hero of the sword and plow;
On the borders of his own Ohio,
  Weave a laurel for the veteran's brow,
While attuned until the murmuring waters
  Flows the burden of thy pastoral lay,
Bid the fairest of Columbia's daughters,
  O'er his locks of silver, crown John Gray.

Slaves of self and serfs of vain ambition—
  Toilful strivers of the city's mart,
Turn awhile and bless the sweet transition,
  Unto the scenes that soothe that careworn heart,
Turn with me to yonder moss-thatched dwelling,
  Wreathed in woodbine and wild-rose spray;
While the muse his simple tale is telling,
  Tottering on his crutches, see John Gray.

When defeat had pressed his bitter chalice
  To the lips of England's haughty lord—
Bowed in shame the brow of stern Cornwallis,
  And at Yorktown claimed his bloody sword;
At the crown of the siege laborious—
  At the triumph of the glorious day,
Near his chieftain, in the ranks victorious,
  Stood the youthful soldier, brave John Gray.

17

While he vowed through peace their love should burn on—
  While he bade his tearful troops farewell,
One alone unto thy shades, Mount Vernon,
  Called the chieftain with himself to dwell;
Proud to serve the father of the Nation,
  Glad to hear the voice that bade him stay,
Year by year, upon the broad plantation,
  Unto ripened manhood, toiled John Gray.

Sowed, and reaped, and gathered to the garner
  All the summer plenty's golden sheaves—
Sowed and reaped till Time, the ruthless warner,
  Whispered through the dreary autumn leaves:
" Wherefore tarry? Freedom's stars are o'er thee;
  Winter frowneth ere the blush of May;
Lo! is not a goodly land before thee?
  Up and choose thee now a home, John Gray."

Thus he heard the words of duty's warning,
  And he saw the rising Empire-star
Dawning dimly on the Nation's morning—
  Guided westward Emigration's car;
Heard, and saw, and quickly rose to follow,
  Bore his rifle for the savage prey,
Bore his ax, that soon in greenwood hollow
  Timed thy sylvan ballads, bold John Gray.

Blessed with love his lonely labors cheering,
  Blithe the hearthstone of that forest nook,
Where rose his cabin in the "clearing,"
  Near the meadow with its purling brook;
Where his children from their noonday laughter
  Turned at eve and left their joyous play,
Hushed and still, when the great hereafter
  Spake the Christian father, meek John Gray

Oh, the years of mingled joy and sadness!
  Oh, the hours—the countless hours of toil,
Shared alike through sorrow and through gladness
  By loved hands now moldering in the soil!

Oh, the anguish stifled in the shadow
  Of the gloom that bore her form away!
'Neath yon mound she slumbers in the meadow,
  Waiting, meekly waiting thee, John Gray.

All day long upon the threshold sitting,
  Where the sunbeams through the bright leaves shine—
Where the zephyrs, through his white locks flitting,
  Softly whisper of "the days lang syne."
How he loves on holy thoughts to ponder;
  How his eyes the azure heaven survey,
Or toward yon meadow dimly wander—
  Yes, beside her shall sleep, John Gray.

In the tomb thy comrades' bodies slumber—,
  Unto heaven their souls have flown before;
Only one is "missing" of their number,
  Only one to win the radiant shore,
Only one to join the sacred chorus,
  Only one to burst the bounds of clay;
Soon the sentry's trumpet sounding o'er us,
  To their rank shall summon thee, John Gray.

Peace be with thee—gentle spirits guard thee,
  Noble type of heroes, now no more!
In thine age may gratitude reward thee,
  In thy need may bounty bless thy store;
Care of woman, gentle, true, and tender,
  Strength of manhood be thy guide and stay;
Let not those who roll in idle splendor,
  To their shame forget thee, lone John Gray.

Five-score winters on thy head have whitened—
  Five-score summers o'er thy brow have passed;
All the sunshine that the pathway brightened,
  Clouds of want and hardship have o'ercast;
Thus the last of those who won our glory,
  Lonely traveler of the weary way,
Poor, unknown, unnamed in song or story,
  In his western cabin lives John Gray.

Three more years of weariness and aging,
    Of growing weakness, yet of patience strong;
Years of strife with penury waging,
    Till a grateful nation rights neglected wrong.
Live now, John Gray, enjoy thy meed of glory,
    A grateful people soothes thy weary way;
Alas! five-score and five! here ends my story,
    For in his western cabin died John Gray.

Beneath the willow in the flowery meadow,
    Where daises bloom and clover scents the air,
Kissed by morning sun and twilight shadow,
    Is a grave intrusted to dame nature's care;
Here, full of years, the long march ended,
    A weary soldier at life's closing day,
One who with men in gallant strife contended,
    Beside his western cabin sleeps John Gray.

Sleep on, but not forever, weary mortal,
    No bugle call shall rouse thee for the fray;
But trumpets' voice, from heaven's open portal,
    Shall summon thy dust from earth away,
Where stands the Chief to welcome thee in glory;
    Where, in the brightness of celestial day,
All earth's great ones, unnamed in song or story,
    With golden crowns, are waiting thee, John Gray.

CHAPTER I.—INTRODUCTION.

It seems as though there is an element of hero worship in every one, and I confess to a full share of it. My hero is a private soldier. Having embarked in this line so early in life, and after devoting a quarter of a century and more to elaborating it in every form in the

public press, it seems to me that I can see but one
course for me to pursue, and that is, on, right on in the
line in which I have started. In the year 1868 I wrote
and published some memories of John Gray, the last of
the "men of '76" to leave us, which work was received
with much interest. Aside from the many copies sold,
copies were placed in most of the more prominent libraries in this country. Two thousand copies of this work I
published at my own expense. When the edition became exhausted, there seemed to be no demand for a
second edition, until this centennial year of Ohio's history, which has revived interest in such matters, and
has demanded a new, and enlarged, and revised edition,
which is now sent forth with the modest hope that its
pages may be read with interest. In 1876, Hon. F. W.
Green, Secretary of the Ohio Centennial Commission, requested me to furnish him with a copy of my original
history of John Gray for exhibition at Philadelphia. As
I had placed copies in the principal libraries in the
country, I had no difficulty (though the book was then
out of print) in forwarding a copy according to his request. This copy he suspended by a ribbon just inside
the main entrance of the Ohio house, and there it hung
until the close of the Exposition, was inspected with interest by millions of people during this time, and returned to me by Mr. Green, well thumbed, about November 15, 1876, accompanied by the following grateful acknowledgment:

PHILADELPHIA, PA., *November* 13, 1876.
HON. J. M. DALZELL, CALDWELL, O.:

Sir : — I send you by express to-day your book and
picture of John Gray, and a few copies of our catalogue,
and the address of E. D. Mansfield on "Ohio." I regret
that I was absent when you were here.

Very truly yours,

F. W. GREEN, *Secretary.*

When I conceived the idea of venturing this revised
edition, in response to what I believed to be a popular
sentiment favoring it, I wrote to my old friend (and the
friend as well of our departed hero), Hon. John A.
Bingham, our venerable ex-congressman, the greatest
orator Ohio ever produced, and so long our distinguished
Envoy Extraordinary and Minister Plenipotentiary at
the Court of Japan, asking him what he could recollect
of John Gray; and, in reply, he honored me with the
following graceful and eloquent tribute to our vene-
rated hero:

CADIZ, O., February 22, 1888.

MY DEAR MR. DALZELL:

In reply to your kind note of the 20th instant, wherein
you request my recollections of Mr. John Gray, a patriot of our Revolutionary War, I regret to say that I
had but one interview with that venerable man, who, at
that time, had attained the great age of one hundred and
four years. I visited him at his home in Noble County,
O., accompanied by a friend, who had known him for
years, and who regarded him as a man of truth and strict
integrity.

I was much impressed with Mr. Gray's conversation

concerning his early life in Virginia, where he was born,
and the statement of his services, while yet a youth, in
the war for American independence. Satisfied that Mr.
Gray had served the sacred cause as a private soldier of
the Virginia line, and that he participated, in that capacity, in the final conflict at Yorktown, I did not hesitate to draft and introduce the bill of which you speak,
granting him a pension—which bill, I am pleased to say,
passed the House of Representatives with great una-
nimity, and was promptly passed by the Senate. You
doubtless have a copy of this act. It is most gratifying
to record the fact that in his last days this aged patriot
was not forgotten, and was made happy by the generous
acknowledgment of the Nation's gratitude.

> Very truly your friend,
>
> JOHN A. BINGHAM.

J. M. DALZELL, ESQ., CALDWELL, NOBLE COUNTY, O.

But, before proceeding further, I consulted also the
opinions of many of the most distinguished men in the
Nation—among them Governor J. B. Foraker; Governor
Beaver; Samuel Bowles, Jr., editor of the *Springfield*
(Mass.) *Republican;* Governor Young, of Ohio; R. B.
Hoover, Springfield, Ill.; Colonel J. D. Taylor; Frede-
rick Douglass; General Joseph R. Hawley, of Connecti-
cut; Colonel James Washburn; General R. T. Buckland;
Hon. W. S. Capellar; Judges Knowles, and Lawrence,
and Phillips, Generals Brown and Gibson, of Ohio;
General Harrison, of Indiana; Ex-Governor Foster, of
Ohio; Rev. T. J. Dague, my pastor at Caldwell, O.;
General N. P. Banks; Ex-President R. B. Hayes; Sen-
ator Sherman; Hon. Wm. R. McKinley; Generals Leg-

gett, Conger, Cowan, Lee, Dawes, Robinson, Grosvenor,
Hickenlooper, Devens, and Butler, and Corporal Tanner;
besides thousands of the rank and file in all parts of the
country, from Maine to California — and from them, one
and all, received such hearty encouragement, that I ventured to proceed. And the result is before the reader.

CHAP. II.—HOW I BECAME INTERESTED IN JOHN GRAY.

My first knowledge of John Gray dates back to the
year 1847, when, as a boy, I was growing up on my
father's farm in the same neighborhood. My earliest
recollections of him are associated with muster days,
mass meetings, and Fourth of July celebrations, when a
number of venerable men — ex-soldiers of the war for
independence — were invited to conspicuous seats upon
the platform. John Gray was always seen to be among
them. These, however, were commonplace affairs, and,
even among his nearest neighbors, very little was known
concerning him, except the bare fact that he had seen
service, which was sufficient to fill my boyish mind with
wonder. A quiet, unassuming farmer, without avarice
or ambition, there was nothing in his outward life to
attract public attention. In this capacity, he was sober
and industrious; as a citizen, quiet and unostentatious;
as a Christian, earnest, faithful, and devout, and, though
six miles from any church, he was always there whenever possible, and was invariably one of the first present
whenever the itinerant preacher of those days would
announce service at any of the farm-houses in the neighborhood. But, though hard-working, he was always
poor, and, as he grew older, found himself in great

danger of coming to want. In these later days, his
strength having in a measure failed, rendering him un-
able to work, he spent much of his time in reading his
Bible in quiet devotion. During these declining years,
he lived mostly alone, with his step-daughter, Nancy
McElroy, a lady also of advanced age, and unmarried.
From the rental of his little farm, supplemented by a
cow and garden, cared for by themselves and the kind
attention of thoughtful neighbors, they managed to keep
the wolf from the door, and, by a mere trifle, to escape
the journey " over the hill to the poor-house."

Apart from this, no one seemed to pay any attention
—certainly he received no public recognition, all seemingly forgetting, at least ignoring the fact that he had
been one of those who marched at the front at the time
that tried men's " souls," and who, in the sacred cause
of freedom, so dear to every American, took upon himself, under the leadership of our own loved Washington, the deliverance of our heritage from the hands of
our oppressors. In politics he was, by his religious con-
victions, trained and developed in the Methodist Episco-
pal Church, an uncompromising Abolitionist, and when
that extremist party collapsed, he became a staunch Republican. As such, he took a lively interest in the war
of the rebellion, and many were the prayers that ascended from that cabin hearth for the success of the
Union cause. If it seems strange, that from the beginning, I have taken such an interest in John Gray's history, I explain this by saying that John Gray was my
neighbor in Ohio for well-nigh twenty years, and that I
loved the old man as if he had been my father. I admired him—who could help it—for his rare and excellent

qualities of mind and heart. I loved him, because he had fought for the same flag that I had, and I loved him because he was so much like Washington—plain, simple, honest, and good.

I bow down not to genius and rank; I worship only the heroes of the true and good. He was such a hero. His name should not and can not rot in oblivion. Through all coming time his name will be like that of Washington. I looked upon him as preserved through four generations to show his children and his children's children what a noble type of men were our revolutionary fathers. He was a worthy sample of that good old stock. Ask the people of Ohio and they will tell you that there never lived in Ohio a better man than old John Gray. He was always a poor man and a Christian. He never attempted any kind of speculation or business, but literally earned his bread by the labor of his hands as a farmer all his life. For four-score years he was a consistent member of the Methodist Church, and never missed a single Sabbath from church when it possible to attend. He joined church at twenty-five. He lived a sober, regular, and industrious life, in so much that he was for half a century and more a model of piety to his church in a degree not excelled by any of his brethren in Christ. His hours of rising, working, and sleeping were regular as the clock. He retired early and rose before the sun. Seldom is any Christian permitted so long and so well to be a "living epistle known and read of all men." More than three-score and ten years he lived to adorn the doctrine of the Savior by a daily walk with God. Schooled as he was in that pure and honest school which made Washington a good man, learning his lessons from the

father of the church and state who formed that beautiful
system of government under which we live, John Gray
was ever a model man. Not one man was ever heard to
doubt John Gray's sincerity as a Christian and as a
patriot. On visiting the old man, he said to us, in reply
to the question "why he enlisted so young." "I lived
and was born near Mount Vernon, the home of Washington:
how could I do otherwise?" Such an answer
speaks volumes for the old patriot.

CHAP. III.—EARLY HISTORY AS GLEANED FROM HIMSELF.

He was born at Mount Vernon, Virginia, January 6,
1764. He was but a mere boy when the war began, and
his father being in the army, he, the oldest of eight
children, remained at home to help support the family.
He said that he and his brother would go to the forest
and fields to catch rabbits, and that was all the meat that
they had. At one time he worked a whole week at plowing
for two bushels and one-half of corn. His father fell
at White Plains, and he, then only about 16 years of age,
promptly volunteered, took up the musket that had fallen
from his father's hands, and carried it until the war was
over. He was in a skirmish at Williamsburgh, and was
one of the one hundred and fifty men on that dangerous,
but successful expedition of Major Ramsay. He was
also at Yorktown at the final surrender, which event occurred
in his eighteenth year. He was mustered out at
Richmond, Virginia, at the close of the war, and returned
to field labor near Mount Vernon, his first day's work
after his muster out being performed for General Washington
at Mount Vernon. Mr. Gray married twice in

Virginia and once in Ohio. He survived his three wives
and all his children, except one daughter, who has since
died over eighty years of age, and with whom he resided
in Noble County, Ohio, at the time of his death. Let it
be borne in mind that John Gray was not illiterate. His
parents were poor, and lived with much difficulty by their
daily labor, but they took pains to give John the best
education at their command. John could read and write
when he went into the army. He said about the greatest
pleasure he had while in the army was in writing home
to his poor old widowed mother. He told me that he
went to school two winters to Joseph Ross, a gentleman
who kept school at his own house, about four miles from
where John lived. He used to be up bright and early,
chop wood, kindle the fire, feed the stock, and be off on
his four mile of a morning walk to school, before seven
o'clock in the winter time. Little did he or his teacher
think that these humble studies that he then pursued
were to be useful to him for well nigh a hundred years
of after life. Certain it is, that, for the last ninety years
of John Gray's life, the little reading and writing that
he learned of Joseph Ross were John Gray's greatest
comforts. He read but few books, but with great care,
and remembered almost every word. The Bible, Pilgrim's Progress, the Plain Man's Pathway, and the Constitution, he could repeat off the book, almost word for
word. For more than three-quarters of a century, after
the close of the war of the Revolution, John Gray lived a
life of quiet and retirement upon or near the banks of the
beautiful Ohio. He left his native Virginia, the banks of
the Potomac, the home of his childhood, in 1795, the state
for which he had done battle service in no less a cause

than the independence of that state. He left her because
she denied and refused the right of suffrage to those of
her sons who had not "caught Dame Fortune's golden
smile," and made his home where—

> "An honest man, tho' e'er so poor,
> Is king of men, for a' that."

He wended his way over the mountains and rivers,
through the then almost unexplored wilderness of what
is now West Virginia, and coming out on the borders of
western civilization, at Morgantown, Va., he constructed
a rude craft, on which he descended the Monongahela
to its junction with the Allegheny, and thence down
the Ohio to the flats of the Grave creek. Here he made
his first settlement, and entered with ardor upon the duties of frontier life, having for his companions in toil,
privation, hardship, and frontier warfare such men as
the Poes, Wetzel, Hughs, Wheeler, Boone, Kenton, and
others, who have made their names conspicuous in the
annals of the west. Time rolled on, and the beautiful
region "north-west of the river Ohio" was, in the year
1802, erected into a state, and John Gray, after changing
his residence once or twice, settled down on the waters
of Duck creek, a tributary of the Ohio, within the present limits of Noble (then Washington) county, in the new,
free, and prosperous state of Ohio. Here, for nearly
three-score years and ten, he lived and labored. He
lived to see the almost unbroken wilderness "blossom
as the rose," and Ohio proudly take position, the third
state in the American Union. He lived to see men born
upon the soil grow up and take the highest positions, military, civil, and ecclesiastic, in the land—men of whom

any state or nation might well be proud. He lived to
witness the most wonderful achievements of science of
any age or any nation in his own country. He saw the
majestic steam-boat take the place of the frail canoe
upon her lakes and rivers. He saw the giant locomotive drag the ponderous train over the highest peaks of
the Alleghenies, through tunnels under mountains, over
rivers and plains, through forests and prairies, and to
the very summit of the Rocky mountains. He lived to
see the inventions of Franklin and Morse distance time
in the transmission of intelligence from London to New
York, and, crossing the continent to San Francisco, return the answer to New York just as old father Time
reached the shores of America.

CHAP. IV.—JOHN GRAY SECURES A PENSION.

During all this time John Gray had neither sought
nor obtained from the government any recognition of
his services in the war of the Revolution. Never rich,
indeed poor in purse, he was yet too proud to ask a
richly-merited annuity, and it was not till the frost of a
hundred winters had whitened his locks, and age, de-
crepitude, and want invaded his citadel, that he gave a
reluctant consent for his friends to apply for a pension.
In 1866, while a law student in Washington, D. C., I was
in correspondence with Matthew McCleary, Esq., who
lived at Hiramsburgh, Ohio, almost in sight of the old
patriot's cabin. He was deeply interested in the venerable hero, and often wrote to me in his letters concerning
him. I had just passed through the war of the rebellion myself, and was now better able to sympathize with his

deplorable condition than in my younger and boyhood days. I made several inquiries of my friends about him, and soon found myself intensely interested in his condition, and began to write him up in all the available newspapers, and to besiege Congress, then in session, to bestow what I believed to be a worthy pension, that he might not become a common pauper, then a likely thing. Most of these communications found their way to the waste basket, or were ridiculed by the clever paragraphers. Congress, as a matter of course, paid no attention to my appeals. Some of my communications, however, found their way into print. One of these, published in the *Waverly Magazine*, of Boston, in December, 1866, is given in full, as follows:

"The Last Man of the Revolution."

"By the report of the Commissioner of Pensions, but one of the revolutionists is now living. The immortal army of Washington, all but one solitary veteran, has gone to the grave! The honor of the old guard has been sung by more than two billions of human tongues that long since have gone to the dust. And yet this old hero lives on to hear a new billion of tongues trumpeting the fame of the army of which he is the only living representative. In the third generation, he is still living to see the glory which Washington and his comrades achieved by valor and patience. But the writer knows of one revolutionary soldier whose name was never on the pension rolls of the United States: John Gray, now 103 years of age, who resides with his daughter in Noble county, Ohio. He was born at Mount Vernon, Virginia, January 6, 1764. He was but a mere boy when the war

began, and his father being in the war, he, the oldest of
eight children, remained at home to help support the
family. He says that he and his brother would go to the
forest and fields to catch rabbits, and that was all the
meat they had. At one time, he worked a whole week
at plowing for two bushels and one-half of corn. His
father fell at White Plains, and he, then only about 16
years of age, promptly volunteered to take up the musket that had fallen from his father's hands, and carried
it until the war was over. He was in a skirmish at Williamsburgh, and was one of the one hundred and fifty
men on that dangerous but successful expedition of
Major Ramsay. He was mustered out at Richmond,
Virginia, at the close of the war, and returned to field
labor near Mount Vernon. Mr. Gray married twice in
Virginia, and once in Ohio. He survived his three wives
and all his children, except one daughter, who is now
nearly eighty years of age, and with whom he resides in
Noble county, Ohio. He has always been a poor man
and a Christian. He never attempted any kind of speculation or business, but has literally earned his bread by
the labor of his hands as a farmer all his life. For
seventy-eight years he has been a consistent member of
the Methodist Church, and never missed a single Sabbath
from church when it was possible to attend. He joined
church at twenty-five. He has lived a sober, regular,
and industrious life, in so much that he is now, and has
been for half a century and more, a model of piety to
his church in a degree not excelled by any of his
brethren in Christ. His hours of rising, working, and
sleeping are regular as the clock. He retires early and
rises before the sun. Seldom is any Christian permitted

so long and so well to be a living 'epistle known and
read of all men.' More than three-score and ten years
has he lived to adorn the doctrine of the Savior, by a
daily walk with God. Schooled as he was in that pure
and honest school which made Washington a good man,
learning his lessons from the father of the church and
state who formed that beautiful system of government
under which we live, John Gray has ever been a model
man. Not one man was ever heard to doubt John Gray's
sincerity as a Christian and a patriot. On visiting the
old man recently, he said to us, in reply to the question
why he enlisted so young: 'I lived and was born near
Mount Vernon, the home of Washington; how could I
do otherwise?' Such an answer speaks volumes for the
old patriot." Also, I published about the same time the
following little poem, which attracted some attention:

THE LAST MAN OF THE REVOLUTION.

In the chill and snow of winter,
  A dark and bitter night,
While the wind is mourning sadly,
  Like a lone and ruined sprite,
In a cottage in Ohio
  A poor lonely man
Sits counting o'er the hundred years
  Since first his life began.

In that cabin is one window
  With a broken many a pane,
Through which the snow keeps drifting
  With all its might and main;
And the old man sits and shivers,
  For his fire is very low,
And his blood has lost the fervor
  Of a hundred years ago.

18

His gray head bows in sadness,
  His prayer is murmured low,
But God can hear him now as well
  As a hundred years ago.

Call the roll of the noble old heroes
  Who battled at Washington's side,
And only this voice in the cabin
  Will answer—for all the rest died
In poverty, sick, in distress, and alone,
  Forgotten, neglected, yet he
Adorns the fair banner he fought for of yore,
  And prays for the " Flag of the Free."

These, with others, I had copied and sent to every congressman, and followed them up with earnest letters and
personal appeals to Hons. John A. Bingham, Ben. Wade,
Benj. F. Eggleston, Speaker Colfax, Senator Willson, Chas.
Sumner, and Thaddeus Stevens, all of whom received me
courteously, and some of them expressed themselves
more emphatically than piously with reference to the old
veteran having been neglected so long. Accordingly, on
the first day of the second session of the Thirty-ninth
Congress, December 3, 1866, Hon. John A. Bingham, a
member of the House of Representatives from the sixteenth district, than whom Ohio has not a brighter star
in her galaxy of living statesmen, arose in his place and
introduced House Bill No. 835, for the relief of John
Gray, a soldier of the Revolution, which was read a first
and second time, and referred to the Committee on In-
valid Pensions. (See page 6, Congressional Globe, second session, 39th Congress.) On Thursday, December
13, 1866, ten days after the introduction of the bill, Mr.
McIndoe, from the Committee of Revolutionary Pen-

sions, reported back, with a recommendation that it do not pass, House Bill No. 835, for the relief of John Gray, and the bill was laid on the table. (See Congressional Globe, second session, 39th Congress, page 3.) Nothing daunted, the patriotic and indefatigable Bingham, after introducing the most incontestible proofs of identity of which the case would admit after the lapse of so many years, in which the old patriot had "outlived the generation born with him," on Friday, January 25, 1867, succeeding in getting a bill reported (No. 1,044), by Mr. Price, from the Committee on Revolutionary Pensions, " for the relief of John Gray, which was read a first and second time. It directed the Secretary of the Interior to place the name of John Gray on the pension roll at the rate of $200 per annum, payable semi-annually."

"Mr. Delano, of Ohio, inquired whether the bill had the approbation of any committee."

He was answered by Mr. Price, "that it had the approbation of the Committee on Revolutionary Pensions." " This applicant," said Mr. Price, "is one hundred and three years old, and I have another similar case to report, in which the applicant is one hundred and seven years old (referring to the case of F. D. Bakeman, of New York, since deceased), and both these men are supported by public charity."

Mr. Spalding, of Ohio, moved to amend the bill by striking out " two hundred dollars" and inserting, in lieu thereof, five hundred dollars, and the amendment was agreed to. The bill was then ordered to be engrossed, and it was accordingly read a third time and passed.

" Mr. Bingham then moved to reconsider the vote by

which the bill passed, and also moved to lay the motion to reconsider on the table. The latter motion was agreed to." (See Congressional Globe, second session, 39th Congress, page 754.)

On the same day, January 25, 1867, a message was received in the Senate from the House of Representatives, by its chief clerk, Mr. Lloyd, announcing, among other things, that the House had passed Bill No. 1,044, for the relief of John Gray, a Revolutionary soldier, which, with others, was twice read by its title, and referred to the Committee on Pensions. (See Congressional Globe, second session, 39th Congress, page 754.)

On Wednesday, January 30, 1867, in the Senate, Mr. Lane, from the Committee on Pensions, reported, without amendment, House Bill No. 1,044, for the relief of John Gray, a soldier of the Revolution. (See Congressional Globe, second session, 39th Congress, page 853.)

On February 14, 1867, "in the Senate, on motion of Mr. Lane, the Senate, as in Committee of the Whole, proceeded to consider House Bill No. 1,044, for the relief of John Gray. The bill directs the Commissioner of Pensions to place the name of John Gray, of Noble county, Ohio, upon the pension roll, and that there be paid to him the sum of five hundred dollars, payable semi-annually during his natural life, commencing on July 1, 1886.

Mr. Lane said: "The bill, as it passed the House, was wrongfully drawn. I move to amend it by striking out the words ' Commissioner of Pensions,' and insert Secretary of the Interior, so as to make it conform to our legislation." The amendment was agreed to. (See Congressional Globe, second session, 39th Congress, page 1309 et seq.)

The bill was reported to the Senate, as amended, the amendment concurred in, and ordered to be engrossed and read a third time. The bill was then read a third time and passed.

On the 15th of February, 1867, the bill, as amended and passed in the Senate, was sent to the House, where, on the motion of Mr. Price, the amendment of the Senate was concurred in. (See Congressional Globe, second session, 39th Congress, pages 1262 and 1275.) A motion to reconsider the vote concurring in the Senate amendment was laid on the table, and a message sent to the Senate, announcing that the House had passed Bill No. 1,044, for the relief of John Gray, a Revolutionary soldier.

In the House of Representatives, on the 16th of February, 1867, Mr. Trowbridge, from the Committee on Enrolled Bills, reported that the committee had found, upon examination, Bill No. 1,044, for the relief of John Gray, a Revolutionary soldier, truly enrolled by its proper title; whereupon, the Speaker signed the same. (See Congressional Globe, second session, 39th Congress, page 1285.) On the same day, a message was received in the Senate, announcing that the Speaker of the House of Representatives had signed the bill as engrossed, and thereupon it was signed by the President pro tem. of the Senate.

Thus John Gray was placed on the pension roll at the rate of five hundred dollars per annum. In the meantime, I had written to Governor J. D. Cox, of Ohio, calling attention to the matter, from whom I received the following letter, which indicates the spirit with which those in authority regarded the matter at this time:

STATE OF OHIO, EXECUTIVE DEPARTMENT, }
    COLUMBUS, *February* 2, 1867.   }

Dear Sir:—Yours of the 29th ultimo is received, and the letter to the *State Journal* has been delivered. My duties are inconsistent with my acting as the trustee of a fund for the benefit of any private citizen, and I must beg you to find some business man or firm of known character, in the vicinity of the residence of the veteran, John Gray, of the Revolution, to do that work. It would involve a good deal of correspondence, which only could be intelligently done by those who are near enough to be personally cognizant of the wants and necessities of the old patriot. Earnestly sympathizing with the spirit which induces your action, I am

Very respectfully yours, etc.,
            J. D. COX, *Governor of Ohio.*
J. M. DALZELL, ESQ.

To say that I was happy over the final result, is but a poor and feeble way to express it. I fairly boiled over with delight, and could scarcely contain myself at all, after the triumph which had been achieved in behalf of the old veteran, and the sudden turn public opinion had taken in his favor. The clever paragraphers, who had ridiculed me, and the stupid editors, who had thrown my communications into the waste-basket, now filled their columns with eulogies of John Gray, and were very ready to extend to him the sympathy now no longer needed.

Many of the leading editors of the country now wrote me concerning the particulars of his life, and their communications were always respectfully considered, and the facts thus became widely published. Among others, Frank Leslie wrote me to procure and send to him a photograph and historic sketch of the old patriot, which I did, and which he printed in fine style, in the *Frank Leslie's Illustrated Newspaper*, one of the finest illustrated papers in the world. I placed copies of this on file in all the leading libraries, and preserve one to this day, among my own selected relics, with religious care.

It is time to prove the leading statement of this history—namely, that John Gray was the last soldier of the Revolution. That he was a Revolutionary soldier is proved elsewhere in this book ; but here we are to show that he was the last Revolutionary soldier. Two days after the pensioning of John Gray, February 18, 1867, Samuel Downing, of New York, was placed on the Revolutionary pension roll. From the report of the Commissioner of Pensions for the year 1867, it appears that the names of John Gray and Samuel Downing only remained upon the roll; the rest were dead. Of that noble band of patriots, they alone survived. Late in the fall of 1867, Samuel Downing died at Edinburgh, Saratoga county, N. Y. John Gray still lived, unquestionably the last soldier of the Revolution, till the 29th of March, 1868, when he died. The soldiers of the Revolution are extinct.

> "This was the noblest Roman of them all—
> The last of all the Romans. Fare thee well!"

Wishing to be entirely certain in the matter, I wrote

to the Commissioner of Pensions at Washington, D. C., to settle this. He replied with an indorsement on my letter, stating that "John Gray, of Ohio, and Samuel Downing were the only two left. The question came up, is Samuel Downing dead? If he is, then John Gray is the last soldier of the Revolution, beyond a doubt." So I wrote, and received the following letter, which settles the question forever:

POST-OFFICE, SARATOGA SPRINGS, }
                 April 16, 1868.   }

Sir:—In answer to your letter of the 12th instant, I have to say that Samuel Downing died last fall, at his home in Edinburgh, this county.

Yours respectfully,
M. A. PIKE, *P. M.*

[NOTE.—It will be remembered that John Gray died afterward, March 29, 1868, and was, therefore, the last survivor of the Revolution. And thus the question is settled forever.]

The following from the Pension Office, which was attached to the Centennial copy of the first edition, fixes also the same fact:

DEPARTMENT OF THE INTERIOR. }
       PENSION OFFICE, *June* 14, 1876. }

J. M. DALZELL, CALDWELL, OHIO.

Sir:—Yours of the 9th inst. is received, requesting information as to who was the last surviving pensioner who served as a soldier in the war of the Revolution. As it may be of public interest in the centennial year, you

JOHN GRAY'S CABIN, BUILT 1795, AS IT APPEARS, 1888.
Sketched by M. W. Horn, Caldwell, Ohio.

will have annexed the names of the last survivors on the pension rolls, with their age, date of death, residence, and so much of their military services as they gave in their applications for pensions.

J. A. BENTLEY, *Commissioner.*

J. M. DALZELL, Esq., *Caldwell, Ohio.*

Waldo, Daniel.--Born in Windham, Conn., September 10, 1762, and died July 30, 1864, aged 102 years. He entered the service in June. 1779, and December 20, 1780, at Horse Neck, in the south-east corner of Connecticut. Colonel Levi Wells. himself, with twenty others, were taken prisoners by refugees, carried to New York City, and confined in the notorious Sugar House. After the war, studied for the ministry; a Presbyterian clergyman; officiated in Lebanon and Suffield, Conn., particularly at the latter place, for many years. In 1837, removed to Wayne county, then to Owondago county, where he deceased. At the session of Congress for 1855-6, when the Hon. N. P. Banks, after a protracted struggle, was elected Speaker of the House of Representatives, Mr. Waldo was appointed chaplain to it, the duties of which he faithfully performed, besides repeatedly officiating in the churches in the city on the Sabbath, his age at the time being over 93 years.

Hutchins, William.--Born in York, Maine, in 1764, and died May 3, 1866, aged 102 years. He enlisted at New Castle, Maine, 1780-1, in the Massachusetts regiment commanded by Colonel Samuel McCobb. The 4th of July previous to his decease, he attended the celebration of that day at Bangor, in which he was an active participant.

Downing, Samuel.--Died February 18, 1867, age unknown. In 1828, resided in Edinburgh, Saratoga county, New York, and, it is understood, died there. His military service was in one of the New Hampshire regiments.

Gray, John.—Born in 1764, and died March 29, 1868. While residing in Fairfax county, Virginia, he enlisted, in 1781. Removed to Ohio in 1795, and has lived in Noble county since 1829.

BIRTHDAY ODE ON THE LAST SOLDIER OF THE REVOLUTION.

Nearly a hundred years ago—
  A hundred years to-day—
Our fathers met the British foe;
  In that immortal fray.
At Yorktown then old John Gray stood,
  Gave Britain her last blow,
And struck to drive the British off,
  A hundred years ago.

Nearly a hundred years ago,
  Our hero in his prime;
But now his head is white as snow,
  His limbs grow weak with time;
But let us gather around John Gray,
  The last man now alive,
And not forget this glorious day
  Make him one hundred and five.

CHAP. V.—MY LAST VISIT TO JOHN GRAY.

The success of my efforts to see the old hero comfortably fixed naturally awakened a renewed interest and a desire to visit him once more at his home. So, on a bright day in June, 1867, I visited John Gray, of Mount

Vernon, Va., for the last time. I felt a deep interest in
the old hero, because I knew him long and well, but
chiefly because I knew he was the last living man who
could say of a truth—

"I have shaken hands with Washington, and fought
under him. I was born at Mount Vernon, and was his
warm personal friend."

I know no mortal man except John Gray could say
these words. I sought for his history. He had a history worth knowing. To fill out the volume of our
colonial and Revolutionary history only one name more
was left; it was the name of John Gray, of Mt. Vernon.
But to get his history was no easy task. He had been
a common man. His deeds were not in print. Only
from his lips could I gather up the raveled threads of his
life. To him, therefore, I went, and to his neighbors;
and from them gleaned the fragmentary points presented
in this volume. If the reader will read as patiently as
I have written, he will lay down this book satisfied that
John Gray was the last survivor of Washington's army.
If the reader finds any discrepancies or contradictions,
let him remember that the field from which I gleaned is
one a hundred years old, grown over thickly with weeds
of forgetfulness, and covered, for the most part, with the
fog of oblivion. John Gray did not figure in public
life. He was a plain man, like Lincoln. From such a
life it is hard to gather strange incidents. I give the
facts as I got them from time to time from an old man
nearly in his grave. He had no writings. He had no
records. You can see John Gray's humble connection
with great events, without putting on my glasses, so I
merely drop these facts. You may elaborate. I deal

with points. You may detail. I profess to tell the
world a new and wonderful story of a wonderful old man.
This is all I claim. I point to the evidence in the acts
of Congress, and in the letter of the governor of Ohio.
A vast crowd of witnesses attest the truth of this history. The proof is plain. It is given in fragments.
You can pick them out. It will interest you as story
never interested you before. Such is the plan of this
history of the last man of the Revolution. A plain tale
of truth. If I take my own way of telling the old man's
story, you can not blame me after you have heard it.

Washington is in the clear upper sky, and John Gray,
his last soldier, has joined him in the land of spirits.
Eighty-nine years ago Washington died; John Gray died
March 29, 1868. Washington was the first soldier of the
Revolution, John Gray was the last soldier of the Revolution. The whole army had died before John Gray
died. Alone John Gray remained as a venerable monument of that noble generation. Washington was a Virginian, John Gray was a Virginian too. Washington was
a patriot and a Christian, so was John Gray. Washington fought for our liberty and independence, so did John
Gray. One after another the Revolutionary soldiers
dropped off, until John Gray alone survived. Like the
sentinel of Pompeii, John Gray remained sublimely res-
olute at his post of duty until God had removed all his
companions in arms by death, and then he folded his
hands quietly over his patriotic heart and fell asleep in
Jesus, in his 105th year. Washington's home was Mount
Vernon. John Gray's birthplace was Mount Vernon.
It would seem as if this coincidence worked a charm to
preserve John Gray alive. It would seem as if to be

born at Mount Vernon were to inherit immortality, as of one bathed in the fabled stream whose waters were said to confer immortality. It seemed as if born at Mount Vernon he could not die. And here we submit material for a grander history of John Gray, for this history is an *unhewn boulder of truth*.

Whoever may hereafter visit Mount Vernon, let him remember that Washington's last soldier was born upon its ample acres. Let him remember, too, that John Gray was a dear personal friend of Washington. That hand crumbling to dust in that white coffin there has often pressed the hand of John Gray. Wherever hereafter you go about the dear shades of Mount Vernon, remember that John Gray's sturdy arm felled trees here, and his skillful hand helped to adorn Mount Vernon for his chieftain's eye. Washington little thought, when last he pressed the hand of his soldier John Gray, that John Gray was to outlive him by nearly three generations, and speak his fame to another century. Washington was only thirty years older than John Gray. His chances to live as long as John Gray seemed fair and flattering. But John Gray outlived his chief well nigh three-quarters of a century. It is of this wonderful old man this book speaks. His fame should keep company with the venerable fame of Washington forever. Washington, the first soldier—John Gray, the last soldier. Worthy every way is John Gray of a place beside the name of Washington, for his life was pure and good. The volume of the history of the Revolution remained open till John Gray died. The volume now closes. This book finishes the history of the Revolution. Nothing more remains

but that we forever revere the memory and imitate the
virtues of such men as Washington and John Gray.
My last visit to Mr. Gray, as before intimated, was in
June, 1867. At this interview I was determined, if possible, to get more definite information in regard to his
parentage and early life. My friend Matthew McCleary,
of Noble county, Ohio, was with me. I transcribe the
notes which I then and there made of that interview. I
am sorry I could not make them more full and accu-
rate. Let future historians do so. It is my duty to
give these facts just as John Gray gave them to me,
without addition. Near Hiramsburgh, Ohio, in the midst
of a meadow, is a cabin; in front of the door is an old-
fashioned well; on the hill just above, and in full view,
perhaps two hundred yards off, is a little enclosure grown
over with weeds, where sleep the remains of John Gray's
people. As I approached the cabin, the old man's dog
ran out and barked fiercely at me. As I entered the
cabin, a sweet girl of perhaps fourteen years met me
with a smile and invited me in. There before me stood
John Gray on his crutches, an old man, the oldest I ever
saw and the most reverend. On his crutches leaning,
his hair falling in snowy showers about his shoulders;
his hands large, for he had lived by hard labor: his feet
as small as a woman's: he was five feet eight inches
high: broad, very broad of chest, and with a massive
head of perfect symmetry. He looked up at me with
his two sweet, blue eyes and smiled. He was not ugly.
His smile made him look handsome. His voice trembled
a little but was pleasant; a subdued and musical treble
like that of a child. I expected him to sit down exhausted. He had been moving about on his crutches,

and was indeed tired. But, on sitting down, he at once began to talk to us. His dog walked around and lay down quietly beside Mr. Gray, the sentinel of the old revolutionist. Thus appeared John Gray in his 105th year, in his home in Noble county Ohio. Doubtless artists will yet set the picture in a beautiful frame in the Capitol of the Nation, and thus for the first time do honor to a private soldier. I came in. The old man looked up, and hardly knew me at firse. My friend, Matthew McCleary, Esq., called to the old man, and told him who I was. Instantly he recognized me, and reached out that hand which had so often grasped the hand of Washington. I seized his hand and kissed it, and felt that I was blessed to have the privilege. The old man's hearing was quite dull, and his eyesight very dim. But he could both see and hear a little. He told me he was five feet eight inches high, though as he sat doubled up in an old man's way, he appeared much shorter. He had grown heavy but by no means corpulent. He laughed as I remarked that he was not much fatter than he was the last time I had met him. "Oh, no," said he, laughingly, "we old men don't fatten much on hog and hominy, and the poor tobacco we get now-a-days." He had a large spittoon by his side—a wooden box that would hold half a bushel—contents thereof better imagined than described. He had chewed tobacco for about a hundred years, and could not leave it off. Mr. Gray had grown quite infirm, and could hardly hear us speaking. His memory, of course, had somewhat failed. So this may account for some discrepancies in this book. I will try to explain them. In the main they are not such as to give the reader any trouble, satisfied as now his mind must be

of the general truth of my story. So here are the fragmentary facts elicited by that last interview. Mr. Gray's
father enlisted in 1777, and fell at White Plains. Mr.
Gray belonged to the militia under Captain Sanford, and
they were called out in the fall, in October prior to the
year the war closed. I now give his words: " I was a
mighty tough kind of a boy in them days I tell you. I
saw big, heavy men give out, but I never lagged a foot
behind. We started from Fairfax C. H. and went to
Fredericksburg, and from there to Yorktown. When we
were near Williamsburg orders came to send out a scout-
ing party to feel of the British; we were then trying to
come up to Williamsburg. We were too weak to fight
them. But our captain called for volunteers to go out
on a scrimmage, and I volunteered with sixty others
We had gone only two or three miles when we came upon
the red-coats in large force. Just as we got near
enough to fire, I could see day-break.

"It was pretty hot for a little while, I tell you. They
had cannon, we had none. They fired grape-shot at us;
but it was on rising ground, and they fired over us. But
we had to fall back, and so we then marched to Richmond. In the next year, Cornwallis surrendered. Our
time was out the day we came in sight of Yorktown. I
went back to hard work, near Mount Vernon, when the
war was over. My people were mighty poor, and there
was a big family of us. So, as I was the oldest of a large
family, I had to go to work to support them. There was
eight children of us. · I used to take my dog, and go
out and catch rabbits. It was about all we had to eat
sometimes. I was married to Nancy Dowell when I was
twenty years old. I first moved to Morgantown, Va.

We had our things in a wagon. I took a notion I would go down to Kentucky. So I built a boat, and put my family and horses aboard, and went down as far as Dilly's Bottom. There I stopped for nine years. From there, I went to Fish Creek, took a lease to clear some land, and stayed there seven years. I came up through these parts in them days. There was a salt-lick up on Duck Creek, and we used to come up and hunt of winters. I saw Indians, plenty of them. I remember the year of Wayne's defeat. I tell you, the settlement was badly skeered then. I may have shot one or two red-skins—no matter.

" I was married to my second wife at the Flats of Grave Creek. Her name was Mary Regan. I don't know where my children is now : I am afeerd they are all gone, except my step-daughter. I have my crutches and a pension to support me. I am very well satisfied. God bless Judge Bingham for getting that pension he got for me! He was always kind to me. I always voted for him, because I have always known him to be a good man. I tell you, we haven't many more such men. He is a soldier's friend. I saw all that through the war. He is always ready to do a good turn for a soldier. No wonder the boys all like him."

Mr. Gray narrated to me the following anecdote of General Washington. I believe it has never before been published, and, as it gives a new view of General Washington's characteristic kindness, it is worth preserving :

At this time (after Mr. Gray had returned from the Continental army) he lived near Mount Vernon. There was then a saw-mill — running by water power, of course — on a stream called Dog Run. The General's negroes came there, with whip-saws in their hands, one bright

May morning, and with them also came John Gray, with
a whip-saw, too. Sawing was a slow business then.
What could not be sawed with the large saw, Mr. Gray
and the slaves easily sawed with the whip-saws. As he
was busily sawing, one day, and musing over his Revolutionary experience, who should ride up but General
Washington himself. With characteristic kindness, the
great man called to John Gray, for he knew him well.
John dropped his saw, and, in a twinkling, was shaking
hands with the General. The General inquired kindly
for his health, and, telling him not to work too hard, bade
him good-bye, and rode away.

It did me good to hear the old gentleman tell it. I
might fill a volume with similar anecdotes, for Mr. Gray
never tired of speaking of General Washington. His
want of property excluded him from voting, in Virginia,
for his beloved Washington. And he often said, had it
not been for that, he might have lived and died in Virginia. But he was a Republican at heart, and could not
well get over the insult thus leveled by aristocratic distinctions against his proud manhood. Saving this, John
Gray was a true lover of Virginia. He often mourned,
and even wept, over Virginia's wayward course in the
Rebellion — for John Gray was loyal. But when the war
was over, all his feelings against Virginia left him. He
remembered that Washington and he were born in Virginia, had fought a common foe in Virginia, and had
returned in triumph from a war that closed so grandly in
Virginia. No Virginian need ever blush to acknowledge
John Gray's fame. He was a true Virginian, proud of
the Old Dominion — with all her faults, loving her still.
I asked him if he would hang Jeff Davis.

"Oh, no," said the old man, "that would do no good.
The war is over. It would only raise bad feelings against
us. He can't do us any harm. Let him live." I asked
him if he thought the South would come back all right.
"Oh, yes, I guess so," responded the old soldier, "when
she cools off a little. You know those Southern folks
are pretty hot-blooded; but they'll come around all right
by-and-by." I asked his opinion of Grant. "Well,"
said he, musingly, "he is a great general. but I can't see
into him very well. But he will be our next President,
though." This was June, 1867. one year before General
Grant was first nominated. Mr. Gray was very fond of
dogs. He said he had always owned a dog or two.
"Though," said he, with a merry laugh, "I sometimes
have had nothing else but a dog;" and, musing a moment, he added: "A plug of tobacco, of course, for
without a dog or tobacco I should feel lost." A little
white dog lay coiled up near his chair. "What is the
name of your dog, Mr. Gray?" I inquired. "Nice," responded he. "Is that not a nice name?" he naively inquired, while his sides shook at the witticism. He told
me the biographies of several of his canine friends. I
remember one only. When Mr. Gray's father first
went into the army John was but thirteen years of age;
but, being the eldest of eight children. the care of the
family devolved upon him. They had no meat. They
had nothing but a little cornmeal—rather a spare larder,
my fair reader of the nineteenth century's fullness; so
John went out and caught rabbits to feed the family. His
dog, "Lade," always was his companion upon these ex-
peditions. What John's gun failed to bring down, Lade's

flying feet brought low. I am glad that Mr. Gray has left us a picture of Lade. She was a red female hound, with a white ring around her neck. He told me that he never cried harder than he did that day that he last saw Lade, except when he was leaving home to enter the Continental army He told me that she died old and full of years, and he laid her down gently to sleep in the deep recesses of the woods of Mount Vernon. Thus closed the old man's story There he sat alone. He had outlived his generation. His white hair, still abundant, flowing down over his bent form, made him seem a patriarchal hero. We bade him good-by.

LINES ADDRESSED TO JOHN GRAY.

The frosts of five-score,
And many years more,
Have whitened your blessed old hair;
Of glory a crown,
By heaven sent down,
Now, Father, you solemnly wear.

O, this is a crown,
By heaven sent down,
More beautiful far than a king's;
For angels in glory
Have made it so hoary,
And kissed all its silvery strings.

Then wear the white crown
By heaven sent down,
For your feet shall soon press the bright shore;
When yonder in glory
Your hair no more hoary,
Will wave in the skies evermore.

O, fair is the crown
By heaven sent down,
For righteous old fathers in age;
A promised reward
From hands of the Lord,
Laid down in the Bible's sweet page.

Chap. VI.—Closing Scenes and Remarks.

The 29th day of March, 1868, closed the earthly career of the last known survivor of the War for Independence, at the ripe old age of nearly one hundred and five years. But in those years he had seen great changes. Independence was established, which was but the beginning of the mightiest revolution in matters of government that the world had ever seen. The War of 1812 had been successfully fought, settling forever certain great principles essential to our national prosperity. The Mexican War had made large additions to our territory, and greatly strengthened and improved matters on our southern boundary. The War of the Rebellion had been successfully finished, setting forever at rest the right of property in human bodies and souls; and between the first and the last of the heroes of the first great struggle he had seen the mightiest development in church and state, science, literature, art, and invention of any age in the world's history. Like old Simeon in the Temple, well might he exclaim : " Lord, now lettest thou thy servant depart in peace, for mine eyes have seen thy salvation." Surrounded by his old friends and neighbors, among whom he had lived in peace and harmony for three-score or more years, he was laid to rest in the family burying-ground near his homely cabin. There he rests in peace, a man worthy of a monument whose top shall pierce the skies. A truly great, heroic man ; great in his simplicity and humility, heroic in the performance of simple known duty without expectation or hope of recognition or reward. The following letter from the postmaster at Hiramsburgh is here inserted as showing the interest taken by his friends and neighbors in the old veteran in his last days :

HIRAMSBURG, NOBLE COUNTY, OHIO, *April* 1. 1868.
MR. J. M. DALZELL.

Dear Friend :—The last Revolutionary hero is gone. Those eyes that saw the infant colonies engaged in deadly conflict with the mother country are now closed. The tongue that helped to swell the notes of victory is now dumb The heart that for more than one hundred and four years kept the blood coursing through the veins has ceased to beat—John Gray is dead. Sunday, March 29, A. D. 1868, at fifteen minutes before nine o'clock, the spirit took its flight. The mortal remains now repose in the family vault. I take the liberty of writing to you to inform you of his death, knowing that you have felt a great interest in the old hero. I am sorry to inform you, and I know that you will be sorry to hear, of the death of Dr. N. P. Cope. He was buried on the 12th of March last. These things speak for themselves. I will make no comments. We have had no mail to pass through here for the last ten days. You will see the difficulties under which we are laboring, but I suppose we can not look for any change for the better for the next four years. Truly yours,

P. BURLINGAME, *P. M.*

It was a fortunate circumstance, that, during my visit to John Gray, in 1867, I conceived the idea of securing his photograph, else no authentic picture of him could ever have been produced. I managed to have a photographer on the ground, and thus, only a few months before his demise, secured what must at some day become exceedingly valuable. The following letter explains the matter fully.

CUMBERLAND, OHIO, *April* 8, 1868.

J. M. DALZELL.

Dear Sir:—You have doubtless heard, ere this, of the death of John Gray. He died Sabbath eve, March 29th, aged 104 years, 2 months, and 23 days. I have his photograph and autograph copyrighted. They will be ready for delivery soon. I want you to send me the precise date of the act of Congress making him a pensioner, as I wish to place a few items of the old man's history on the back of the pictures. How would you like to secure a picture of the Gray residence for your history? Please reply by return mail. Yours truly,

I. N. KNOWLTON.

The following appeared, soon after his death, first in the *Washington Chronicle*, and afterward in many other periodicals:

"THE LAST SOLDIER OF THE REVOLUTION.

" *To the Editor of the Chronicle:*—I have just learned, through a private letter from Ohio, that John Gray, the last soldier of the Revolution, expired, at his residence in Noble county, Ohio, on the 29th of March. I knew the old man well, having lived for nearly twenty years within sight of his house, and frequently met and conversed with him. There never lived a purer or better man. During the twenty years that I knew him, I never heard one word against his character. Greater praise than that is impossible. Every citizen of Noble county, Ohio, knew and loved the old man. John Gray was born at Mount Vernon, January 6, 1764, and was consequently in his one hundred and fifth year when he died. He told me that he worked many a day on the Mt. Vernon estate for General Washington. At sixteen years of age, John Gray entered the Continental army, and served till the close of the war for our independence. He was at the surrender of Yorktown. Mr. Gray removed to Ohio before it was a state, and remained there till his death. His history will be written, but I give these few facts as they come to my mind to-day. Hon. John A. Bingham, of Ohio, knew old John Grey well, and did much to help the old hero in his declining years. The last soldier of the Revolution was an earnest friend of Mr. Bingham's. Mr. Bingham found the old man in very destitute circumstances a few years ago, and determined to do all he could for him. For some reason Mr. Gray never received any pension, so Mr. Bingham gave the old man some money to relieve his most urgent necessities, and afterward prevailed upon Congress to grant him a pension of $500 per annum. This act of generosity and patriotism to Washington's last soldier was remembered gratefully by old John Gray to the last hour of his life. The people of the Sixteenth District will never forget it.

Yours, etc.,   DALZELL.

" WASHINGTON, D. C., *April* 4, 1868."

Eulogy on John Gray.

" Eulogies turn into elegies." Indeed, the eulogy and elegy come properly at one and the same time. The final judgment can not be pronounced, either in this world or the next, until the man is dead. "Well done, good and faithful servant," has already welcomed John Gray to heaven. The welcome of the skies may well find a welcome here. A life of virtue, in its fullest sense, was the the life of this grand old man. Listen. John Gray was a citizen of Ohio for three-score years and ten, and you can not find in that state one man, woman, or child who can recall one evil word he ever said, or one bad act he ever did. Nay, more. Not one man, woman, or child in Ohio has ever so much as said that such a rumor ever was heard. This would be great praise. But we can go farther. Until stricken by the infirmities of age, he labored hard with his hands, and led a life of noble usefulness, prayer, and virtue. Because he was inoffensive, it does not follow that he lacked mental capacity. By no means. But he sought to do good and be good, and he accomplished it. What an example to hold out to the rising generation. This man was a patriot—he fought for your liberty. This man was a Christian during a long, long life. He never injured his neighbors in thought, word, or deed. Was he not worthy to be Washington's last soldier? He was not as great, but he was as good, as Washington. And are there not purposes of God plainly seen in his life? Did God prolong John Gray's life until John Gray alone remained of all the Revolutionists, and this without a purpose? Verily, no. God had a purpose in it. Might

it not be that, by his pure life, he might forever stand as
an example to coming generations? And has not labor
her heroes? There are heroes who marshal armies and
rule nations; are there not heroes, too, in humble life?
To be good as John Gray was, and do his whole duty to
his God and fellow man, is such heroism as stands high
above that of Napoleon. Therefore, I honor John Gray.
Therefore, I gather up what I can of his life and write it
here, that coming generations may see and admire the
pure and unpretending virtues of Washington's last
soldier.

Following is a copy of John Gray's will, extracted
from the records in the office of the probate judge of
Noble county, Ohio. It is not less remarkable for its
simplicity and brevity than for the noble spirit of gratitude which pervades it.

Copy of John Gray's Will.

In the name of the benevolent Father of all, I, John
Gray, of the county of Noble, and State of Ohio, being
now in the 104th year of my age, of sound mind and
memory, though my limbs are feeble, and I am the last
survivor of the Revolutionary War.

Item 1. I give and devise to my only daughter, Nancy
McElroy, and heirs, forever, all moneys, goods, chattels,
and effects, of whatsoever kind or nature, that may be in
my possession at the time of my decease, only asking
that she, the beloved Nancy, will still continue to take
care of me while I live, as she has done heretofore.
And the above devise is made to compensate, so far as I
am able, the said Nancy McElroy for the care, kindness,
and attention that I have always received at her hands.

Item 2. I do hereby revoke all former wills by me made. In testimony whereof, I hereunto set my hand and seal, this 14th day of February, 1867.

JOHN GRAY. [SEAL.]

Signed and acknowledged by said John Gray, as his last will and testament, in our presence, and signed by us in his presence. PHILIP BURLINGAME, JOHN W. SCOTT.

Here we close the history proper of John Gray, the patriot, friend, and companion of Washington. The details of his life, as the reader has already seen, are meager, and yet enough is known to secure him the lasting friendship of angels, patriots, and men. He was a Christian, having perhaps a longer church record than even a few attained—eighty years. He was a patriot, daring, not for himself, but for posterity. He was a man, than whom there are few more manly. He was the last of a noble and grand generation. Those who read this brief history in other states will pardon me for saying that I am proud to say that the old hero sleeps in my own State of Ohio, near the spot where I now write.

Herald it to the world that the last soldier of the Revolution died in Ohio. Rear a marble column, to tell coming generations that John Gray, Washington's last soldier, sleeps in Ohio. Men of the Sixteenth District of Ohio—aye, of the whole great Commonwealth of Ohio—bestir yourselves, to honor Washington's last soldier. Strike some plan, by various and early subscription, to raise a marble column to his memory. Washington's last soldier died in Ohio. Governor Cox wrote me that he sympathized deeply with a scheme to rear a monument to John Gray's memory. All good citizens of Ohio will contribute to it. Set me down for a dollar. Are there not ten thousand other dollars?

> Let a column rise to heaven,
> Till sky and marble meet,
> And sunlight of the morning
> All its pallid beauty greet."

Consequently, upon the revival of interest in the old patriot's history during this Centennial year of Ohio, the idea recurred to me to revive my original appeal of twenty years ago to Congress and the people, to take some action looking toward the erection of a monument of our venerable hero, and, to tell the truth, to procure by any honorable method the means necessary to push and complete the enterprise in hand. In pursuance of this end, early in March I addressed letters to our Congressman, Colonel J. D. Taylor, asking him to urge Congress to take suitable steps to secure the erection of a monument, and, at the same time, I wrote the Secretary of War concerning the matter, as above stated. Colonel Taylor at once introduced the bill, at my suggestion, and I have received the following letters in reply:

WAR DEPARTMENT,   }
WASHINGTON CITY, *March* 27, 1888. }

Sir:—I have the honor to acknowledge the receipt of your letter of the 8th instant, requesting that the Government pay you $1,000 for time, labor, and money expended by you in preparing a sketch, with portrait, of the life of John Gray, the last soldier of the Revolutionary War, who died in 1868. In reply, I beg to inform

you that your letter has been referred to the Department
of State, where the records of the Revolutionary War
are on file.

Very respectfully your obedient servant,

S. V. BENET,

Brigadier-General. Chief of Ordnance, and
Acting Secretary of War.

MR. JAMES M. DALZELL, CALDWELL, O.

DEPARTMENT OF STATE, }
WASHINGTON, *March* 22, 1888. }

JAMES M. DALZELL, ESQ., CALDWELL, OHIO.

Sir:—Your letter of the 8th inst., addressed to the
President and Secretary of War, has been referred to
this department. In reply as to the propositions stated
therein as to the material compiled by you for a memoir
of John Gray, a soldier in the army of the United States
during the War of the Revolution, which you wish to sell
to the government, I have to inform you that Congress
has made no provision to enable this department to ac-
quire your collection. You also state that you have
brought this subject to the attention of certain members
of Congress who will, I assume, duly consider it, and
take such action upon it as may seem to them to be
proper.   I am, sir,

Your obedient servant,

G. RIVERS,

Assistant Secretary.

WASHINGTON. D. C., *March* 26, 1888.

HON. J. M. DALZELL, CALDWELL, O.

Dear Sir:—I will introduce the Gray bill in a few days.
I have it ready. I would have got it in to-day, but I had

some very important matters to look after at the Post-
office Department. and was detained on the way, and I
found, when I got to the House, that they had omitted
the reading of the minutes, and called the States for bills,
before I got there. I will likely get it in to-day by unani-
mous consent, and I will push it as fast as possible. I
wish you would write some of the members about it, and
get them to take an interest in it. I think it would be a
splendid thing to l. e the old man's grave marked by a
suitable monument. Thousands of people would go
every year to see it. I am sorry we did not think of this
at the opening of the session, so as to get the bill earlier
before the committee. It is so hard to get a bill out of
a committee, but I think this will be an exception.

Yours truly.
J. D. TAYLOR.

Mr. Joseph D. Taylor. of Ohio, introduced the following bill in the House of Representatives, April 2. 1888:

A BILL to provide for the erection of a monument to John
    Gray, the last survivor of the Revolutionary War.

Whereas, John Gray, who was born at Fairfax, Virginia, in
the year seventeen hundred and sixty-four, and died in Noble
county Ohio, in the year eighteen hundred and sixty-eight, at
the unusual age of one hundred and four years, was the last living soldier of the Revolution: and,

Whereas, The said John Gray was pensioned as the last surviving soldier of the Revolution by the Thirty-ninth Congress, at
the rate of five hundred dollars per annum ; and,

Whereas, This aged veteran died the year after his pension
was granted, very poor, and left no means with which to mark
his grave: Therefore,

Be it enacted by the Senate and House of Representative of the United
States of America. in Congress assembled, That the sum of two thou

sand dollars be, and is hereby, appropriated out of any moneys in the treasury not otherwise appropriated, for the purpose of erecting a monument to the memory of Private John Gray, the last survivor of the Revolution, whose remains now rest in an unmarked grave in Noble county, Ohio.

Sec. 2. That the secretary of state shall have the management and control of the erection of said monument and the selection of the spot where it shall be placed, and all other matters in relation thereto.

THE REVOLUTIONARY TRIO.

WASHINGTON.

First in War.

Foremost among the mighty names that make
The times of Revolution brilliant yet.
Chief of all that patriot host that won
For us our freedom and our glorious flag—
" First in war "--the brightest spirit of them all,
Behold the Chieftain Washington ;
A man not molded in a lordly hall,
Nor reared in splendor near a kingly throne,
Nor taught to jabber in a classic shade.
Nor trained for war by printed rules ;
But in the wilderness of this fair land
Born and nurtured in the plainest scenes
That plain and rugged nature can produce,
To manly independence every thought attained,
And every act conformed to nature's plan,
And all the men controlled by love of right,
His great heart full of love to God and man,
He grew up strong in body, strong in mind ;
In purpose strong and armed with right,
God and the people holding up his hands,
And guiding and supporting him through all,
He took the Army, and Victory loved
To leave the tyrant and come to him.

First in Peace.

And, when the war clouds rolled away,
And all the Nation's sky was bright with **peace**,
He, the " First in war," the conquering chief,
The brave, resistless general, became
Again the first, the " First in peace,"
And at the Nation's helm again,
Saul-like, with head and shoulders over all,
The grandest President he stood;
And words of wisdom from the cherished chief
Still guided our young Nation's early plans,
And every danger he foresaw, and turned
The Ship of State around ere she had touched
The rocks of discord lying near.
His farewell to the people, whom he loved,
His farewell words still linger yet, and oft,
With tender memories rushing through the mind,
Do millions read those farewell words;
Words of counsel caught from heaven,
Words of hope, and words of cheer,
The last words of the great immortal chief,
While Americans still love the land he loved,
And still revere the flag to him so dear.
Will his words linger in the peoples' hearts,
And guide the peoples' hands, and keep
Still sacred and secure the liberties
Wrung for us from tyrant's hands
And first made safe by Washington?

First in the Hearts of His Countrymen.

Millions have lived and died since the tomb
Closed first upon the corpse of Washington.
The corpse in marble wastes, and dries to common dust,
And ashes now are all we have of Washington.
Though he is dead and gone to the dust,
His spirit lives and breathes in all our laws,
And is the talismanic word that makes **these states**
In harmony and Union ever one.

The Declaration, Constitution, Laws,
The Union, Flag, and Nation's Arms,
Are bound in volumes with a golden thread
That reaches through the peoples' hearts,
Is fastened through the throne of God, and runs
All through the fame of Washington.
Let marble blush if it would tell
How dear is Washington to every heart;
His memory is not encased in solid stone,
Nor pent up in your marble monuments—
It lives in living men, and every tide
Of warm life-blood in every heart
Still murmurs sweetly as it courses on,
And all its crimson streams are vocal
With the praise of Washington.

GRANT.

O, come
Ye lofty spirits from the fields of song,
In all your singing robes and flowing train,
And voices chanting out melodious verse,
And us inspire with fitting thought and words
Aglow with some of that seraphic fire
Which made such glowing harmony on the lips
Of Otis, Henry, Adams, Jefferson,
When they with fervent praise of Washington,
With kindling eloquence in Freedom's name,
Proclaimed the leader of their glorious cause.
And there is one, another Washington,
Whose fame with his the hand of fate has joined;
And, while the name of Washington is named
By patriots' tongues, another mighty name
Shall ring with grandeur through our fair domain,
And Freedom's sons can ne'er forget the chief
Who saved the flag from rebel hands, and now
Is still defending with a heroic might
The flag of Washington, of you and me.
Need I repeat in blind and staggering verse

And accents rude and illy tuned,
The Chieftain's name which echoes now
In verse and prose throughout the land?
Need my imperfect muse repeat his name
Who flung our banner to the breeze of war,
And by it stood through all the fiery storm,
Thundering with might of Jove at treason's gates
Far down the Mississippi's bloody stream ;
Or, turning to the East, when Vicksburg fell,
To drive the traitor from his last foul den,
And wrest the bloody sword from traitors' hands,
And Appomattox, and so close the war?
Ah, no; that name is written on the nation's heart;
That name is sacred to the army yet;
And freedom stands with victory now,
And, smiling, both are crowning him with fame,
And all the comrades dear repeat Grant's name.

JOHN GRAY.

And now another name, a third,
   A private soldier of heroic mold,
Shall close the burden of my lay,
   And laurels deck the brow of Private Gray.

———

For there are those unknown to song or story,
Whose deeds, though brave and great, are never told
To individual praise—the humble ones
Who fill their spheres with patriotic glow
Of soul known but by heroes moved by zeal
For country's good—without ambition for a
Higher place, yet face the cannon's mouth,
And yield their lives a cheerful gift
To save her from her deadly foes.
All hail the private soldier—highest type
Of love, disinterested and pure—
Who lives not for himself, nor seeks renown,
But only for the sake of those he loves,

Pours out his blood a willing offering.
Such were the men of '76 and '61,
Who, brave and strong, on many a bloody field,
Bared their bosoms to the fatal shaft,
And in the stern crisis of the Nation's life,
Withstood the shock, and marched to victory.

At midnight, or at morn's gray drawn,
They answered to the long roll's fearful call.
Thus, when the call of duty, stern and cold,
Was heard, each answered name was known.
But in the hour of victory and triumph,
The individual name, amidst the throng
Of souls heroic who have braved the storm,
Is lost, where all were true and brave alike.

Yet one there is whose name shall long survive,
Who, when the story of the cause he served,
And of the chieftain by whose side he stood
Is named, shall, too, be named as one of those
Who, in the hour of her darkest night,
Their country saved from death and made her free.
Who, though not greater nor e'en yet more brave
Than thousands, comrades on the tented field,
Laid down his arms only at call of peace
When Yorktown's fall declared the struggle o'er;
Who, though no longer needed for defense,
Yet lived to see his country, grand and great,
The foremost of the nations of the earth.
Saw one by one his comrades pass away,
His wife and children, age, and fall on sleep;
Yet living on he saw a second war,
A third, and yet a fourth, each adding more
Of glory and of strength—a nation tried
By fire, and for her giant sins
Scourged, and baptized in a sea of blood.
He lived to see her from her trials come
Bright as the sun, and clear as is the moon,

With strength, with majesty and beauty clothed.
All this he saw through five score years and five.
Thus, having shared the triumphs of an age,
The greatest age of all the world's great life,
The last of all that noble band of men—
The sires of '76—his head adorned
With hoary locks, his eye grown dim,
And marks of superadded years upon his form,
Yet brave of soul and strong of mind and heart,
Sustained by grace, and cheered by Christian hope,
He, too, passed over to the great beyond.

Who shall be left from out the last great strife,
To linger longest in this earthly way?
Who shall behold the wonders yet to be
Within the century that is dawning now?
Whose name shall be enrolled as last of those
Who saved our country from her rebel foe?
Mayst thou dear reader in that future day
Bear fitting news of country's weal or woe
To that assemblage where on equal ground
Are Washington, and Grant, and Private Gray.

THE END.

JOHN GRAY'S NEGLECTED GRAVE, 1888.

THE NATION'S SHAME.

[Photographed by M. W. Horn, Caldwell, O.